A Fine House in Trinity

'Written with brio, A Fine House in Trinity is fast, edgy and funny, a sure-fire hit with the tartan noir set. A standout debut.'
MICHAEL J. MALONE

'The storyline is strong, the characters believable and the tempo fast-moving.'
Scots Magazine

'This is a romp of a novel which is both entertaining and amusing . . . the funniest crime novel I've read since Fidelis Morgan's The Murder Quadrille and a first class debut.'
Crime Fiction Lover

'Razor sharp Scottish wit . . . makes *A Fine House in Trinity* a very sweet shot of noir crime fiction. This cleverly constructed romp around Leith will have readers grinning from ear to ear.'
The Reading Corner

'A welcome addition to the Tartan Noir scene, Lesley Kelly is a fine writer, entertaining us throughout. This is a book perfect for romping through in one sitting.'
Crime Worm

Lesley Kelly has worked in the public and voluntary sectors for the past twenty-five years, dabbling in poetry and stand-up comedy along the way. She has won a number of writing competitions, including *The Scotsman*'s Short Story award in 2008, and was long-listed for the McIlvanney Prize in 2016.

She lives in Edinburgh with her husband and two sons.

DEAD
MAN
DRIVING

A HEALTH OF STRANGERS THRILLER

LESLEY KELLY

SANDSTONE PRESS

First published in Great Britain in 2023 by
Sandstone Press Ltd
PO Box 41
Muir of Ord
IV6 7YX
Scotland

www.sandstonepress.com

ISBN: 978-1-914518-36-2
ISBNe: 978-1-914518-37-9

Sandstone Press is committed to a sustainable future. This book
is made from Forest Stewardship Council ® certified paper.

Cover design by David Wardle
Typeset by Iolaire, Newtonmore
Printed and bound in Great Britain
by TJ Books Limited, Padstow, Cornwall

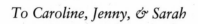

To Caroline, Jenny, & Sarah

MONDAY

RESERVATIONS

I

Bernard McDonald had always prided himself on his ability to heed a warning. To the best of his knowledge he hadn't ever eaten food that was past its *Best Before* date, never mind playing fast and loose with the dangers of an expired *Use By* sticker. When forced to consume medicines of any kind, he not only read and reread the caveats on the accompanying leaflet about potential side effects, but also conducted his own internet research on peer-reviewed websites. On his rare trips to London he was fastidious about Minding the Gap.

After checking for traffic, Bernard stepped off the pavement to allow a woman pushing a buggy to get past. She was the only pedestrian he could see who was heading away from Edinburgh's town centre, as the whole population of the city seemed intent on making its way up the cobbles of the Royal Mile and joining the 'Food for All' protest taking place outside the Castle. The woman nodded her thanks.

'Bloody disgrace, this,' she said, waving an arm at the crowds. 'Have they all forgotten about the Virus?'

He smiled, but she wasn't wrong. The protestors had thrown caution to the wind, flouting health precautions that discouraged people from meeting in large groups where the influenza Virus could easily be passed on. Given that the Virus killed a substantial minority of the people it infected, such gatherings were a considerable risk. At least they were for the moment: the news had been full of talk of a potential vaccine that might give at least some limited protection against the worst aspects of the Virus. Bernard was treating these news reports with a degree of scepticism. There'd been talk of a vaccine almost as long as there had been a Virus, but no-one had yet come up with a workable version. One of the unworkable versions had resulted in the death of several of the participants in the clinical trial, so it was safe to say that there were some concerns among the population about the whole concept.

Bernard had no particular concerns about being in a crowd, as he had previously contracted the Virus, survived, and consequently now had complete immunity. Neither he, nor any of his similarly immune colleagues at the North Edinburgh Health Enforcement Team, needed to worry about catching the Virus at today's event. There were a number of other things he *was* concerned about, not least the fact that he was running five minutes late for a briefing at the City Chambers regarding the HET's involvement in the proceedings, but today's anxiety levels were quite manageable.

Joining the HET had been a substantial challenge to Bernard's natural risk-averseness. Situations arose so quickly that he didn't have time to reflect on the pros and cons of a course of action, and before he knew it, he'd rescued a prostitute from a homicidal drug dealer or clubbed an armed man over the head or been caught up in some other HET imbroglio that would have been unthinkable two years ago. Caution-wise, he was definitely, if not a completely changed man, at least a man who was open to the possibility of change at some point in the future, after due diligence was undertaken.

His mobile beeped to alert him to an incoming text, three lines of properly punctuated writing that Bernard recognised as the texting style of his girlfriend, Lucy.

Dinner with my parents and me on Thursday evening 6 pm. The Sizzling Pepper. PLEASE DON'T MESS THIS UP! I just want a nice meal for my birthday and to put the last couple of weeks behind us.

Bernard prided himself on his ability to heed a warning, and he was in no doubt at all that this was one. Sometimes life sent you a signal that you just could not ignore, a heads up that, if disregarded, would change your life for ever. And sometimes life sent disaster without any kind of advance notice. Like the elbow that was currently making its way directly towards Bernard's nose.

'What happened to you?' Paterson, the head of the North Edinburgh Health Enforcement Team stared at Bernard in dismay.

'He got elbowed in the face, Mr Paterson.' His colleague Carole spoke up on his behalf. 'It's getting pretty crowded out there.'

Maitland, the youngest member of the HET, leaned in towards him for a better look at the damage. 'I don't fancy Bernard's chances on the front line today if he can't even make it to the Command Centre without getting beaten up.'

'Shut up, Maitland. It's just a slight knock. The bleeding will stop in a second or two.' He sniffed, hoping this was true. 'Although I have to say, Mr Paterson, that we really shouldn't be doing this. It's quite a stretch of our job descriptions to say we should be marshalling an event of this kind. We haven't even had any formal training.'

'It's not my idea, Bernard, I can assure you. I'd be quite happy if the G8 came to Edinburgh, discussed whatever Virus nonsense they have to, then left, with my only input being shouting at the television from the comfort of my own home. Unfortunately, due to every left-wing loony in town lining the streets out there complaining because they can't get access to a crate-load of chicken nuggets every time the urge hits them, we need all the community officers we can possibly get.'

'It's the V8, not the G8 – they're all Virus Ministers. And the concerns that people have about rationing are a little bit more realistic than that. *And*', Bernard returned to his original theme, 'we're not police, Mr Paterson. We're HET officers. We're supposed to be tracking down people who miss their Health Checks, not providing policing services on the cheap.'

'Well, you can tell that to Fraser Mauchline when you meet him.'

'Who?' asked Maitland.

'The Scottish Health Enforcement Partnership's Deputy Chief Officer, AKA Stuttle's second in command, who is now first in command, while Stuttle is on gardening leave.'

Maitland looked puzzled. 'Garden—'

'It's a euphemism. It means he's on an enforced holiday while everyone's favourite government minister, Carlotta Carmichael, works out a way to give him his jotters.'

Stuttle, their ultimate boss, was currently accused of being to blame for a security breach at the Parliament. It was widely seen as a convenient way for the Minister for Virus Policy to sack him, having crossed swords with him on a number of occasions. The North Edinburgh HET staff were very upset about their boss's situation; Stuttle was their preferred leader in a 'better the devil you know' kind of way.

'What's this Mauchline guy like, Guv?'

Paterson shrugged. 'Can't say I know him particularly well, but pretty competent from what I have seen. Stuttle certainly rated him. But it doesn't really matter, because he's only acting up for a couple of days while they get some proper replacement in. Temporarily, of course, while they investigate the accusations against Stuttle.'

'Yeah, of course.' There was a murmur of agreement, although in reality nobody was holding out much hope of Stuttle coming back.

Out in the street the PA system crackled into life and they could hear a message being shouted at the crowd.

'What's it saying?' asked Bernard.

'Upstairs,' Paterson pointed an index finger at the ceiling, 'have set a message to go off every ten minutes reminding people that this is an illegal demonstration, as under the terms of the Health Enforcement Act people are not allowed to meet up in groups larger than twenty.'

'So why aren't they all being arrested?' asked Maitland.

'Believe me, if they had the resources, that's exactly what they would be doing. As it is, they're prioritising the arrest of anybody stupid enough to bring their kids with them into germ central out there. The rest of us are just focusing on crowd control. Right,' he said, looking round the room with a sudden sense of purpose. 'We should get moving. All the other HET officers are already out there, as *their* teams managed to turn up on time.'

Bernard recognised this as a jibe. 'It's not my fault—'

'So, the jist of the briefing which you missed, due to being late—'

'I was injured!'

'Is that you, the marshals, are on the road side of the metal barriers, keeping the scumbags well away from the

5

diplomatic cars as they drive up the High Street. Any attempts by anybody to climb over the barriers, you press the button on your radio and call in your position. Police reinforcements will be dispatched immediately. Take this.' Paterson handed him a bright yellow vest, and a walky-talky.

'I'm not doing it,' said Carole suddenly.

There was an uncomfortable silence, which Paterson eventually broke. 'I know you have some concerns, Carole, about work.'

Some concerns was an understatement. A clause in their contract of employment had been invoked recently, outlining the specific circumstances under which they could leave the HET workforce. Currently, the number of acceptable reasons for quitting had been narrowed down to one – death. Carole had responded to this in a number of ways, including beginning legal proceedings against the Scottish Health Enforcement Partnership, instigating a solo protest of working to rule, and generally making Paterson's life miserable. Bernard hoped that for her sake the court found in her favour, as Paterson now had a stack of Carole-related grudges he would be looking for payback on.

'I know you're upset, but you do need to do the work we require of you, and today we're helping out as marshals.'

'I get that, Mr Paterson.' She shot him a withering look. 'But I'm not wearing one of those.' She pointed at the high-visibility vest.

'What's wrong with—'

'Or carrying one of those ridiculous radio things.' She talked over him. 'I couldn't agree more with what the "left-wing loonies" out there are complaining about, so I'm perfectly happy to be attending an illegal demonstration on work time. But I'm not doing any of this marshalling nonsense, and if you disagree with that, why don't you sack me?'

Paterson's eyes followed her as she walked out. As the door closed on this challenge to his authority, he snapped round to face the two remaining members of his team.

'Has either of you clowns got anything to say?'

'About agreeing with the left-wing loonies or about not wanting to be marshalling?' asked Bernard, for clarification.

'Oh, shut up and put this on.' Paterson shoved a vest at him.

Bernard hesitated but, not having Carole's appetite for confrontation, acquiesced. A dribble of blood fell from his nose onto the front of the vest.

'Gross,' said Maitland. 'Guv, look at his face. You can't actually expect him to go out there looking like that? He'll scare people.'

Before their boss could offer a response, a young man appeared in the room. 'Mr Paterson? You're wanted upstairs by Mr Mauchline.'

Paterson sighed. 'OK, Maitland, time you were out marshalling. Bernard, you'd better come with me.'

Upstairs turned out to be a room on the first floor given over entirely to a bank of computers, each of which appeared to have a young man with a ponytail seated at it. Bernard was reminded of the HET's IT Officer, Marcus, who seemed to have been left off the invite list for the day's duties.

'Interpol,' muttered Paterson in his ear. 'Scanning the crowd with facial recognition software to see if any European troublemakers have joined us for the day.'

'John!' A thin man in a suit headed in their direction. 'You got the message. Excellent.'

'Fraser. Good to see you.'

'What the hell happened to him?' Mauchline stared at Bernard.

'Hit in the face,' said Paterson.

'So they're assaulting us out there now, are they?'

'No, no,' said Bernard hastily, not wanting to be the misplaced cause of a crackdown on the protesters. 'It was an accident due to the crowds.'

Paterson ignored him. 'Well, what do you expect with those types? Anyway, you wanted to see me?'

'Yes, I've got a job for your team. Nothing too complex, and it shouldn't take them long.'

Bernard's heart sank. The only plus point in Stuttle not being around was the fact that he couldn't involve them in any of his off-the-books investigations, which generally turned out to be both complicated and time-consuming, indeed occasionally life-threatening.

'Sir!'

They all turned in the direction of the call.

'I think we have one.' One of the young men gestured them over. French, thought Bernard, if the accent was anything to go by.

'We've got intel that there's a group of anarchists got something planned for today,' explained Mauchline.

'Anarchists?' asked Bernard.

'Well, troublemakers, you know the sort.'

'Here, sir.' The young man tapped the screen. 'That is Florian Boucher.'

'Boucher.' Mauchline frowned. 'He's one of the ring-leaders, isn't he?' He peered at the screen. 'Is there a marshal nearby?'

'There is one here.' The Frenchman pointed to the screen. Bernard saw he was pointing at Maitland's image.

'Nobody closer?'

The Frenchman brought the camera back to Florian Boucher. Bernard stared at the image on screen then turned to Paterson. His boss's face revealed several fleeting emotions, before it settled reluctantly on honesty.

'The woman standing next to him is also a marshal. She's from my team.'

'Why isn't she wearing a vest?' Mauchline demanded. 'And she doesn't seem to have a radio?'

'Well—'

'What is she doing now? Is she *waving* to somebody?'

Carole did appear to be signalling very enthusiastically. She then blew a kiss.

'I think she said her sons were also coming down to the demo,' said Bernard.

In response, Paterson stood discreetly, but heavily, on his foot. Bernard internalised a yelp.

'Oh, for Christ's sake, Paterson. Is this some kind of family outing for your guys?'

'I don't quite know what's, ehm ... I'll radio Maitland and get him to move closer.'

'Something's happening.' The French IT man sounded concerned. 'Boucher is covering himself in liquid.'

'This is Marshal Point 76.' Maitland's voice came over the radio. 'There's a guy down here shouting about setting fire to himself.'

'Move into standard evacuation procedure,' Mauchline said. 'Reinforcements are being dispatched.'

Bernard caught sight of the screen again. There wasn't any need for Maitland to commence evacuation, as everyone seemed to be stampeding away from Boucher; everyone, that is, apart from Carole.

'Bernard – let's go.'

Paterson gestured to him to follow, so he ran after his boss, out of the Chambers and back to the High

Street. The other marshals had obviously all got the message to clear the area: there were numerous arguments going on as they tried to persuade the people who had turned back to watch proceedings to move further away. Paterson pushed his way to the front of the crowd and vaulted over the crash barrier with a surprising degree of grace, given his bulk. Bernard followed as quickly as he could, and the two of them raced up the centre of the Royal Mile until Paterson ground to an abrupt halt. He held out an arm to Bernard to stop him moving.

Florian Boucher was six feet away from them on the other side of the crash barrier. His clothes were dripping, and his hand was aloft, clutching what seemed to be a lighter. Carole was holding tight to his arm.

'Everyone OK here?' asked Paterson.

'Yes, thank you, we're just having a chat,' said Carole, her voice high-pitched but controlled.

Bernard saw someone move towards them on his left. *Maitland.* The two of them exchanged a quick glance before turning back to the tableau in front of them.

Marshals were still attempting to get people away to a safe distance. Most had fled the scene apart from a few ghouls who were capturing it all on their mobiles.

'It's very important that you don't use your lighter,' said Paterson, slowly.

Florian looked around at the remnants of the crowd. 'Are you filming this? Are you getting all this on camera?'

Nobody answered.

'Yes, they're filming you. Don't do anything stupid,' said Paterson. 'Carole?' He lowered his voice. 'You might want to walk away now.'

A number of police had arrived. In the distance he could see some of their number toting bright red fire extinguishers, hurrying over the cobbles in their direction. If Carole could just keep Boucher talking for another few minutes, she'd be safe.

'If I move, he'll set fire to himself,' she said.

'I will!' shouted Florian.

'Why aren't there more police?' whispered Maitland to Bernard.

There was the sound of shouting from further up the street. They couldn't hear the words but it had the feel of a challenge to authority.

'Maybe this isn't the only protest?'

In the distance a wail of sirens could be heard.

'I think you're right,' said Maitland. 'I'm going to try to edge closer to Carole.'

Before he could put his plan into action, Carole brought Florian's arm crashing down onto the metal barrier. He yelled as the lighter bounced out of his hand and onto the cobbles. It bounced twice and landed by Paterson's foot. He immediately bent down and pocketed it.

Two of the police officers jumped on Boucher, twisting his arm up behind his back and wrestling him down to the ground.

'Are you getting this?' Boucher was still yelling, despite the fact that he was now horizontal. 'Capture this police brutality on your phones!'

A young policewoman with an extinguisher ran up beside them and enthusiastically sprayed all three of them with foam. She then turned the hose onto Carole, the force of the spray shoving her up against the crash barriers.

'Are you OK?' Paterson shouted. Carole waved a hand in his direction, then drew it across her face in a not entirely successful attempt to remove all the foam from her eyes and mouth.

Paterson's radio broke into life, broadcasting Mauchline's message to everyone around. 'Everyone OK down there?'

'I think so,' said Paterson. 'Everyone's still alive and no-one's on fire.'

'Thank God you're all safe.' Mauchline's voice echoed. 'But please tell me that the woman down there who tackled Boucher isn't the one who's trying to sue us?'

Carole wiped the remaining foam from her face. 'Why don't you all just—'

Paterson's hand made it to the mute button on his radio in the nick of time.

2

'Do you think we can go?' asked Maitland. They were back in the City Chambers, having spent the best part of the last two hours being interviewed about the recent events by the Scottish Health Enforcement Team, Police Scotland, and several other large men who hadn't bothered to explain to them who they were.

Bernard looked round the room. It was the same one he had started the day in, and people were still rushing to and fro, talking into mobiles, shouting and waving across the room to the long-haired guys on computers, occasionally stopping to listen to the messages that were being broadcast over the loudspeaker system. There was no sign of Paterson or Mauchline, or anyone else who could officially give Maitland an answer to his question. 'Probably? I think everyone who could possibly have wanted to speak to us has spoken to us by now.'

'Well, almost everyone. We haven't had a visit from your mate.'

'My mate?'

Maitland grinned. 'Yeah, Ian Jacobsen. Don't he and Bob Ellis usually pop up in situations like this?' He attempted to mimic Jacobsen's voice. '*We're here from HET/CID Liaison to patronise you about how you're doing things all wrong.*'

'I don't think you can really call Ian Jacobsen my mate. Quite the opposite.' Bernard shuddered. Even the thought of being in the same room as the HET/CID Liaison Team was terrifying. Jacobsen and Ellis were a two-man team who assisted the HET with any chasing of Health Defaulters who strayed into potentially criminal territory. His colleagues had had to call on the HET/CID Liaison far more frequently than Bernard liked; he hated the bits of his job that brought him into contact with Edinburgh's criminal fraternity. If he'd wanted to work with criminals, he'd have joined the police force or the probation service instead of the HET, where he had hoped to put his degree in Health Promotion to good use. This was only part of his dislike of working with the HET/CID Liaison, however. His other issues with them were that they were both bloody terrifying, and that nobody, not Mona, not Paterson, not even Stuttle, really believed that they were serving members of Police Scotland.

Ellis was a large man, broad and cheerful, whose bonhomie Bernard always thought was a front to disguise an utterly ruthless temperament. Jacobsen was smaller and slighter, and considerably less charming. While the HET were united in their dislike of the CID officers, they each had a different theory as to who their actual paymasters were. Maitland favoured Secret Service, either MI5 or MI6 (his colleague was unclear on the difference between the two). Mona thought they had something of the military about them and had them pegged as an elite army unit. Paterson's money was on some brand-new government unit set up as a response to the pandemic.

These were all good theories, although no-one had answered the burning question of what the actual purpose of any of these agencies was in relation to the HET, beyond turning up and poking around in their business, usually at the most inopportune moment. There were only two things about them that Bernard could say with absolute certainty. The first was that they were very good at ensuring that Carlotta Carmichael MSP got her own way. The second was that however much he disliked the CID officers, the feeling was definitely mutual.

'I can totally understand why Jacobsen hates you.' Maitland was warming to his theme. 'After all, you did beat him unconscious with, what was it? A lump of wood?'

Briefly, Bernard closed his eyes, the memory of that evening coming back to him. 'It was the wooden pole they used to open the skylight at the Plague Museum.' The thought still made him feel sick. 'And in my defence, I thought he was trying to kill Mona at the time.'

Maitland nodded, sagely. 'And still no-one at SHEP has considered giving the three of you any workplace counselling. Just a pat on the back, whoops, these misunderstandings happen, off you go and work happily together.'

'Well, maybe if we had been offered counselling, he wouldn't have felt the need to push Mona down a flight of stairs.'

'His word against hers, Bernie. Do you want me to suggest to Stuttle's replacement that he organise some mediation?'

'Please don't.'

'Probably wouldn't work anyway, not with all the other grudges he has against you.'

Bernard felt his heart rate speed up. 'What other grudges?'

'Well, I don't think he ever bought that you didn't know Bryce was a spy.'

Bernard put his head in his hands. Bryce was a former member of the HET's IT department, who as it turned out had been spying on them on behalf of, well, no-one was exactly sure who Bryce had been aligned to. What they did know, without a shadow of a doubt, was that Bryce had had a lot of weapons at his disposal and had been extremely willing to use them.

'And I suppose I can see where he was coming from.' Maitland was enjoying himself. 'After all, you and Marcus were really good friends with Bryce. He must be assuming that the only reason that you didn't rat him out to CID was that you were all in on it.'

Bernard looked up. He couldn't quite read the expression on Maitland's face. 'But *you* don't believe that, do you?'

'I think that both you and Marcus are such morons that you wouldn't spot a spy if he sat on you. Anyway,' Maitland said, looking round the office again, 'I'm surprised not to see the pair of them here.'

'I'm not.' Bernard immediately realised his mistake. He knew exactly where the HET/CID Liaison Team were. They were busy following up a lead on Operation Trigon, a lead that he, Bernard, had given them. A lead that Bryce had insisted he pass on to them, in order to give Bryce himself a bit of extra time to make a getaway. Bernard had no idea what Operation Trigon was, but the effect on the Liaison Officers had been extreme. The words had barely been out of his mouth when Ellis and Jacobsen had abandoned him and headed off to deal with whatever horror this operation referred to. He had had several sleepless nights since trying to work out how much damage he'd done with this false tip.

He'd tried to say no to Bryce. He tried very hard to say no, but Bryce's threats had been both extravagant and strangely believable. He didn't want to risk Bryce shooting his colleagues if he refused or, God forbid, making good on the intimation that he knew where Bernard's mother lived, and wouldn't hesitate to kill her either if Bernard didn't do this one little favour for him. So he'd obliged, although due to some really bad timing on his part, by the time he had passed on the message, Bryce was already dead. And when Jacobsen found out he'd been lied to, Bernard would probably be joining him. He got to his feet. 'I mean CID will be really busy, and I don't think we're doing much of use here.'

'They know where we are if they want to speak to us again. Come on, let's get gone before anyone says otherwise.'

'I'm surprised you're so keen to get back to the office.' It wasn't like Maitland to be rushing back to work when there was the opportunity to laze about, doing nothing, on work time. In fact, his ability to spin out simple tasks was legendary. Bernard had witnessed him on many occasions effortlessly turning a ten-minute task into something that involved several hours of concentrated skiving.

'I'm starving. Aren't you?'

Bernard realised, with a slight feeling of surprise, that he was, in fact, very hungry. Despite the near constant discussion of food all day, no-one had offered them anything to eat. He followed Maitland, looking round as he went, waiting for one of the people with clipboards to shout at him, but no-one batted an eyelid. It would appear they were free to go.

'Can you believe the price of a …' Maitland contemplated his lunch. 'A pretty common-or-garden sandwich these days?'

'Well, if you buy something on the Royal Mile you end up paying tourist prices.' He looked at the poster in the window of a shop they were passing. It illustrated a large BLT, a fine-looking one, admittedly, with a great selection of lettuce, and probably some quality tomato, but the price quoted in the corner of advert was eye-watering. Since when did buying a sandwich leave you with no change from a tenner?

'Even so, I reckon this is, what, double the price of what it would have been pre-Virus?'

'Yeah, that's probably about right.' The Virus had led to staff shortages in just about every walk of life, but the food sector had taken a particular hit. Fruit and veg had ended up rotting in the fields, lorry drivers were in short supply, and consumables prices had rocketed. Wages, on the other hand, had not.

Bernard downed the last of his vegan bake and speeded up his pace. 'I'll catch up with you back at the office.'

Maitland hurried after him. 'Why? Where are you going?'

Bernard tried not to answer. 'Just got something, to, ehm ...'

His colleague walked in front of him, forcing him to stop. 'You're off to the Museum aren't you, popping in to see your bird on work time?' He shook his head, grinning. 'Shame on you, Bernie, mixing work and private life like that.'

Bernard took a large step to the side and continued walking. 'Don't call Lucy *my bird*. It's sexist.'

'Whatever.' Maitland grinned. 'Have you told the woman who you respectfully call your *girlfriend*—?'

'I actually prefer the term *partner*.'

'Have you told your *partner* about your ex-wife possibly being up the duff with your child?'

Bernard was torn between breaking into a run or grinding to a halt and telling Maitland to F Off. His indecision resulted in his pace slowing down, which his colleague took as a sign to continue his interrogation.

'Are you even sure that your ex-wife is actually carrying your kid, and not someone else's?'

'She's not technically my ex-wife. We're still married.'

'Oh well, that'll reassure Lucy. The woman that you are still legally attached to may be having your baby. That won't make her insecure at all. Anyway, I still don't understand why you think the child is anything to do with you. You've been separated for ages, and it wasn't like you were still, you know...' He made a graphic hand gesture that Bernard did his best not to look at. 'I say the kid's not yours.'

'I don't know. She was so into having another child, and I wasn't, so maybe she kept some of my sperm and used it.'

'With a turkey baster?' Maitland grinned.

'Why am I even talking to you about this? It's none of your business.' He resumed his previous speedy pace. 'Don't ever raise the subject with me again.'

'Can't promise that. Impregnating one woman while being with another is literally the only interesting thing you have ever done in your life. If we don't talk about this, you bring absolutely nothing to our conversations.'

'Then don't talk to me at all! Anyway, the office is in that direction.' He pointed back up the High Street.

'Go back on my own? What am I supposed to tell Paterson? I came running back but Bernard's caught up in some urgent heritage work? No chance. I'm coming with you. Anyway, it'd be nice to catch up with Lucy.'

Bernard ran through possible scenarios that would stop Maitland following him to the Museum, and decided that, regrettably, nothing short of pushing his colleague under a bus would stop him. 'OK, but just keep your mouth shut about exes and babies, right?'

'Soul of discretion, me.'

The Edinburgh Museum of Plagues and Pandemics was located on York Place, in a three-storey Georgian town house. The Museum had had a key role in one of their previous investigations. The HET's involvement had resulted in damage to several of the exhibits, and the arrest (and subsequent sacking) of Lucy's then boss. Lucy didn't seem to be bearing any kind of grudge against the HET, but then she had been given her boss's old job, which might have made the interference easier to bear.

He stepped into the foyer and looked up. A wrought-iron staircase wound its way skyward, leading up to a cupola that flooded the hallway with light. The building was truly beautiful, yet much as he loved visiting Lucy here, he couldn't quite shake off a feeling of dread every time he set foot on the premises. For him, it would always be the building in which Ian Jacobsen had tried to kill Mona.

'Bernard!' Lucy stepped out from behind a large pile of boxes. 'I wasn't expecting you.'

'We were passing.' He reached for her hand and gave it a quick squeeze.

'Hi Lucy. Remember me?' Maitland stepped into the hall and rested his elbow on top of the pile of boxes.

'Of course.' She smiled, much to Bernard's annoyance. 'Maitland, right?' She turned back to Bernard and perused his face. 'Is something wrong with your nose, it looks kind of bruised?'

'Your boyfriend was very brave,' said Maitland. 'Took on a bunch of rowdy protestors single-handed.' He winked at him.

'Really?' Lucy's eyes were wide.

'No. Well, anyway, it's not important.'

She put her arm round him. 'I'm just glad you're OK.' She lowered her voice. 'Do you think it will have faded by Thursday? I'm sorry to be so shallow, it's just that it will be the first time you've met my parents, and—'

'It'll be fine by then,' he said quickly. 'Anyway, you look busy. We probably shouldn't disturb you, but I just wanted to let you know that I got your message about Thursday night and I'm really excited.' He needed to get to a mirror and see how bad the damage to his face was. Was he going to have to buy some make up to cover up the bruise? Or maybe he should stick with Maitland's lie that he went down in the line of duty?

'Oh, wonderful. Look, we're just putting the finishing touches to our latest display.' The Museum housed a wide range of standing exhibits about pandemics through the ages. There was a room documenting the role of animals in spreading various diseases to humans, a room which featured a wide range of human interventions in response to illness, including some truly gruesome prophylactics and remedies for the Black Death, and an exhibit about the use of big data in tackling outbreaks. However, as Bernard had learned since meeting Lucy, the large room on the ground floor housed a topical exhibition which was updated every three months. Today, it would appear, was changeover day.

'What's the new exhibition?'

'Well,' she beamed, 'strange as it seems we've never actually had an exhibition about our current virus. This exhibition is all about the H1N1 strain of influenza. Why don't you take a look? I'd appreciate your feedback.'

Bernard looked at his watch. 'I don't know. We probably ought to—'

'We'd love to.' Maitland hustled him through the doorway, past a volunteer who was busy pinning a display board in place.

'Paterson might be looking for us by now,' Bernard hissed.

'Not as important as keeping your good lady wife-stroke-partner happy, under the circumstances,' said Maitland quietly, although not quite as quietly as Bernard would have liked. 'Get some Brownie points in the bag before you tell her about—'

'OK, OK, OK,' he looked back over his shoulder, and was relieved to see that Lucy hadn't followed them in. 'Just shut up. We'll have a quick look then head straight back.'

'Course.'

Maitland headed off, taking in the room in an anti-clockwise direction. Bernard sighed. If he was going to look at this exhibition, he was going to do it properly, and read it from beginning to end. He turned round and looked at a display board that had 'Introduction' in large red letters at the top. He skim-read the information ...

The H1N1 influenza strain was responsible for Spanish Flu ...

The current strain has caused the death of over 1 million people in the United Kingdom since its first appearance on these shores ...

He skipped over a few boards then stopped in front of 'Government Response'. It outlined in detail the various departments that had been established in response to the crisis. There was a picture of Cameron Stuttle next to an explanation of the Scottish Health Enforcement Partnership, and underneath that, a brief description of the Health Enforcement Teams.

In an attempt to control the pandemic, the Government instituted a monthly Health Check for all Citizens who had not yet had the Virus. The information on Citizens' Health Status is held on a database, and each individual has a card with a unique identifying number on it – commonly referred to as a 'Green Card'. If a Citizen fails to attend a Health Check, this will be followed up by the Health Enforcement Team (the 'HET') who will track the individual down. The HETs have considerable powers of enforcement.

It wasn't a bad summary of how the HETs worked, it just missed out on a few of the realities of their work. It didn't mention that most of their time was spent tracking down drug addicts and alcoholics, whose chaotic lives meant that they struggled to make the regular monthly date. It skipped over the fact that many of their regular customers objected to their presence in their lives, and generally expressed their annoyance through the medium of violence. And it also didn't mention the tendency of Cameron Stuttle to use the North Edinburgh HET as his own personal task force, roping them in to do whatever task Police Scotland was too busy to do, or more likely, to do whatever task Stuttle wanted to keep private.

He turned round to see what his colleague was looking at. Maitland appeared to have given up on the display boards and was staring out of the window, his tolerance limit for culture apparently reached after five minutes. In fairness, this was longer than Bernard would have predicted. He resolved to look at one more panel, then hit the road. He shuffled along and found that the next section looked at Young People and the Virus. It was a sobering read.

H1N1 can result in a huge overstimulation of the immune system, meaning that young, fit people are most at risk of dying from the Virus ...

He stopped reading. If he read further, it might talk about the impact of influenza on babies. He didn't need to read about the impact of influenza on babies. He'd lost his infant son to the Virus back in its early days, when no-one, not doctors, not researchers, not politicians, actually knew what they were dealing with. His marriage had never recovered, and if he was honest, he wasn't sure that he had either.

'Maitland.' He nodded towards the door. His colleague loped over to join him, and they headed back to Reception, where Lucy was stocking Perspex leaflet holders with promotional information.

'Did you enjoy it?' She spun round to face them. 'Be honest.'

'I thought it was brilliant, really reminded me of lots I'd forgotten.' Maitland nodded thoughtfully, and Lucy looked delighted. Bernard resisted the temptation to ask him if he had actually read any of it.

'The exhibition was great, Lucy,' he said. 'I'll be back to have a proper look at it as soon as I can. I'll ring you later.'

'Do you want to meet up this evening?'

'Ehm, I'm sorry I can't there's a, ehm, work thing I need to attend.'

'OK, give me a ring when you're done.' She waved to him, and they headed back through the grand entrance.

'Work thing?' Maitland ran down the steps and stared back up at him. 'What work thing?'

'Shut up.'

'Did you just lie to your girlfriend?'

Bernard ignored him, walking determinedly past him in the direction of the office.

'You did, didn't you?' His colleague swivelled round and started to follow him. 'You know what, Bernie? I think you're finally growing up and turning into a proper man, in all our lying, cheating glory.'

Before Bernard got a chance to tell Maitland to mind his own business, his phone rang. He looked at the screen and grinned.

'Mona! Where are you?'

3

'How was Bernard?'

'Good,' said Mona, shoving her phone back in her pocket. 'The HET's been dragged into marshalling the food protests. Bernard said they got caught up in a bit of excitement.'

'Oh yeah?' Greg Paterson turned from the passenger seat and stared at her. 'When you say excitement ...?'

'An activist called Florian Boucher attempted to set fire to himself on the Royal Mile and was only stopped when my colleague Carole grabbed hold of him.'

'Florian did that?' Liz, Greg's girlfriend, took her eyes briefly off the road and looked at her in the mirror.

'You know him?' Mona was surprised, then when she thought about it, unsurprised. Liz was active in the trade union movement; she'd come across a wide range of activists. They might all share a vision, but their views on how to achieve it would vary.

'Yeah, met him a few times at meetings and demos and things.'

'Have I met him?' asked Greg.

His girlfriend laughed. 'Where would you have met him? You don't go near any of the meetings I attend.' She caught Mona's eye again. 'He thinks that policemen aren't supposed to get involved with that kind of nonsense, whatever their actual feelings might be.'

Mona smiled. Greg took after his father: conservative,

no nonsense, but definitely someone you'd want around in a crisis. When she'd taken ill and Paterson senior had wanted to send her somewhere she'd be safe, it was no wonder his son had been his first choice. That his girlfriend was a registered nurse had been a bonus. She'd had a magnificent time recuperating at Liz's flat in London; cake and wine had figured large in her recovery. 'Why were you surprised that Florian Boucher threatened to set himself alight?'

'I don't know . . .' Liz thought for a minute. 'I guess I'm just astonished that he did something so risky. I'd always thought he was a bit of a lightweight, you know? All talk but no actual action. Maybe I was just biased because . . .' She laughed.

'What?' asked Greg.

'Well, he's a good-looking guy and several of our female activists get all starry-eyed whenever he's around, so maybe it was just some prejudice on my part that he was only coming to meetings to meet women, rather than really being into the cause.'

'He sounds like a bit of a dick,' said Greg.

'Well, he's going to be Police Scotland's problem now, not the HET's,' said Mona. Greg snorted, a sound that could have been a laugh or could have been an expression of disbelief. 'What's that supposed to mean?'

'You're right. Attempted self-immolation in a public place sounds like a breach of the peace to me, and firmly in Police Scotland's remit. However,' he turned to face her and grinned. 'You've spent the last two weeks moping around Liz's flat, looking like the world was ending. Now you've got an interesting case to get your teeth into, and suddenly you've perked up no end. I don't see you leaving this one alone, whether it's any of your business or not.'

'I wasn't moping. I was sick.' She said it with a smile, which Greg returned, unaware of the nerve he had touched.

He was right. She *had* been moping.

He was right. She *was* worried that the world was ending.

'I think I might close my eyes for a minute or two,' said Mona.

Greg turned round again, his earlier flippancy replaced by worry. 'Are you OK? Do you need us to stop?'

'Fine, still just tiring easily,' she lied.

'Have you got enough room back there?' asked Liz. 'If that stuff is in the way, throw it on the floor.'

The back seat was crammed full of banners and leaflets that Liz was taking with her to the V8 demonstration, all of them emblazoned with the logo of the Health Collective, a trade union-backed pressure group of health staff, who were often at loggerheads with the government over official Virus policy. There was no way the Collective was going to miss out on a chance to get their message out when leaders from across the world were gathered in one place. Whether they would actually get a hearing was debatable. There hadn't been much evidence of it so far.

'I'm fine, really.'

By Mona's reckoning, she had less than two hours until she was in Edinburgh, and she still hadn't worked out what she was going to say to her colleagues about Bryce. As soon as she was back at work there was bound to be a debrief, and she needed to be clear what she could say to her bosses. Whoever her boss now was.

She'd had a certain understanding with Stuttle. She wouldn't go as far as saying she could rely on him, but he had certainly shown himself to be well aware of the realities of their work. Stuttle would have understood that nothing that had happened with Bryce was their fault, and that they had reacted as well as they could. She could have been honest with Stuttle, but now she had to deal with someone new. How would her new boss react if she gave him the unvarnished truth?

You remember Bryce, sir, that rogue IT officer, who was really a mole in the heart of the Health Enforcement Team? Well, he made it clear he's not working alone. Apparently, he has plenty of fellow travellers, some of whom are probably still bugging our communications. No, sir, he didn't tell us what it is he's actually trying to achieve, but to be honest he's not going to share that with the likes of me, is he? Anyway, the big news on the Bryce front is that he's dead, at least I think he is, you know how it is with brain trauma, leaves you a little uncertain about everything.

But one thing we do know is that things got a little out of hand with Bryce, and some people, some very unpleasant people, ended up dead. The only other person who knows about this, Blair Taylor, is the exception to the rule of Bryce working only with consummate professionals. Blair is the world's least competent terrorist, you'll know him if you see him, as he managed to destroy half his face with a home-made incendiary device. I don't know what I'm going to tell you, sir, but whatever it is, if Blair turns up, I could be in trouble.

'Is she asleep?' she heard Liz say softly to Greg.

She lay still, hoping that they wouldn't try to engage her in conversation. A debrief with Bernard and Paterson would be good for her. Keeping secrets was stressful and having her boss's view about what she should do would be very useful. She'd love to sit down with them both and offload onto them every single thing that Bryce had said to her. But she wouldn't.

Paterson and Bernard were good people, and she cared about them. She couldn't burden them with the knowledge that Bryce had given her. Bryce had told her things because he wanted to hurt her, and because he wanted her to be scared. Maybe he had lied; maybe what he had told her had no basis at all in real life. She hoped so.

She pictured Bryce's face, smug and smiling as he told her the fact that would ruin her life.

The Virus, Mona, it's man-made.

She'd told him he was wrong, shouting at him that he was making it up. It had to be a lie; it couldn't have even the smallest element of truth in it, because if it did, it meant that none of them was safe. No vaccine or immunity would protect the world against a virus that could be mutated at will.

But Bryce had just smiled his lazy, irritating smile, and told her to watch out for interesting developments in the developing world.

Keep your eye on Haiti, Mona.

Now all she could do was wait and watch the news. And pray.

4

'Where have you been?' Paterson glared at them, his head sticking out of his office door, all flat-top and fury.

'We had to stay for questioning about our experiences, Guv.' Maitland wandered towards his desk at a leisurely pace. 'Mauchline's colleagues interrogated us for ages about the stuff on the Royal Mile. What had we seen, was Boucher with anyone, and what had he been up to before it all kicked off? It took forever. We got out of there the second that we could.'

Paterson snorted. 'And hurried back here as fast as your legs would carry you, no doubt.'

'Is there something you need us to do, Mr Paterson?' asked Bernard, before his boss delved any further into their whereabouts for the last hour.

'Apart from the job that you get paid for?' He disappeared into his office and reappeared with his jacket in his hand. 'Well, actually, Bernard, yes, there is. Mauchline has summoned us all to a meeting.'

'Here or at the City Chambers?' asked Maitland.

'Neither. We're meeting him at St Ignatius' church.'

'Oh no, Guv. Have things got so bad that the only answer left to us is praying?'

'No, Maitland. Things have got so bad that it's the only venue left in Edinburgh that we can be sure hasn't been bugged by Bryce or his mates. Mauchline's mother is a key-holder for the church hall.'

'What does Mr Mauchline want to talk to us about that's so top secret?' asked Bernard.

'Who knows? But in my experience secret meetings never end particularly well for the North Edinburgh HET.'

St Ignatius was an imposing church on the Cowgate, its steeple towering above the surrounding tenements. A spacious stone-built structure, it was renowned for the quality of its internal acoustics. The hall, on the other hand, was a brick-built construction, its dimensions confined to a small footprint at the side of the church. It might have been considered cosy, were it not for the fact that the heating didn't appear to have been turned on in months. Bernard shivered and zipped up his coat.

Bryce and his colleagues would have to have been particularly zealous in their scoping out of the HET's connections to identify the parish church attended by the mother of the Deputy Chief Executive of the Scottish Health Enforcement Partnership as worthy of bugging. Bernard thought it highly unlikely that it would have been one of their priorities, but this didn't stop Mauchline and Paterson checking the underside of all the chairs and tables laid out in the hall. Once Mauchline had finished his security check, he gestured them to sit and opened the meeting.

'Thanks for getting everyone here, John. Mona is—?'

'Not back from her sick leave until tomorrow. I'll see she's fully briefed.'

'And Carole . . .?'

Paterson's eyebrows shot skyward. 'You really wanted her here?'

'No, definitely not. I was just checking she wasn't about to appear.'

'Credit me with some sense. She's having the afternoon off to recover from this morning's excitement.'

'OK. Well, guys, we have a problem.' He frowned. 'Or more exactly Carlotta Carmichael has a problem, which she's passed on to us.'

Carlotta Carmichael MSP was chair of the Virus Parliamentary Committee. When it came to making decisions about Virus policy in Scotland, she was second only to the First Minister. Bernard, and he assumed the rest of his colleagues, thought her a bully and borderline corrupt, wheeling and dealing for personal gain with the assistance of her husband, Jonathon. Carlotta, for her part, had made no attempt to disguise how much she loathed the North Edinburgh Health Enforcement Team, who had thwarted her schemes on several occasions, usually more by accident than design. It would appear, however, that her hatred didn't stop her calling on them when she needed to.

'The V8 are here for the week, as you know, staying at a variety of venues across the city, before all getting back on their private jets on Friday. Thursday night, Ms Carmichael is supposed to be bringing the proceedings to a close with a formal dinner – you know the kind of thing, nice food, lots of self-congratulatory speeches about how much they've all achieved.'

'Which in reality, will have been bugger all,' said Paterson.

'Anyway, given the current sensitivities around food—'

'You mean the price of food?' asked Bernard.

'Price, yes, but more than that. The inequalities of access to food, kiddies going to school hungry, that kind of thing. The protests we saw this morning are one extreme, but there's plenty of *Daily Mail* readers mouthing off about the government not doing enough to sort the situation out too. And people who really know about the issues aren't just worried about food *prices*, there's a whole food security issue as well. As a nation, we don't produce all the food we need. We import food, sometimes considerable distances. So, it's a massive issue if we fall out with one of our supplier countries, or if there's some issue that impacts on our distribution systems, you know, driver shortages or bad weather. All in all, access to affordable food is a massive political shitstorm. And ...' He laughed, shaking his head as he did so.

'What's so funny?' asked Paterson.

'I'm just experiencing an emotion I've never felt before. I'm feeling sorry for Ms Carmichael.'

'Really, sir?' Maitland's tone was one of disbelief, a feeling Bernard wholeheartedly shared.

'Yup. You've got this food disaster going on, protests, papers all over it, and Ms Carmichael somehow has to work out a way to feed the leaders of the V8 in a manner that isn't going to offend anyone in her home country but isn't going to make her look cheap in front of her counterparts. It's an impossible task.' He grinned, happily.

'My heart bleeds for her,' said Paterson. 'It really does.'

'Well, you're going to have to dig deeper into your reservoir of compassion, John, because there's more. The V8 are due to have their farewell meal at the City Chambers on Thursday. On Sunday afternoon, a refrigerated lorry full of food for the event left a warehouse facility in Glasgow. It never arrived in Edinburgh.'

'That's not possible. Surely these things have tracker chips in them?' asked Paterson. 'They must have measures to stop them getting nicked.'

'The tracker was disabled somewhere outside Bellshill. Since then, there's been no word of it.'

'A rogue lorry gone dark,' said Maitland. 'Very James Bond.'

'Our working theory is that it's less James Bond and more crusty. We think it's probably connected to the protests. And I don't have to tell you how embarrassing all this could be for Ms Carmichael, given the current regime of Consumable Purchase Restrictions.'

'What's Consumable Purchase Restriction?' asked Maitland.

Not for the first time, Bernard wondered if his colleague had ever watched a news bulletin in his life. 'What do you think the people this morning were protesting about?'

'Rationing,' he responded, promptly.

'They're the same thing!'

'Ah, Bernard, I have to correct you there,' said Mauchline. 'Ms Carmichael is very much at pains to say that we have not introduced rationing. Rationing involves everyone in the country being given a set amount of food that they have access to, giving them coupons or vouchers allowing them permission to purchase items. The country is very far from needing that kind of state intervention, and in fact all the Government has done—'

'—is give the supermarkets a huge bung to get them to place a limit on the number of items that each person can purchase.' Paterson finished his sentence for him, although not in the way that Bernard assumed it had actually been heading.

'That's a very cynical point of view, John. The Government has merely worked in close partnership with supermarkets to ensure that consumables are distributed in the most efficient and effective manner until this temporary upset in food distribution is resolved.'

'It's a bloody disgrace.' Paterson shook his head. 'People's lives being policed by checkout cashiers.'

'I do feel for the staff at Asda being on the sharp end of all this. But, back to the matter in hand. Nobody, even Ms Carmichael, could spin the loss of a lorry full of high-end food stuffs as an efficient and effective distribution of consumables. So, we need to track down the lorry.' Mauchline paused. 'And its driver.'

'Its driver?' Paterson's face had the expression it usually wore when Maitland was trying to explain his monthly timesheets to him. He looked suspicious, and Bernard couldn't work out why.

'Currently AWOL.'

'And let me guess, has missed a Health Check,' Paterson said. 'How convenient for Carlotta Carmichael.'

As usual, their boss had worked out what was going on long before they had. They would be tracking down this lorry driver under Health Enforcement law.

'Will we be working with Police Scotland on this?' Bernard asked.

'Good question, Bernard. I'm having difficulty getting an answer to that. Your usual CID colleagues seem, I don't know, preoccupied? I thought they'd be falling over themselves to help out but they're not prioritising it.'

Bernard felt his palms turn sweaty. *Operation Trigon.* Please God let the HET/CID Liaison not work out that he'd been spinning them a line.

'They're braver men than me if they're going to tell Carmichael that they're too busy to look for her food,' said Paterson.

'She's not got time to yell at anyone at the moment. She's running the whole V8 thing, trying to rearrange the catering, and doing it all without her Parliamentary Assistant, who everyone knows was the one who kept the whole show on the road.'

'Yep. We all miss Paul.' Paterson sighed.

Paul Shore, Carlotta's long-term assistant, had been shot by Bryce and had died in hospital. Paterson was firmly of the opinion that his injuries hadn't been life-threatening, and that his death had been more to do with his threat to spill the beans on some of his boss's dodgier schemes. People who upset Carlotta Carmichael did have a bad habit of ending up either dead or disgraced, and Bernard didn't fancy either option. He just didn't want to be anywhere near the woman, but here they were, yet again, doing her bidding.

He unzipped his coat. He was starting to feel hot, and maybe even a little faint. He could do with a glass of water and looked round to see if there was a kitchen.

Maitland elbowed him. 'Oi, loser. Pay attention.'

'I feel bad dumping this on you.' Mauchline passed over a sheet with the missing lorry driver's details, a cheery grin belying his words. 'I know you're busy with the holiday Defaulters.'

'Damn right we're busy. As soon as the government reopened international travel, everyone decided that a little thing like a scheduled Health Check wasn't going to stop them hitting the Greek islands the first second that they could.'

It was true. Every Health Defaulter they'd tracked down in the last week had had a glowing tan and a risible story about an unexpected illness that had prevented them from attending their Health Check.

'Well, this will be something a bit more interesting to get your teeth into.'

Paterson was skim reading the notes. 'Adam Stone. Couple of now spent convictions for shoplifting and breach of the peace as a teenager, then a blameless life. Never missed a Health Check until ...' He stopped and pulled his phone out to check the date. 'Until last week.

So, he missed a Health Check the week before he went missing?'

Mauchline shrugged. 'If that's what the paperwork says.'

'That's a bit risky, isn't it? If you're a protestor who's an essential part of a high-profile heist aimed at embarrassing the government, you'd keep your nose clean in the run-up to it. You wouldn't miss a Health Check and risk us landing on your doorstep just as you were setting off to pick up the lorry.'

'Good point.' Mauchline nodded thoughtfully. 'Ms Carmichael's going to be impressed with the fine quality of the investigative minds working on this.'

'Shut up. When are you wanting us to report back to you on all this?'

'Actually, I'm not.' He looked slightly rueful. 'Cameron's replacement has been identified.'

'Temporary replacement, I assume?' said Paterson.

'Of course, of course. Temporary until the investigation is at an end, and Cameron is vindicated.'

'This replacement then – who is he?'

'She. Jennifer Hunter.'

Paterson frowned. 'I don't recognise the name. Is she police?'

'No, career civil servant.' A look of mutual disgust passed between them, to Bernard's amusement. Personally, he thought it would be no bad thing if there was a more diverse range of people involved in SHEP's management structures. It might result in fewer people barking orders at him as if he was a trainee police constable.

'Rumour has it that she's very much one of Ms Carmichael's protégés, so tread carefully, John.'

'Noted.' Paterson sighed. 'Right, let's make a start on this nonsense.'

'Actually, can I have a word with you before you go?'

Paterson passed the paperwork to Bernard, who folded it carefully and placed it inside his jacket.

'You pair get the lorry driver's address checked out. And don't give me any of your *oh it's nearly four o'clock it's barely worth starting on this tonight*. I'm going to expect to see an update and a plan of action first thing tomorrow.'

Bernard followed Maitland towards the door, his colleague muttering, as predicted, about how close it would be to knocking off time by the time they got started. He ignored him and focused on trying to hear what Mauchline was saying to Paterson. Despite his best attempts, he couldn't make out the conversation beyond a couple of names.

Mona and Stuttle.

5

Mona stopped to catch her breath, leaning one hand against the nearest building. Someone turned round to stare at her, and she realised she was looking directly into a café. A couple of middle-aged women with plates of toasted sandwiches in front of them were giving her the evil eye, so she waved an apology, and walked on until she identified a less controversial resting place.

She found a blank bit of wall and leaned back against it, closing her eyes. When Liz had dropped her off at her flat, she'd given her strict instructions not to overdo it. *Give your body time to heal. Take it easy.* Mona had smiled and promised she would, her fingers firmly crossed behind her back. As soon as the car had pulled out of the street, she'd unlocked her front door, thrown her bag into the hall, and immediately set off to make a couple of house calls.

She needed to find Professor Alexander Bircham-Fowler. Until recently, the Professor had been the leading Scottish authority on the Virus. A decent man, he had insisted on cutting through the politicians' grandstanding on healthcare and attempted to keep them focused on facts rather than politically expedient fictions. This approach had very nearly cost him his reputation, if not his life. He had recently retired, prompted not just by disillusionment with the political environment but also by the fact that his Virus study had been going nowhere.

Over the last year his research had yielded results that made no sense, throwing up contradictory findings that had the Professor questioning his abilities.

Mona thought his departure had been premature. Amongst the many nuggets of information Bryce had imparted to her, he had implied that the Professor knew something that made him dangerous to the politicians. The only problem was, Bircham-Fowler hadn't worked out what the gold buried in the dirt actually was. Somewhere in the muddled findings of his research was a clue to what was really going on. If anyone could stop the bad thing that Bryce was predicting in Haiti, it was the Professor.

Unfortunately, her first attempt at finding him had drawn a blank. She'd headed directly to the Professor's former PA's house. Theresa Kilsyth watched over the Professor like a hawk, protecting him as best she could from the malevolent forces that surrounded him. Mona wasn't sure whether Mrs Kilsyth considered her to *be* one of these malevolent forces, but either way, there was no engaging with the Professor without getting her onside first. Mona had gone to her flat to talk to her, half hoping that the Professor might be there as well. Instead, she got a closed door, and a discreet peak through the letter box showed a pile of mail lying on the hall floor. Theresa clearly hadn't been there for some time.

So, now she was heading, slowly and breathlessly, in the direction of the Professor's house, deep in the Grange area of Edinburgh. She turned into his street, lined on either side with solid stone-built villas. It was deserted, so she walked up his garden path and hammered on the door. This brought no response, and after a quick look round to check she wasn't being watched, she knelt down to look through the letter box.

'He's not there.'

A woman's voice came from behind her, and she scrambled to her feet, her head swimming slightly with the sudden movement.

'I'm a neighbour.' The woman was around Mona's age, casually dressed in jeans and a long, beige woollen cardigan. 'I've not seen him for a while. I think he's gone on holiday.'

'Oh, I see.' From the pile of post she'd seen she'd figured as much. The Professor had gone somewhere, probably with Mrs Kilsyth. But was it a vacation, or was he hiding from something?

'I could pass on a message if you like?' The woman tilted her head to one side, her long dark hair falling forward as she did so.

'No, it wasn't anything important.' She joined the woman on the pavement, closing the gate firmly behind her. 'Thank you anyway.'

She gave the woman a bright smile, which was returned in kind, then walked as swiftly as she could to the corner of the street, steeling herself not to look back. Once she turned the corner she stopped, gave it a minute then peered round. The woman was on her mobile, staring back at the Professor's house. After a second she hung up and crossed the street, getting into a blue Mondeo parked diagonally opposite. Mona watched the woman get in, waiting for her to turn the engine on and pull away from the kerb. The car didn't move.

Neighbour, my arse, thought Mona. The Professor's house was under surveillance. He wasn't on holiday, and unfortunately, it looked like she wasn't the only one looking for him.

She walked on, ignoring the dull ache in her head that was threatening to turn into a full-blown migraine. Her phone beeped, and she saw that Paterson had been in touch with an instruction to phone *our mutual friend*, complete with a mobile number and a cryptic instruction to *use BF.*

Use BF? she texted back.

Burner phone, obviously.

She'd have a talk to the Guv about phonetics when she got back, but she got the point he was making, and pulled out the cheap pay-as-you-go mobile she'd been using for any sensitive conversations.

Stuttle answered on the first ring. 'Mona, lovely to hear from you.'

This was not the usual response she got when she phoned him. His customary method of answering calls was to snap *this better be murderously urgent.* She felt a momentary sadness about his change of circumstance.

'Mr Paterson told me to give you a ring.'

'Yes, I was hoping you might be free for a bit of a powwow tonight.'

'OK, no problem.' She'd no plans for the evening, beyond an early night. 'Any particular focus to our discussion?'

He laughed. 'Getting me my job back! And tackling corruption at the highest levels etc. etc.' His tone became serious. 'I'll be sure to remember any help that you give me here, Mona. I haven't forgotten our earlier conversations about getting you improved security clearance. Everyone can see you're wasted chasing down junkies for Health Checks. I could use you here.'

It was going to have to be one hell of a good powwow to get Stuttle back to being in a position to bribe her with job offers. And history had shown that Stuttle wasn't great at delivering on his promises. He'd already promised her improved security clearance, which had not, as yet, materialised. Yet in spite of her misgivings, she found herself agreeing to meet. 'Am I coming to your house, sir?'

'No. We thought some discretion might be in order. I'll text you the venue details.'

He hung up, and a second later her phone bleeped. She read the address in disbelief.

Really? she thought. *We're meeting there? What am I supposed to wear?*

6

'You really think this is it?' Maitland's head was bobbing between looking at the white terraced council house in front of them, and the paperwork that Mauchline had given them.

'Yes, why wouldn't it be?' Bernard was doing his best to keep a lid on his irritation. Maitland had whinged non-stop since they'd left St Ignatius, keeping up a steady diatribe outlining how unfair it was that they were being sent on a mission that was clearly going to run on past five o'clock. Bernard wondered how Maitland had ever survived his time in the police, a profession not generally noted for clocking off on the dot of five. When the Virus eventually ran its course and his colleague resumed his police career, he was in for a rude (re)awakening.

Maitland went on staring at the paperwork, so Bernard opened the gate and walked in. If he was honest with himself, part of the irritation wasn't aimed at Maitland. He too, was irked that tonight, of all nights, it was going to be a late finish. His plan for the day had been: get marshalling gig over and done with, find some paperwork that needs shuffling, keep head down, get out of the office by five at the latest, go home, rehearse Riot Act to be read to estranged wife. It was going to be bad enough when he landed unannounced on Carrie's doorstep, without his being less than a hundred per cent sure of what he was going to say.

'Bernie, wait.' Maitland hurried to catch up with him, looking round the garden as he walked. 'This can't be it.'

'Why not?'

'Because we're looking for a crusty, and whoever lives here, it's not one of them.'

'We're not looking for a "crusty", as you so inelegantly put it; we're looking for someone who is potentially an activist, or at the very least sympathetic to the aims of the V8 protestors.'

Maitland snorted. 'Bit more than just sympathetic. The guy was willing to hijack a lorry on their behalf.'

'OK, fair point, but activists come in all shapes and sizes, and they don't all live in inner-city squats or rambling country farm houses . . . .' He looked round the garden. It was extremely well maintained.

'Adam Stone is a 54-year-old lorry driver, living in a house he's bought off the Council; his garden has an immaculate lawn, a bird feeder, a water feature, there's even a gnome over there, for Christ's sake . . . .'

Bernard followed his gaze. There was indeed a red-hatted gnome with a fishing rod sitting next to the miniature fountain.

'Where's the posters in the window complaining about things? Where's the solar panels on the roof? Where's the—'

'You have a very narrow idea of what an activist looks like. And the Virus has brought all kinds of people out on the streets who wouldn't normally get involved.'

Maitland let out a cry of frustration. 'We're not talking *get involved*. We're talking *steal a lorry!*'

'Well, whoever he is, I don't think he's in, otherwise he'd have appeared to see what we were arguing about.' Bernard pressed the doorbell, which played a jaunty metallic tune.

Maitland stepped off the path and pressed his face up against the window.

'Oi, what are you doing?'

They turned to see a heavy-set man at the end of the path, staring at them in a manner that suggested he considered them Up To No Good.

'Official business.' Maitland waved his ID in the general direction of their questioner, who paused for a moment before taking to his heels. Bernard suspected there was about to be an urgent phone call made to Mr Stone about the goings on on his garden path.

'Let's go,' he said. 'Adam Stone clearly isn't here.'

They turned out of the street to see a bus speed past them. Maitland took off after it at a run. Bernard followed his example, and much to his annoyance did not manage to overtake him before they reached the stop. One of the few pleasures that Bernard had in his dealings with Maitland was the fact that he was so much fitter than his colleague, due to his previous career as a professional badminton player. Obviously life at the HET was taking its toll on his fitness as well as everything else. He no longer trained every day, and alcohol and junk food had slowly and persistently worked their way into his life. He needed to get on top of things again.

They climbed the stairs. Bernard found a window seat, and Maitland took the chair in front, turning round to face him. Bernard had the horrible realisation that his colleague intended to chat all the way back. Judging by the thoughtful expression on his face, Maitland had something he wanted to discuss. Bernard hoped to God it was nothing to do with how his ex-wife's baby had been conceived. Maitland had never really mastered the concept of an indoor voice, and he didn't want the whole

47

of the upper deck of the Number 8 treated to his theories about artificial insemination.

'What's your thoughts about the stuff in the news about vaccines, Bernie?'

He heaved an internal sigh of relief. This was safe ground. 'I'm a little sceptical that they've actually developed a working model.'

'But you do think they'll get there?'

'Oh yes. I think they've come on leaps and bounds. I'd imagine they'll come up with something workable pretty soon.'

'Hmm.' His colleague tapped the metal top of the chair, sending little reverberations along it. 'So, what does this mean for the HET? Will they still need us?'

This thought had occurred to Bernard as well. 'They're still going to need us for a while. But, I suppose, if this vaccine does actually work, eventually we'll be out of business. Which, personally, I'm quite looking forward to.'

Maitland grunted.

'Aren't you looking forward to it? I thought you'd be desperate to get back to the police.'

'I am. I'm just a bit out of practice with proper police work.'

It looked like Bernard wasn't the only one who was worried about being match fit.

'You'll soon get back into the swing of it.'

'Yeah, but the lucky bastards who weren't seconded into the HETs will have two years' head start on me when it comes to promotion and things. Nobody's really going to value the experience we've had in the HET, are they?'

He shrugged. 'I don't know. You'd probably be better talking to Mona.'

'So, Mona is back tomorrow then?'

'Yes, that's what she said earlier. Hopefully she's feeling better.'

'Well, I for one will be pleased to see her.'

Bernard looked at him in surprise. He hadn't thought that Maitland was much of a Mona fan. For one thing, he had to do a lot more work when she was around to nag him.

Maitland continued on his theme. 'Yup, once she is back I want a conversation with her and Paterson about tying up all the things coming out of Bryce's death.'

A knot of fear formed in Bernard's stomach. The last thing he needed was any further discussion of what had really happened with Bryce. 'What things?'

'What really went on in the factory between Mona and Bryce. What all the gunshots were that we heard. And most importantly, what we're going to say to Blair Taylor's parents. You saw the state they were in when we interviewed them. They don't know if their son is alive or dead, and we do know that he's alive, and I think someone needs to tell them that.'

Bernard's heart was beating so fast he had to slow down to be able to speak. 'We can't tell them that.'

'Why?'

'Because he might still not want to see them, or they might be even more horrified to find out what he's done. He's on the run, remember? He's going to be up on terrorism charges if the police catch up with him.'

All of this was true, although none of it was his real motivation. His main concern was for his own skin. The last thing he wanted was any involvement with Bryce's friends, to whom Blair was their only remaining link. He hated what he had become since he joined the HET. The kind of person who would let two grieving parents suffer.

49

'Whatever. I'm still taking this up with Mona.'

'OK, but she won't be happy. Why have we stopped moving?'

Maitland twisted round and looked out the window. 'Roadworks.'

'I wish the bus would get a move on. I need to get home.'

His colleague grinned. 'Oh yeah, your "work thing". Does it involve your ex-wife by any chance?'

Bernard didn't answer, and his colleague burst out laughing. 'Lying to your girlfriend, you dog. Welcome to the real world of grown-up relationships.'

'Shut up.'

7

Bernard was trying to figure out which of the many uncomfortable things about this situation was bothering him most. There was the uncertainty, of course, a state that he never dealt with well. His wife might be having his baby, probably wasn't, but it remained enough of a possibility for him to need to rule it out completely. There was the possibility of conflict; actually, more like *certainty* of conflict, when he raised the subject with Carrie, and Bernard was nothing if not conflict averse. But at this precise moment, all he could think about was how rude it felt to be turning up unannounced.

If Maitland was here, he would, no doubt, be pointing out that the tenement that Bernard was currently staring at contained a flat upon which he was still paying a mortgage – the whole mortgage, not just a share of it. He would also, no doubt, suggest that, given that fact, it didn't seem unreasonable to be popping by for a chat about the future. But Maitland wasn't here, and all Bernard could do was steel his nerve and resolve not to agree to go away if she didn't want to speak to him. He pressed the buzzer. Carrie picked up almost immediately.

'Uh right, OK, hi, Carrie, it's Bernard.'

There was no response. He was on the point of clarifying whether she could actually hear him when she finally spoke. 'What do you want?'

Her tone wasn't unpleasant, more surprised. Heartened by this fact he pressed on. 'We need to talk. Can I come in?'

'I really don't think that's a good idea.'

Her tone remained gentle, so he pressed on. 'It'll only take five minutes.'

Without responding she buzzed him in. He ran up the stairs and found the flat door open. The hall looked almost exactly the same as when he had lived there, the main change being the *Mamas and Papas* boxes spread across the floor.

'You've been shopping.'

'Well, unless the baby is happy to sleep in a drawer, I needed to buy a few things.'

He wondered where she was getting the money from. Had she got a job? Was there a father for this child who was contributing to its upkeep?

'Do you want a cup of tea or anything?' she asked.

'No, no. I'm OK.' He followed Carrie into the living room, and sat down in what had, once upon a time, been his favourite armchair. It currently had a copy of *What to Expect When You're Expecting* balanced on its arm. He picked it up. 'This takes me back.'

Carrie looked pained, and he felt a sudden stab of anger. 'Are we just supposed to pretend that you haven't already had a child? Our child?'

'I just can't think about that at the moment.'

'You can't think about Jamie? Because I think about him every day.' His tone was sharp. Carrie stared at him for a second, then raised her hand to her face and started to cry. As quickly as it had arrived, his anger evaporated, replaced with a desperate desire to comfort his wife. 'I'm sorry. I wasn't trying to upset you.'

She nodded her acknowledgment of this. 'Please don't think I've forgotten about Jamie. It's just that I can't think about him because if I did, I'd fall apart, and then I'd be no good to this little one.' She stood, awkwardly pushing herself up off the sofa, picked up a box of tissues and returned to her seat. 'I'm just anxious all the time, Bernard.'

'Which is exactly why I didn't want to have another . . . you know what. This isn't the time. We are where we are.' He paused before going in with the killer question. 'Is the baby mine, Carrie?'

She didn't look up. 'We weren't together when I got pregnant, Bernard, you know that.'

'Yeah, but you could have . . . I don't know . . .' He tailed off, unable to quite vocalise the scenario he'd been picturing. The silence between them stretched on. Carrie was crying properly now, her head buried in her hands. Any ideas he had had about laying down the law had disappeared. 'Please don't get upset. I'm just worried about you. Are you OK, Carrie?'

Her shoulders heaved, and without looking up she spoke. 'I'm scared, Bernard.'

With two swift steps he was across the living room and sitting next to her on the sofa, a comforting arm around her shoulder. She cuddled into him for a second, then pushed him gently away. 'My blood pressure is through the roof. If it's not down tomorrow they're taking me into hospital. What if I lose this baby, Bernard? It'll be just like Jamie all over again.'

His stomach lurched as the memories came flooding back. *A hospital room. Kind but exhausted nurses. The slowly dawning realisation that their baby son wasn't going to make it.* 'It's not going to be like that. What time is your appointment tomorrow?'

'8.30.' She sniffed.

'Right, I'll swing by with the car and take you there.'

'What about work?'

'I'll tell them I'll be late. They'll be fine about it.' They wouldn't, but he'd deal with that later. The most important thing right now was to keep Carrie calm. He got to his feet. 'I'm going to head off but promise me that you'll go and have a nice relaxing bath and get an early night.'

'I promise.' She smiled up at him. 'Thank you, Bernard.'

He ran back down the stairs and continued homeward at a light jog. He was halfway to his flat by the time he realised two things. One, Carrie hadn't actually come out and told him definitively that he was not the father, and two, he hadn't made it clear that he was taking Carrie to her appointment just as a concerned friend, nothing more. He hadn't mentioned Lucy at all. It might not have been good for Carrie's blood pressure to learn that he had moved on, so perhaps that was for the best. He could raise the issue of his new girlfriend at some point in the future when things were a bit less fraught. It would all be fine.

Probably.

8

'You're wearing a skirt.' Paterson eyed her with surprise. 'Did I miss a memo on the dress code for this evening's meeting?'

'I just thought that seeing as we were going to an institution that should have died out in the Victorian era I'd dress appropriately.'

'Good. Because if you're dressing to fit in, you shouldn't have bothered. There's not going to be anyone quite like you in there.'

They both contemplated the ornately carved Masonic Hall.

'Have you been in here before, Guv?'

'Would you think less of me if I said, yes, on many, many occasions?'

'I'm going to assume that's because the beer is cheap. Is Stuttle a member of this Lodge?'

'He was a little bit evasive on that point. He said a friend had arranged for us to have a room here. But I would imagine if he's not a member of this Lodge, he's a member of another one.'

'And yet he is where he is.'

Paterson shrugged. 'The Virus has changed things. The people who thought they were in charge are getting a bit of a wake-up call. And cheap beer aside, I'd be very happy to see this kind of place crumble and die. Anyway, are we going in?' He held open the door and gestured her through. 'Ladies first.'

'Very funny.'

Stuttle was waiting in the Reception area. 'John, Mona, good to see you.'

Mona was relieved to see that despite his current circumstances, Stuttle did not look remotely down-trodden. He looked focused and energetic, and was considerably more casually dressed than she was.

'Mauchline's waiting for us upstairs.'

'Do we need to sign in?' Paterson had his Green Card in his hand, looking for the box to validate it.

'Not today.' He grinned. 'Thought it best we keep this meeting on the down low. Come on, this way.'

They followed him up the stairs, and into a function room that was deserted apart from one table in the middle, currently occupied by Mauchline and several empty pint glasses. He nodded to them as they sat down.

'So,' said Stuttle. 'I'm assuming I can rely on your discretion.'

'Of course,' said Paterson. 'As long as you're not planning to involve us in anything that is actually criminal.'

'As if, John, as if.' He grinned. 'This is all strictly above board. I'm not intending to give in to Ms Carmichael's plans to hang me out to dry without a fight, but I'm also keen to avoid giving her any chance to put me in prison, as opposed to just putting me out to grass. So.' He thumped the table, and Mona wondered exactly how much real ale had been consumed before she arrived. 'We need a plan to get me reinstated.'

'And we need to move quickly,' Mauchline chipped in. 'Cam is currently on gardening leave, while he's being investigated.'

Stuttle snorted. 'And by investigation, we mean giving Carlotta time to come up with a reasonable explanation as to why her parliamentary assistant getting shot was my fault.'

'True.' Mauchline nodded. 'And our colleagues at the Parliament may be assisting with her enquiries in a way that ensures that no-one on their team takes any of the blame for Paul getting shot during an evacuation of their building. But it's much easier for Cam to keep his job if we can resolve all this while he is still technically in the post, rather than him being found at fault and sacked. It's not impossible that we could get an investigation finding overturned if we can identify that it was carried out inappropriately, but that would have to be done publicly. Our best chance is to put some pressure on Carlotta while the investigation is still live.'

'Put some pressure on?' queried Mona.

'Blackmail her,' said Paterson. 'That's what you mean, isn't it?' He sat back in his chair, shaking his head. 'I'm not sure I'm happy with this, Cam. Blackmailing a member of the Scottish Parliament? That's got the potential to get us all sacked, at the very least, if not imprisoned. Carlotta's pretty good at defending herself. The last person we know who fell out with Carlotta is now enjoying a "promotion" in one of the less developed bits of the developing world, and I don't know about you, but my other half is not going to take kindly to being relocated to the Democratic Republic of Africa.'

Mona had never met Mrs Stuttle, but she was pretty sure that a move to Africa was not going to be welcomed by her. She shared this point of view, but unlike Paterson she was intrigued enough to want to know more. 'I'm not in favour of "blackmail", obviously, but I'm assuming you were planning something a bit less blatant?'

'Of course.' Stuttle grinned. 'And the one good thing about Carlotta is she does give us plenty of opportunity for identifying areas where a bit of pressure could be applied.'

'And you have some particular area in mind?' she asked.

Stuttle nodded. 'Paul Shore, God rest his soul, was very helpful in identifying what Carlotta was up to with regard to the development of a vaccine for the Virus.'

Paterson was looking increasingly agitated. 'And that's what got him killed! As soon as he decided that he was going to make a clean breast of his dodgy dealing in the development of the vaccine, his non-life-threatening injuries took a sudden turn for the worse.' He got to his feet. 'I'm out. Come on, Mona.'

She didn't get up.

'Mona. See sense.' Paterson stared at her.

'I hear what you're saying, Guv, I just think that under the circumstances it wouldn't hurt to—'

'Fine.' He turned on his heel. 'But leave me out of this.'

She watched him leave, torn between the common sense of what he had said, and the excitement she felt at being part of Stuttle's plan. When she turned back both Stuttle and Mauchline were staring at her.

'I'm in, sir. What did you have in mind?'

'I'm thinking we use the Paul Shore stuff.'

Mauchline frowned. 'I don't actually know the ins and outs of Shore's involvement.'

'Apologies, Fraser, I was forgetting you weren't in that particular loop.' Stuttle grinned. 'One of the key bits of information that Paul Shore gave us was that both him and Carlotta, and Carlotta's immediate family, had all been given an early dose of the vaccine. To me this shows a very inappropriate use of resources. Why should they have access to the vaccine when the rest of the population still hasn't been given it? Why has Carlotta's husband been given this potential lifesaver, when we've got individuals out there at much higher risk? It's not going to play well with the electorate. I say we put the pressure on her about us going public with that fact.'

'Sounds a good plan, sir,' said Mona. 'What do you need us for?'

'I believe you have built up a good relationship with one of the other people who received the vaccine?'

'You mean Catriona McBride?'

'Exactly. We need her onside. A sworn testimony from her about the circumstances under which she was given the vaccine would greatly strengthen our case.'

Mona thought back to the Guv's comments about people ending up dead. 'Would we be putting her in any danger, do you think?'

Stuttle's face betrayed a slight irritation. 'No, no. Your boss, as usual, is overstating the implications. I'm not as convinced as he is about Paul's death being suspicious.'

'Can I think about it overnight?'

The irritated look deepened briefly, before being replaced by Stuttle's usual courteous mask. 'Of course, of course. I don't want to pressure you. But, as Fraser said, time is of the essence?'

'Absolutely, sir.'

She headed back towards the entrance, playing the conversation over again in her mind. She could have done without having to make difficult ethical decisions on her first day back; her head was seriously aching now, a sure sign that despite all the warnings she had been given, she had definitely overdone it. She'd go home, take two of the heavy-duty painkillers she'd been given and hopefully sleep solidly for eight hours. Come morning, Paterson would have plenty to say on the issue, she was sure, but she was clear on one thing. She wasn't letting Carlotta get away with sacking Stuttle. Mona hadn't managed to save Paul, but if anyone had a plan for stopping the Minister for Virus Policy, she wanted to be part of it.

TUESDAY

À LA CARTE

I

Mona bounded up the stairs of the Cathcart Building, eager to get to her desk. After two weeks' sick leave, she was anticipating several hundred emails, most of which could safely be deleted unread. Also, according to Paterson, Stuttle's replacement started today, and was planning an early morning visit to the HET. Why they were so high on her list of priorities she wasn't quite sure, but no doubt it related to the missing lorry driver that Paterson had mentioned. Whatever Jennifer Hunter's motivation in visiting them, it wouldn't do any harm to be in the office, looking keen, when she turned up.

The sound of female voices floated out into the landing. *Crap.* The new boss was already here, and as the only other female on the team was Carole, she would be getting a less than positive introduction to the team. Picking up her pace, Mona did a quick mental preparation of how she could undo the damage and opened the door with a cheerful but also professional smile. She managed two steps into the room before her carefully positioned smile gave way to an expression of surprise. There were two women in the room, just not the two that Mona had been expecting. Carole wasn't talking to their new boss, but she was talking to someone that Mona knew very well indeed.

'What are you doing here?' She threw a quick panicked look over her shoulder. 'You can't be here.

Seriously, we can talk later or something, but you just can't be here at the moment. Carole, you shouldn't have let her in.'

This provoked sighs from the other women. Carole walked behind her and closed the door.

'Honestly, Elaine,' said Mona, 'our new boss is coming over this morning, and however much you want to talk to me it's just going to have to wait.'

'Darling, lovely as it is to see your face again, I'm not actually here to see you.'

Mona felt confused, annoyed and a tiny bit disappointed, all at the same time. These emotions were quickly overtaken by her continuing anxiety about Stuttle's replacement arriving. 'OK, but you still need to get out of here, because if our boss walks in to find Cassandra Doom, shock jock, columnist, and all-round scourge of the HETs hanging out in our office, she's going to have us all shot!'

'I don't care,' said Carole. 'Anyway, I invited Cassandra—'

'Call me Elaine, darling. Cassie is strictly for print and radio only.'

'I invited Elaine to come and talk about my situation.'

Elaine smiled and levered herself up onto Mona's desk. She sat there swinging her legs and revealing several inches of thigh. Mona tried and failed not to look, catching Elaine's eye as she did.

'Have you missed me then, Mona?'

'There was never anything to miss,' Mona said, quickly. 'And please don't go interfering in the work of the HETs. Life is hard enough as it is.'

'I can't help it! Poor Carole here has been enslaved by the Health Enforcement Team. The world needs to hear about it.'

Carole nodded. 'Sorry, Mona, but my picture was in all the papers yesterday, with loads of people saying I should get a medal or something, but nowhere in any of the stories was there a mention that I don't want to be here.' She shrugged. 'I don't want a medal, I just want to leave. So, I got in touch with Cass— Elaine, to put my side of the story.'

'Couldn't you do the interview in a coffee shop?'

'But it's so much better to see Carole here engaged in her servitude. Do you want to give me a quote for the story?' She smiled sweetly.

Without a word, Mona fled back into the hallway. She headed to the ladies and resolved to stay there until Elaine was safely off the premises. She'd rather be late than get caught up in Carole's Machiavellian schemes to get out of the HET. After a couple of minutes, she heard the office door slam, followed by Elaine's heels clattering down the stairs. She waited a moment to be sure they were gone, then headed back to the office, relieved that she now had the place to herself.

She finally made it to her desk, turned on her PC, and the device slowly began to download a fortnight's worth of correspondence. There was a lingering fragrance in the air, which she recognised as Elaine's signature perfume. Well, it was good that she was gone. Mona had already passed on the opportunity to have a relationship with Elaine, due to her reluctance to get involved with someone who wrote a tabloid column every week which decried asylum seekers, benefit cheats, and any government agency that attempted to restrict the liberty of the British public, by, say, ensuring they had a monthly Health Check. She was pretty sure that Elaine didn't believe everything she wrote, but Mona wasn't sure if that made her behaviour better or worse.

Elaine was definitely trouble. She might have helped them out with the occasional problem in the past but in general she was no friend to the HETs, and judging by her current engagement with Carole, it didn't look as if she was planning to give them any positive coverage in the near future. So, she should put all thoughts of Elaine out of her mind, which was actually quite difficult with the scent of Chanel No 5 pervading the office, and focus on her emails. She wouldn't be seeing her again.

Her eyes had strayed over to where Elaine had been sitting and alighted on a notebook with a striking green and blue William Morris cover lying on the table. She picked it up and leafed through it but found herself unable to read the contents, hampered by her lack of knowledge of Pitman's shorthand. She'd probably be doing the world a favour if she threw it straight in the bin, but her conscience wouldn't let her do that. Would Elaine still be on the premises? She grabbed it and ran, making it down the first flight of stairs before pulling up as she heard Paterson talking to someone. A second later he appeared, two steps ahead of a woman in her late thirties. She was small, with brown hair pulled into a bun, and dark brown eyes that were looking at her surroundings as she climbed.

'Mona,' said Paterson. 'Going somewhere?'

'Ehm, no sir, just heading to the office. You must be Ms Hunter.' She held out a hand, and after a second her new boss took it.

'Good to meet you,' she said. 'Let's get up to the office and meet the rest of the team. I need to be back out of here by 9.15 at the latest.'

Mona let them pass, then sneaked a discreet look at her phone. It was already after 9 – where was everyone?

Paterson ushered his new boss into their office, keeping up a steady monologue as he did so. 'And this is the North Edinburgh HET office. We only have the one room in the building – apart from us it's all health staff based here. My office, such as it is, is here.' He gestured to the MDF structure that cordoned off approximately a quarter of the room into a private space for their Team Leader. 'Not very pretty, but it does the job.' He laughed. Jennifer Hunter did not.

'Where is everyone?' She pulled back the sleeve of her jacket to check the time on what appeared to be a very nice watch. 'Are you the only one here?'

Behind Ms Hunter's back she could see Paterson silently urging her to come up with some reasonable explanation for the absence of staff.

'Carole was definitely here earlier, and Bernard is never late, so it may be that he's out looking for a Defaulter, and, oh, here's Maitland now.'

'You're late,' snapped Ms Hunter.

Mona silently willed Maitland not to make some smart-arse reply. Fortunately, even he seemed to grasp that now was not the time and muttered an apology. He looked round the office. 'Where's Bernard? He's never late.'

'Well, I'm absolutely delighted that the first time your reliably punctual colleague is late it's on the day that I'm due to meet you all.' She shot another look at her watch. 'I have literally three minutes now until I have to leave for my next meeting. John, I think we need to have a discussion about how this team is being managed.'

Paterson muttered something not quite audible, and threw a dirty look at Maitland, who shuffled from foot to foot.

'Can I at least have an update on where you are at finding the lorry driver?'

'Ah, yeah,' said Maitland, clearly delighted that he at last had a question he could answer. 'He wasn't in.'

'And?'

Maitland returned to looking uncomfortable. 'And we don't know why.'

'Where else have you looked for him?'

'Ma'am, if I may,' said Paterson, making a desperate attempt to regain control, 'we were only given his details late yesterday afternoon, and we haven't had time to meet to discuss possible options—'

'Well, discuss it now,' she snapped. 'What's your next move?'

There was a brief silence. 'We go to his place of work?' said Maitland, wavering between a question and a statement.

'Yes, you go to his place of work! And do it now. Ms Carmichael has been very clear that finding the lorry driver, and the lorry, are her key priorities.'

'So, she's got Police Scotland looking for him too?' Mona knew the answer to this, but wanted to see what Hunter said.

'The lorry driver is first and foremost a Health Defaulter, so the HET will be leading on finding him.' The answer came quickly, obviously pre-prepared. 'And you should talk to me before involving anyone outside this team in the search.'

'But—' began Maitland.

'I need to go.' She turned to Paterson. 'I need to speak to Carole Brooks. Tell her to get in touch, if she actually bothers to turn up at any point.'

'I'll show you out,' Paterson opened the door.

'Don't bother. It's more important that you stay here and try to turn the remnants of your workforce into something approaching a team.'

Without any further leaving taking, she was gone. Mona prepared herself for a bollocking, undeserved in her opinion, but Paterson looked more fed up than furious.

'God save me from civil servants.' He disappeared into his office, leaving Maitland and Mona staring at each other.

'Thought we were for it,' Maitland said.

'I don't think the Guv can even be arsed to yell at us anymore.'

Maitland smiled. 'I'm going to head out to the lorry company. I'll phone Bernard en route, unless you fancy a trip?'

'No, thanks.'

'What's this?' He picked up Elaine's notebook. 'Are you keeping a diary?'

'No.' She grabbed it back. 'It's not mine. I need to return it.' The thought of returning it to its owner gave her a tiny thrill of anticipation, before common sense reasserted itself. It would probably be for the best if she just dropped the notebook back to reception at Elaine's office.

The door opened, and Bernard appeared. 'So sorry I'm late. Did I miss anything?'

2

'So, that was our new boss? I can't believe I was late.' Bernard's stomach churned and he stopped for a moment to catch his breath, before hurrying after his colleague. 'Was she annoyed?'

'Furious is the word I'd use. Where were you, anyway? You're usually irritatingly punctual all the time.'

'I don't see how being punctual could be considered irritating. It's just good manners. Being late on the other hand...' He'd spent more time than he cared to remember waiting for Maitland to turn up.

'So, what happened this morning? Did you sleep in?'

He could have agreed with this, and, aside from a lot of sarcasm, that would have been an end to the matter. But there was some part of Bernard that wanted to unburden himself, and, unfortunately he couldn't think of anyone else to discuss the matter with. 'I went with Carrie to an ante-natal appointment.'

'What the—' Maitland stopped walking and spun round. 'Why? Are you literally insane?'

'I know, it probably wasn't a wise move, but her blood pressure is really high and she's worried about losing the baby. My baby, possibly.'

'And at any point in this lovely family outing, did she actually confirm that the baby is yours?'

'No.'

'So, you're jeopardising your relationship with Lucy in

order to support your ex-wife through her pregnancy with someone else's child?'

'I'm not jeopardising my relationship.'

'Did Lucy know about this early morning trip?'

He didn't say anything.

'Ha! I knew it,' said Maitland, a note of triumph in his voice. 'And I can't believe I'm going to say this, Bernie, but that is a level of arseholery that even I wouldn't participate in.'

Bernard was regretting his earlier candour. 'We're here.'

They had made it to the haulier's firm, which was located surprisingly close to Adam Stone's house. Bernard wondered if he'd moved there to be close to his work or taken the job because it was close to home. As they walked through the yard, a man passed him who looked slightly familiar, although he couldn't place him. He seemed to provoke the same reaction in the man, who stopped to give him a second look before hurrying off.

'Excuse me.' Maitland stuck his head into a door that was open on the side of the industrial unit. 'Looking to talk to the boss. Is he around?'

'She.' A short woman stepped out into the yard. Despite the rough and ready surroundings, she was perfectly made up, and her hair was immaculate. She pointed at herself with a long pink fingernail. 'Julia Conlon. I run this place.'

'We're here from the Health Enforcement Team. We're looking for Adam Stone.'

'He's not here,' she said quickly, eyeing Bernard's ID with a degree of suspicion. 'I can't help you.'

'We need to track him down,' said Maitland. 'Do you have any idea where he might be just now?'

She shrugged. 'Try his home.'

'We already did. When was the last time you saw Mr Stone?'

'Not for over a week. He's been ...' She stopped herself, and her eyes flicked back in the direction of Bernard's ID. He was pretty sure she'd been about to say that he was on holiday before she'd had a sudden thought that maybe her employee had missed a Health Check and she was about to dump him in it.

'Oi!' They both turned, and Bernard saw the man he'd passed earlier running towards him. It fell into place where he'd seen him – at the end of Stone's garden path, asking them what they were doing there. The man was being pursued by a shorter, sturdy individual with a healthy all-over tan, which was already starting to peel at the top of his bald head: *Mr Stone, I presume.*

'You were at my house!' Bernard had a close-up view of the man's bronzing, as he strode past the other man, coming to a halt disturbingly close to his face. 'I've done nothing wrong.'

'Apart from miss a Health Check.' Maitland appeared behind Bernard.

'Oh, you're that bunch of f—'

'Adam!' Julia Conlon also appeared at his side, and he was struck by the irony that despite their being in a very large yard, all five of them seemed to be crammed into a square metre.

Adam Stone looked at the three of them, then turned away, shaking his head. 'I'm saying nothing.'

'Ms Conlon, having Health Defaulters on your staff is the kind of thing that could trigger an HMRC investigation into your organisation.'

Bernard wondered if this was actually true. He had no memory of reading this anywhere in the legislation, and he was pretty sure he had read the relevant statutes in much greater detail than his colleague. The assertion did, however, appear to be having the desired effect. Julia Conlon was looking rather rosy-cheeked, and Adam Stone was busy staring at his feet.

'It's a bloody disgrace.' Stone's colleague put up a last-ditch fight. 'A man and his kids should be able to go on holiday without the bloody police turning up on his doorstep.'

Julia turned on him in exasperation. 'Oh Bert, bugger off and do some work for once in your life!'

Bert reluctantly wandered off, turning to watch them over his shoulder.

'Adam, tell these guys what they want, then they can get off our premises.' The expression on her face suggested that their leaving could not come a minute too soon.

'It was the wife's idea, she's into all that kind of stuff.'

'The environment?' asked Bernard.

Stone appeared to think for a minute. 'I guess?'

'So, your wife is a bit of an eco-warrior then?' Maitland took a step towards the man and loomed over him. 'You do realise that what you have done is a serious crime?'

'Everyone is doing it!' Stone was looking increasingly panicked. 'I thought it would just be a fine.'

Maitland crossed his arms. 'Well, that's for a judge to decide, isn't it? But the theft of a lorry could well result in a custodial sentence.'

Julia Conlon pushed Maitland out of the way, and punched Stone on the arm, with what looked like a reasonable degree of force. 'What have you done this time, Adam? I bloody told you after that fiasco with the cases of Johnny Walker that you were on your last warning. So help me God if you've—'

'I haven't done anything, Jools, I swear!' He rubbed his arm, his eyes darting between the three of them.

'These guys are confusing me. I don't know what they're talking about.'

Maitland sighed. 'Let's start at the beginning. Two days ago, Mr Stone undertook a job for West Coast Hauliers—'

'You were moonlighting?' Julia Conlon took another swing at Stone, who managed to get out of reach just in time.

'Two days ago I was in Portugal!'

Something wasn't right here. Between Stone's holiday tan, and his obvious confusion at their questioning, Bernard was beginning to wonder if he really was their man.

'Two days ago, I was on the Algarve. Ask the wife, or the hotel, or check with bloody passport control when I got back. Check my Green Card check-ins. They'll tell you where I was.'

'Mr Stone,' began Bernard, 'is there any way that someone could have used your details to, I don't know, sign on with an agency as a driver?'

'I don't know. It could be something like that, couldn't it, Jools?' There was a slight pleading tone to his voice. Bernard wasn't sure if he was looking for his boss to get him out of trouble with the HET or was just desperate to hang on to his job.

Julia Conlon was looking less than impressed. The incident of the missing whisky may have been playing on her mind. 'I suppose it's possible. Are you guys going to be checking out Adam's story?'

'Yes, of course,' said Bernard.

'Right, Adam, you can get back to work for now.' She pointed a long pink fingernail in the direction of a lorry.

'Actually, he can't,' said Maitland. 'There's still the issue of his missing Health Check. We're legally obliged to escort him to get one now.'

'Now?' Julia looked horrified. 'We've a delivery due in Lauder in two hours.'

'We'll be quick.' Maitland grinned, which Bernard strongly felt was not going to help the situation.

She tutted loudly and turned on her heel.

'Sorry, Jools,' Stone shouted to her back.

The office door was slammed behind her with a resounding metal clang. Stone eyed them both malevolently. 'Let's get this over with then.'

Somewhere from in between the lorries they heard the thump of a door being slammed, and the sound of muttering. Bernard leapt out of the way as one of the lorries reversed, then pulled up alongside them. He caught sight of Bert glaring down at them, his lips moving behind the glass of the driver's side pane. He wound the window down, and accelerated off, his words echoing behind him.

'Bloody interfering government bastards!'

3

'Hello.'

Mona looked up from her emails to see Marcus, the HET's IT officer, standing in the doorway of the office. He was carrying a laptop and wearing an expression of unadulterated misery. Mona experienced a moment of guilt; Marcus had been carrying a torch for her since she started at the HET, and according to Bernard was still getting over the revelation that men really weren't her cup of tea. She suspected that even if she was interested in men in general, Marcus in particular still wouldn't be her type, but he was a nice guy, and she'd no desire to cause him any pain. She stared at him for a moment and decided that his expression was communicating a more recent sorrow.

'I'm in trouble with our new boss.'

'Are you?'

'Yes.' He ambled into the office. '*Someone*,' he aimed this word in the direction of Paterson's open door, 'someone was supposed to have sent me an email inviting me to a meeting this morning to meet her. But didn't.'

There was no response from within the MDF.

'So she sent me an email telling me how disappointed she was that I hadn't turned up, and now I need to phone her to tell her something, and she's going to shout at me unless *someone* explains that it wasn't my fault I wasn't at the meeting.'

'That passive-aggressive shit doesn't work when Bernard tries it, Marcus.' Paterson appeared in his doorway. 'So, it's not going to work for you either. If you want me to do something, you need to ask me directly.'

'OK, will you tell Ms Hunter it wasn't my fault I missed the meeting?'

'And have her mad at me instead? I don't think so. Man up, and phone her.'

Marcus looked at Mona for help. She was trying very hard not to laugh. 'What do you need to speak to her about anyway?'

'She told me to see if I could get her any information about Florian Boucher's social media activities.'

'Did you find anything?' Mona was genuinely interested.

'No. I haven't looked.'

'Oh, for—' Paterson returned to his office. Over his shoulder he shouted, 'She's definitely going to be annoyed with you if you haven't actually done what she asked.'

Marcus looked torn between following Paterson into his office and staying talking to Mona. He stayed, which was definitely the best option for his health and well-being. 'I didn't get to the social media because I stopped to check Bryce's files first.'

'And found something?' She sat up straighter.

'Yes.' He dropped his laptop onto her desk, landing on the corner of her keyboard, and sending a row of AAAAAAAAAAAAAAAAAAs across her page. 'Boucher was someone he was monitoring.'

'Monitoring? Like surveillance?'

He nodded.

'Did the HET IT department routinely monitor people?'

'No. Where would we have got the time, in between trying to track down where Health Defaulters have got to online, monitoring social media for emerging health myths, and supporting HET staff issues with their IT problems? Dealing with Mr Paterson's attempts to use computer software alone could take up half of my week.'

'So why was Bryce undertaking surveillance work?'

'Well, logic would dictate that there are two possible reasons.' He paused to push his glasses back onto the bridge of his nose. 'One, someone asked him to, most likely Cameron Stuttle.'

'I'm sure Bryce would have mentioned it if he did.' She thought this over. 'At least I think he would. What is your second option?'

'It was part of the wider range of activities that Bryce undertook that might come under the heading of, you know, health terrorism. His campaign of vengeance against corrupt politicians and civil servants. The shooting people, blackmailing them, threatening their mothers stuff.'

'I remember, Marcus. I was there. And I don't think that Bryce ever would have followed through on his threat to shoot your mother.'

There was a jumble of questions in her head relating to the who, what, when, and most of all why of Marcus's revelation. However, she was pretty sure that Marcus wasn't actually the person who could answer any of them.

'Guv,' she shouted. 'You need to see this.'

'Has the IT prick gone yet?'

Marcus looked hurt.

'Ignore him.' She raised her voice. 'Marcus has found something useful.'

'First time for everything.' Paterson was finally dragged out of his lair and joined them at her desk.

'Bryce was monitoring Boucher.'

'Interesting. Did he find anything?'

'Just this.' Marcus pulled up a file.

They stood in silence and read it.

Paterson pointed at the screen. 'Florian Boucher, Dieter Lange, and I can't even guess at that last one.'

'Looks like Polish or some other Eastern European.' Mona tried sounding the letters out in her head. *Ana Procházková*. 'Quite a range of countries. I assume Boucher is French?'

'Belgian, actually,' said Marcus.

'Well, after yesterday's little stunt, he must be the world's only famous Belgian.'

'Oh, no, Mr Paterson.' Marcus looked horrified. 'Belgium has offered many talented people to the world. There's the painters Ruebens and Magritte, Adolphe Sax, inventor of the saxophone, the guitarist Django Reinhardt, Audrey Hepburn, the actress, and of course, Hergé.' He looked at them both. 'He wrote Tintin. And if you want to get more modern, Belgium has had considerable sporting success with.'

'Stop.' Paterson put up a hand. 'I'm probably going to regret asking this, Marcus, but why do you know so many famous Belgians?'

'Funny story. There's a pub quiz in Stockbridge and one of the answers is always either "Belgium" or "Belgian". I've picked up a lot of Fleming and Walloon trivia over the years.'

'That's a fascinating insight into Marcus's social life,' said Mona, 'but to return to the matter in hand, was Bryce of the opinion that these guys were working as a cell?'

Marcus nodded.

'Do you think that these activists were working with Bryce?' asked Paterson.

'No.' Marcus shook his head vigorously. 'Absolutely not.'

'How can you be so sure?' asked Mona.

'Because if they were part of his masterplan, he wouldn't have stored their details on our server, and he certainly wouldn't have stored them in a barely encrypted file. There are files on the HET's system that I've got nowhere near.'

Paterson frowned. 'I thought the pair of you were both equally geeky.'

'I like to think that my digital skills are every bit the equal of Bryce's.' Marcus looked put out at this affront to his abilities. 'But Bryce had the edge on me as he was responsible for setting up our systems. I joined later. Who knows what secrets he built into them.'

Mona thought about this. 'But why would Bryce want us to find the information?'

'Who knows?' said Paterson. 'But I'll tell you one thing. That last sentence isn't going to be good for us.'

She read it out loud. '"All three activists have been consistently avoiding engaging with the Health Check regimes in their home countries." Oh, God.'

'Why is that a problem?' asked Marcus.

'Because at some point, Carlotta, or Mauchline, or this new woman, is going to decide that someone needs to track these people down and get them into a Health Check. And seeing as Boucher is in Edinburgh, there's a large chance that the other two are as well, which would make it our problem.' Paterson sighed. 'Well, Marcus, you'd better crack on and get Hunter phoned.'

Marcus didn't move. 'Are you absolutely sure that you don't want to speak to her first?'

Paterson folded his arms. 'What did I just tell you? If you want me to do something, you need to ask me directly.'

'If I do ask you directly, will you say no again?'

'Of course I will.' He patted Marcus on the shoulder and headed back to his office. 'Grow a pair and get her phoned.'

With one last mournful look at Mona, Marcus finally pulled out his mobile. She listened to him tell the story to their new boss, then was surprised to hear her name mentioned.

'Mona. Mona Whyte.'

She tried to catch his eye, but he was too focused on the call.

'OK, I'll tell her.' He hung up and swung round on his chair. 'Ms Hunter wants you to meet her at Drylaw Police Station. You're to ask for her at Reception.'

'Why? What does she want me to do? Do I need to take anything with me?'

He shrugged. 'I don't know. All she said was who was the blonde woman who worked for the HET, and when I said your name, she said tell her to go to Drylaw.' He packed up his laptop. 'Ms Hunter wants me to keep searching Bryce's files, to see if there's anything else there. I'll be in my office if anyone wants me.'

'OK, whatever.' Her mind had moved on. 'Guv?' She wandered into his tiny office. 'Hunter wants me to meet her at Drylaw Police Station – what do you think that's all about?'

'Don't know.' He leaned back in his chair. 'Some kind of Health Check issue, or maybe she just wants to sound you out about being her pet HET officer, just like you were with Stuttle.'

'That's not fair, Guv.'

He arched an eyebrow. 'Isn't it? I'm never quite sure where your loyalty lies, Mona. I know Stuttle offered you all sorts to keep you onside, not that it looks like he'll be able to deliver on his promises. What did you decide last night?'

'You really want to know?'

He sighed. 'Actually, no, I don't.' He stared at her. 'You are being careful, aren't you? Stuttle could easily take you down with him. It might not be a bad idea for your career if you were to go and lick Jennifer Hunter's arse.'

'I'm not so sure that Stuttle is a spent force. He's got a pretty good plan for dealing with Carlotta.'

He snorted. 'I wouldn't underestimate Carlotta, but that's your business. Just leave me, and the rest of the team, out of it.'

She hurried back to her desk to grab her bag, anxious to find out what was happening at Drylaw.

4

'Afternoon all!' Maitland flung open the door to the office and was met with silence in return. He stuck his head into Paterson's office. 'Nobody home.'

Bernard felt slightly relieved. He always preferred to do his thinking without a background commentary from Paterson about how useless they all were.

'Wonder where everyone's gone?' Maitland flung himself onto his seat. 'Think there's some top-level secret meeting going on that we weren't invited to?'

'Probably. There usually is.' Bernard turned his computer on. 'So, I guess that's our part in all this over.'

'What?' Maitland spun round on his chair. 'Weren't you listening to our brief? We were to find the lorry driver.'

'We did! We took him for a Health Check. That is our job.'

'We found *a* lorry driver, we didn't find the one who was actually driving the missing lorry. That's what Carlotta Carmichael wants us to do.'

Bernard thought back to the instructions they'd been given by Mauchline. Maitland could be interpreting the situation correctly, or he could just have decided that hunting for a missing environmental activist was more interesting than their current work of chasing down people who had been lazing by a poolside when they should have been at a Health Check.

'What do you think we should do now? Should we contact West Coast Hauliers?'

'Excellent idea. You crack on with that.'

'It still feels to me like something Police Scotland should be pursuing, not us. I suppose I can always pass any information we get on to them.'

'Good plan.' Maitland thought for a moment. 'Pretty sure the West Coast guy is going to react in the same way as Adam Stone did.'

Bernard had a moment's relief at the thought that at least he didn't have to face another irate logistics professional face-to-face.

Maitland was looking thoughtful. 'See if the haulier is up for a Zoom call. You'll get a better idea from his body language if he's bullshitting us.'

This was a good idea, and one which he was very reluctant to action.

'Come on, Bernie! Leap to it! Grab a laptop and get yourself down to the Zoom Room. Don't want you getting into trouble by attempting an online call in an open plan office. You know Paterson's view on that.'

'I know.' Bernard had a bitter memory of being shouted at by Paterson for attempting a Zoom call from his desk, ostensibly on the grounds of confidentiality. Bernard thought it was more likely that Paterson just didn't like the sound of human interaction in the office.

He got up slowly. Maitland noticed his lethargy. 'What's the matter with you? I thought you liked video calls?'

'I do. I much prefer to be able to see who I'm speaking to, and if the NHS had supplied us all with a laptop each that we could use to set up the calls, it would be nice and simple. But as it stands, we've got one suitable laptop between us, and if we want it ...'

'We need to brave Marguerite.' He grinned. 'I understand your reluctance now. As admin staff go, she's pretty feisty.'

Bernard would have added a few additional words to that: lazy, incompetent, nosy, overly dramatic, and, all in all, extremely annoying.

'Anyway, word to the wise, Bernie. You'd better take a pound coin with you.'

'Why?'

Maitland dug deep into his trouser pockets and produced two crumpled strips of paper. 'She's selling raffle tickets for her dad's bowling club. This strip' – he held up a thin pink one – 'was when I wanted to borrow the laptop. And this' – he held up a blue one – 'was when I needed her to get something from the File Archive. She tried to stiff me for a third one before she'd hand over our mail. I told her to get stuffed and said I'd send Paterson down to collect it.'

'Did she hand it over?'

'Nah, she said Paterson hadn't bought any tickets yet so she'd be happy to talk to him.'

Bernard tried to picture that particular scene. It would truly be a clash of the titans, with the two of them each bringing their different but equally impressive gladiatorial skills to the arena. 'So, what happened? Did he get the mail without paying?'

'I forgot to tell him. You'd better take two pound coins.'

'This does actually count as blackmail, you know?'

Bernard picked up one laptop, two letters, and an inexplicable three strips of raffle tickets. He was only glad that he'd managed to argue Marguerite down from her starting point of five strips.

'There are some really good prizes. Alcohol, chocolates ... we even got a voucher for a visit to a spa. How much would your girlfriend like that?'

He had no idea whether Lucy liked that kind of thing. 'Maybe she would, but you can't hold our property hostage.'

'Bernard! Shame on you for suggesting such a thing.' Marguerite's eyes twinkled, beneath eyelids that were sporting several different shades of eyeshadow and some unnaturally long false lashes. 'Everyone here is just keen to support a small, grassroots sporting organisation, who've got their eyes on a major Scottish league title this year. It's not blackmail, Bernard, it's community support.'

'Well, whatever, that's the last strip I'm buying.'

'Really?' She smiled. 'And have you got the key for the Zoom Room? You know the policy. You're not supposed to have Zoom calls in an open office.'

'I don't have any more money!'

'Oh, Bernard.' Marguerite got up from her chair, picked up a key from a set that were hanging on the wall, and slowly walked back. She placed it on the desk in front of him and squeezed his hand. 'Consider this one a freebie. But next time, come prepared.'

The Zoom Room managed to be both cold and stuffy at the same time. It had previously been a cupboard, and the boxes of stationery that no-one had yet got round to moving helped it to hold on to its previous identity. The room's lighting combination of a small window set high in the wall and a weak and naked lightbulb had allowed sufficient illumination for staff to assess which colour of Post-it notes they wanted to steal for home use. It was, however, barely adequate for Bernard to read the sticker with the laptop's password handwritten on it. After a moment or two's struggle he had the technology under his command, and really had no excuse not to speak to Edward Harman, managing director of West Coast Hauliers Ltd.

Bernard had half hoped he would refuse to speak to him. He'd dashed off a quick email, fully expecting that he'd get a curt refusal in response, or at least a delaying tactic until Mr Harman could chat to a lawyer about whether he had to bother with the Heath Enforcement Team. However, he'd had an almost immediate response, saying that he was available to chat any time that morning. Bernard sighed and launched the meeting.

Edward Harman was younger than he'd expected, casually dressed in a hoody and woolly hat. It would appear his office was even colder than the Zoom Room.

'Have you found my lorry?' Harman wasted no time.

'Ah, apologies, no, that's not why I'm getting in touch.' Bernard felt a twinge of guilt that he didn't have some better news.

Harman slumped back in his chair, disappointed. 'So, what do you want then? I've already told the police everything I could think of that might be useful.'

'We just wanted to know if you employed Adam Stone directly, or through an agency?'

'I already told the police that. He came through an agency.'

'Did you recruit him specifically for this job?'

The figure on screen shook its head. 'No. We're so short of staff that I have feelers out permanently for any qualified drivers who might be looking for work. One of the agencies we work with emailed to say they had just got a new man on their books who might be suitable for me.'

'Is there a possibility that your emails could have been hacked?'

'I'd say it's odds on. I admit I was surprised – I'd not heard from the agency for months, then suddenly they come up with someone who is perfect. I was delighted to hear from them, though, I was desperate for more drivers, and pretty much said send him straight over. When this Adam Stone guy turned up at the yard, he had all the right paperwork. Nothing that made me think there was anything suspicious going on. After the lorry went missing, I phoned the agency, and of course, they had an Adam Stone on their books, but he's not accepted any work from them for years. They said they'd not sent me anyone recently.'

Bernard wondered if the Adam Stone on the agency's books was the one they'd met. He could have worked for the agency prior to his current job.

'Did they invoice you for the work?' he asked.

'Nah.' The figure on screen shook his head. 'But I don't think they were interested in getting paid for the job – I reckon they were just after the contents. I told all this to the police already. Have they made any progress at all on finding my lorry?'

'I'm sorry, you'd have to ask them directly. But you've been very helpful. Thank you for your time.' He ended the call before Edward Harman could interrogate him any further.

Maitland didn't look up when he returned, intent on staring at his computer. Bernard wouldn't usually disturb a colleague so caught up in their work, but long experience had taught him that when Maitland was so engrossed it was usually the football scores that he was looking at.

'West Coast Hauliers think their emails were hacked. Stone was registered with a recruitment agency that they use and he was offered to them out of the blue. They're so short-staffed they jumped at the offer.'

'Hmm. Probably more likely that the recruitment agency was hacked. You should talk to them.'

'Really? Do you not think we should just hand all this over to Police Scotland?'

'Well, we could do, if you really want to go back to Mauchline and Hunter and tell them that we gave up hunting for their missing lorry driver at the first hurdle.'

'It's not so much giving up, as why are we doing this in the first place? I thought the only positive thing about Mr Stuttle not being in post was that we might get to stop doing things that are completely outwith our remit.'

'Stop moaning.' Maitland sat back in his chair. He had an air of smugness that Bernard didn't quite understand. 'Anyway, I've got something more interesting than email hacking for you. I think I've found the lorry.'

'So that's why you're looking even more pleased with yourself than usual.' He regarded his colleague with scepticism. 'How did you do that then?'

'Simple. I was thinking about what Stone was saying this morning, about how we could check where he was if we wanted to just by looking at his Green Card. So, I decided to look at where "Adam Stone" has been over the past few days—'

'Oh yeah?' In spite of his misgivings, he found his interest growing. 'What did you find?'

'Well, I went back a couple of weeks, and for the first few days it's what you would expect, Adam Stone checking in at work and out again, checking into some pubs that I remember as being well rough when I was in uniform, supermarkets, hotels, other places that look like deliveries. So, I'm guessing the real Mr Stone. Then we have a couple of days of absolute silence before a Green Card Check In at—'

'West Coast Hauliers.' Bernard stared at the screen.

'Pretty smart move of them choosing to clone the card of a driver who was on holiday. At least that way it wouldn't show up at two Check Ins at the same time, at opposite ends of the country.'

Maitland snorted. 'There's nobody monitoring this stuff. You could be Checking In on the moon and no-one would notice. The only people that ever look at this stuff are HET/CID Liaison when they're trying to work out where some ned has been.'

'And us.' Bernard sighed. 'When we are doing work that Police Scotland should be doing.'

'So, I'm thinking he must have had some other cloned Green Card to be able to do all the other Check Ins, I mean, he's obviously in the country illegally.'

'Not necessarily. He could be using his real name. If he's not on any kind of terrorist list, and he has an up-to-date Health Check, there's no reason why anyone would pick him up.'

'Interesting.' Maitland mulled this over. 'Anyway, where it starts getting really intriguing is where he visited after he left West Coast Hauliers, which is absolutely nowhere until he checks in at a petrol station about twenty miles south of Edinburgh at ten past eight on Monday night.'

'He stopped the lorry to refuel?'

Maitland shook his head. 'Possible, but not what I'm thinking. Look at the timing. How long do you think it would take to drive from Bellshill, where we know the tracker stopped working, to Goreton petrol station?'

'I don't know, a couple of hours?'

'My thoughts exactly. But this Check In isn't until twenty-four hours later. I don't think he's stopped off to refuel en route to somewhere, I think he's driven the lorry to wherever it should be, bunkered down, then strolled out to buy some supplies on foot.'

'So, the lorry is somewhere within walking distance of Goreton petrol station?'

He nodded. 'I think it is certainly a possibility.'

'Pretty stupid of him to use his Green Card. It massively narrows down the search for where they are.'

'Beyond stupid. You want my theory on what happened here?'

Bernard found this was one of the very rare occasions when he was actually interested in what his colleague had to say. 'OK.'

'Our Adam Stone impersonator enters the country using his own Green Card, or more likely, a fake card. He also has another fake card in the name of Adam Stone, which he needs to show to the hauliers before they'll let him loose with one of their lorries. I think that is the one and only time that he is supposed to use the Adam Stone card. He's supposed to ditch the Stone card, and go back to using his original card, making himself pretty untraceable.'

'I still don't understand why he'd be careless enough to use the wrong card at a petrol station.'

'I've got two theories there, Bern. One, he gets to his destination, starts to relax, gets drunk or high and his standard of care slips. Nips out to the petrol station for some fags, and due to his inebriated state, whips out the wrong card.'

'Possible, I suppose. And your other theory?'

'He gets to his destination, and something goes wrong. He heads to the petrol station, I don't know, maybe to refuel so he can travel on somewhere. He's distracted, reaches into the wrong pocket, and pulls out Adam Stone's card.'

'Something would have had to have gone massively wrong for him to be so flustered that he gets that careless.'

'True. Anyway, like you said, our next step is to visit the petrol station.'

'I did not say that! All I said is it narrows it down. This is police work, Maitland, not something we should be pursuing. The police will already have looked at his Green Card data.'

'Not necessarily. Police access to Green Card data is heavily restricted. The only coppers who can access it are the HET/CID Liaison Officers, neither of whom anyone can track down . . .'

Bernard had another stab of guilt. *Operation Trigon.*

' . . .and senior management. Hunter's brand new in post, and probably doesn't have clearance yet. Mauchline is Stuttle's man, so he's probably not going to do anything to help Hunter, so I think we have information that Police Scotland don't have yet.'

'Which we could alert them to?'

'I say we go try and find it ourselves. You and me, Bernie. What do you say?'

'I say no, firmly and repeatedly.'

'I'll have to go on my own then, which could be dangerous.'

'It won't be any less dangerous if I'm there, which reinforces my previous no.'

Maitland sat back and sighed. 'I get it, Bernie, you're a family man now, as good as anyway, and you don't want to put yourself in danger now you have dependants.' He stood up, and Bernard watched him warily. 'I'll head off now, but if I'm passing the admin staff and they ask where I'm heading to all on my own, I might just pass the information on to them that I'm risking life and limb in the pursuit of justice, and Bernard is sitting by the phone, awaiting an update about his unborn child.'

'You wouldn't!' Bernard stared at his colleague. The idea of Marguerite being updated about his complicated family circumstances was too horrific to contemplate. It would keep the admin team in gossip for the next six months.

'Probably not, but do you really want to risk it?'

He picked up his coat. 'This is blackmail.'

'No, it's not, Bernie. It's colleague support.'

5

The desk sergeant at Drylaw did not look pleased to see her. Whether this was due to her asking for Jennifer Hunter, or whether it was because the station was going like the proverbial fair and he couldn't deal with yet another enquiry, she didn't know. He buzzed her into the office and barked at her to take a seat, without any clear explanation of what would happen next. She hoped that he was somehow communicating her arrival to Ms Hunter, but from the way he'd distractedly turned back to the next person at the counter without appearing to reach for the phone, he would have had to be doing it telepathically.

She waited until he was fully engrossed, then set off into the station to see if she could find anyone who could assist. She struck lucky with a young female PC who seemed to know what she was talking about, who ushered her into an interview room which contained Jennifer Hunter and a young man who looked vaguely familiar.

'You wanted to see me, Ma'am?'

Hunter looked irritated. 'Please don't call me that. I'm not a police officer. Call me Jen, or if you absolutely must, Ms Hunter.'

'OK, sorry ma— Ms Hunter.'

'We need you to oversee a Health Check. Florian Boucher, whom I'm sure you will remember, entered the country on false papers. He's done a wonderful job of avoiding getting a Health Check in Belgium, so now it's up to us to remedy the situation.'

She glanced back at the other person in the room, and it fell into place who he was. He was a GP they'd taken clients to in the past for an emergency Health Check. He smiled at her, and she tried to remember his name.

'Dr Harrison will undertake the Health Check. I'll see if they're ready for us.' The door slammed behind her.

'Any chance we can get this over quite quickly?' asked the doctor. 'Only I've already been here for an hour and a half.'

'How come?'

'Well, first of all, Florian Boucher staged a bit of a protest in there about his human rights being violated, so we had to make a tactical retreat while Ms Hunter rounded up some police officers to assist.'

'What, to hold him down while you took the blood test?'

'No, of course not. I'm not taking blood from someone against their will without a court order. The police were just there to stop him throwing furniture around the interview room. Once they'd got him to calm down, Ms Hunter was able to talk him round.'

'Really?'

'Yeah, there were quite a lot of threats about how he would have to remain in solitary confinement to minimise any risk to staff, and how they wouldn't even be able to charge him until they'd established his health status. By the end of her speech I think he was imagining never seeing Belgium again.'

'Well, she's right on the law. It's playing havoc with the prison system trying to accommodate prisoners in solitary confinement until they can get a court order to compel them to comply. Nobody is winning in all this except the solicitors.'

'Very true.' Dr Harrison nodded. 'But I wish your boss

was as strong on all aspects of the law, and I could have been out of here an hour ago. I just gave Florian Boucher his Health Check without having a HET officer present.'

Her sudden summons now made sense. 'Why was there no HET officer there?'

'I think Ms Hunter thought that because she was head of SHEP her presence would be sufficient. To be honest, I assumed the same, but then another SHEP officer – Macklin, I think?'

'Mauchline.'

'He said that the legislation was very clear – there had to be a HET officer to sign the paperwork. The two of them had a furious set-to about it. I think they completely forgot I was there.'

Mona grinned. 'Oh dear.'

'I can see why Ms Hunter is reluctant to do another one. I mean, if Boucher was furious about having his blood taken once, what's he going to say when they tell him it's being done again?'

'To say nothing about the fact that it was taken illegally the first time around.' She shook her head. Stuttle was going to love this. 'What a total—'

The door opened and Jennifer Hunter stuck her head into the room. 'They're ready for us now.'

Mona followed her boss to the interview room, a slight adrenaline rush coursing through her veins as she prepared for the worst. If there were any chairs flying around the room, she'd be sure to duck. However, Florian Boucher could not have looked more chilled out. He was leaning back on his chair, his arms folded. Mona thought back to Liz's description of him. She was right; this was a very handsome man. Blonde, dishevelled hair, a deep tan, and grey eyes that flicked over in her direction as she took a seat opposite him.

'Hello, Mr Boucher, my name is Mona Whyte and I am here to oversee you having a Health Check. I'm not sure how this works in France, but in the UK it involves you giving us a pin-prick sample of blood which we use to establish whether you are infected with the Virus. You have the right—'

'I have already given him my blood.' Boucher nodded in the direction of the GP.

Both Dr Harrison and Mona looked round at Hunter, who was hovering behind them. There was no way Mona was about to leap in with an explanation. *Actually, Mr Boucher, we cocked up. Would you like to sue us?*

'And we need you to do it again,' said Hunter.

'Why?'

There was a silence during which Mona tried very hard not to catch anyone's eye. She was already planning the email she was going to write to Paterson to emphasise that she was in no way responsible for what could turn out to be a disaster. Their only hope was if Boucher assumed that there had been some technical hitch with the test, rather than a procedural one.

'This woman' – Boucher pointed at her – 'was not in the room when you took my blood. I think, maybe, your test was not legal without her here?'

And with that, all hope was gone. She and Dr Harrison turned again in unison towards Hunter, who nodded her head curtly in the direction of the door, and the two of them escaped back into the corridor.

'Do you think I can go now?' asked Dr Harrison.

'I strongly suggest we both get out of here as quickly as we can. This is turning into the kind of shitstorm that my boss gets paid to deal with, not me. Ms Hunter can take it up with him.'

With a quick glance over their shoulders to make sure

that the door wasn't about to open, they headed for the exit.

'Mona.' She ground to a halt. Dr Harrison gave her a wave and ran up the stairs as fast as his legs would carry him. She slowly turned round.

'Yes, ma— Ms Hunter?'

Hunter strode towards her, stopping at a distance where she could lower her voice and still be heard. 'You've probably gathered that there was some miscommunication about Mr Boucher's Health Check. I was not informed that I required someone from your team to sign off on it.'

Was not informed. Didn't ask. Maybe didn't listen.

'Yes, Ms Hunter. Will you require me to come back once Mr Boucher agrees to a Health Check?'

'Possibly. I need to talk to Legal first.' She lowered her voice still further. 'I was wondering who you were planning to tell about this, ehm . . .'

'Miscommunication?'

'Yes.'

'Obviously I was planning to keep my Team Leader apprised of the situation.'

Hunter nodded. 'Yes, I can see that would be good practice. However, as the situation is not yet resolved, I think it would be worth waiting until the matter is concluded before we involve anyone else.' Hunter's brown eyes stared up at her, a mute question in them. *Whose side are you going to be on, Mona? Are you Stuttle's pet or mine?*

She played for time. 'I'm not quite sure what you're asking me to say?'

'I'm not asking you to say anything, Mona. I'm just suggesting that John Paterson will get a better view of the situation once I've spoken to Legal and we're all clear on the way forward.'

'With all due respect, Ms Hunter, I usually find it's better to report back while the issues are still fresh in my mind.' *Before the truth is rewritten by SHEP's Legal Department and I'm implicated in whatever bending of reality they suggest.*

'I appreciate that, Mona.' A slight uncertainty showed on Hunter's face. 'I suppose I'm asking for your help here.' *Another mute question, or possibly a series of them. Can I rely on your support, woman to woman? Is there something I can offer you to keep you onside? Who actually are you, Mona?*

'I'm not trying to be unhelpful, Ms Hunter, but I just want to be clear on what my role is here.'

Hunter's expression hardened. 'Covering your back. The typical police response.'

'Not a reaction that's limited to the police, Ms Hunter.'

The two of them glared at each other. Hunter threw a glance over her shoulder to check they weren't being overheard. 'You ought to think very carefully about who your friends are, Mona. I'm offering you a chance to move forward, not get caught up with all the nonsense that's been going on over the past few months.'

'I'm happy with my friends, Ms Hunter.'

She shook her head. 'You want to stick with Stuttle, that's your funeral.'

'I'm not sure anyone's being buried just yet, Ms Hunter. Not even Mr Stuttle.'

'Really?' Hunter smiled, a humourless affair with more than a touch of malevolence to it. 'Perhaps Mr Stuttle isn't on quite as solid ground as he thinks? He's definitely lost the confidence of the Minister for Virus Policy. And she usually gets her way.'

'Well, that might not be the case this time.' Without waiting to be dismissed she headed up the stairs. 'Ma'am.'

6

'Leave me to do the talking.' Maitland gestured at the petrol station. 'This needs a bit of delicacy.'

'Delicacy?' Bernard stared at his colleague. 'The first word that springs to mind when I think of you.' Despite his sarcasm, he was delighted to let Maitland take charge here. He'd no idea what to say to the attendant. *Remember any terrorists popping in?*

The girl behind the counter was young enough to make Bernard feel old. What age did you have to be to work in a petrol station? The girl barely looked sixteen, never mind eighteen. She looked up and smiled as they approached.

'We're here from the HET.' Maitland flashed his ID at her so quickly she didn't really have time to look at it.

'What's the HET?'

'The Health Enforcement Team.' Maitland peered at her name badge. 'Chloe, we're going to need your help.'

'Health Enforce what?' Chloe was clearly struggling to understand what was going on. Bernard wondered if this was part of Maitland's masterplan. He'd had many experiences of Maitland trying to get him to do things by confusing him and bombarding him with information. He'd like to say the technique never worked on him, but he'd be lying.

'The Health Enforcement Team needs your assistance, Chloe. Lives are at stake. You're our only hope.' Maitland shot her a very big smile, which in spite of her confusion she reciprocated. Bernard tried not to roll his eyes. This was Maitland's only other method – rampantly insincere charm. And he was happy to say this technique definitely never worked on him.

It did seem to be having some effect on Chloe, however. 'What do you want me to do?'

'We need to have a look at your CCTV for Monday evening.'

'I'd have to ask the manager. Who did you say you were again?'

'It'd probably just be easier to say we're working with the police.'

Finally, she'd heard something that made sense. 'OK, I'll phone him.'

'What did you say that for?' Bernard whispered, angrily. 'We're not the police.'

'Didn't say we were. I said we were working with them, which is true. Anyway, wheesht.' He nodded in the direction of the camera behind the counter. Bernard decided to keep any further conversation for the car, where he'd be having a strongly worded discussion about Maitland's continuing willingness to pretend to be a police officer whenever it suited him.

After a couple of minutes Chloe reappeared and opened the hatch. 'Mike said I was to show you whatever it was you wanted then get you out of here as quickly as possible.' She said this solemn-faced, and Bernard tried to stifle a smile. Manager Mike probably hadn't intended his words to be repeated verbatim.

'We'll be gone in a flash.' Maitland shot her another of his apparently charming smiles, and they followed her into the back room.

'So, you wanted to look at the CCTV for Monday

evening?' She opened up a fairly elderly-looking laptop and logged on. 'Was there a particular time?'

Bernard did some calculations in his head. 'Could we look at the feed from 7pm onwards?'

'And do you want the feed from the camera in the shop or on the concourse?'

'Could we have a look at both?'

She scrolled through a list of files and clicked on one. 'This is the shop. It'll need to be fast forwarded.'

The door beeped to announce another customer. 'We can do that,' said Maitland. 'You go and see to your customer.'

She frowned, obviously torn between her shopfront duties and keeping an eye on the two strange men who had somehow ended up in the back room. Her duties to her patrons won out. 'Let me know if you need anything.'

Maitland took over the playback duties, stopping the feed occasionally to check the time. Eventually he slowed down the fast forwarding. 'Keep an eye out for him from here on in.'

Bernard watched as people shuffled in and out of the shop at high speed. It was like watching an old black and white newsreel. 'There!'

Maitland stopped the feed and rewound it slightly. He peered in towards the screen. 'What is he buying?'

'Did you find what you were looking for?' Chloe joined them. 'Oh, it's *him* you're looking for.'

'You remember him?'

She nodded. 'Yeah, he was a bit ... you know ...'

'A bit what?' asked Maitland.

'A bit weird. He's foreign, isn't he?'

'Yes.' Maitland produced one of his winning smiles. 'So, Chloe, can you think back to when this man came in. Was he on his own?'

She nodded. 'He was.'

'What did he buy when he came in?'

'Funny stuff.' She frowned, thinking back to the evening in question. 'He bought some plasters and things.' She tapped the screen, where Dieter Lange was freeze-framed hovering in an aisle. 'He got really annoyed with me when I said that was all we had in the way of bandages.'

'Bandages?' Maitland and Bernard spoke in unison.

If Chloe thought there was anything odd about their interest in this, she didn't show it, caught up in her memories of the night in question. 'Yeah, when I said we didn't have any, he kind of ran round the shop picking up stuff, then eventually came back with a packet of, you know, ladies' things.'

'Ladies' things? asked Bernard. 'What kind of ladies' things?'

'A packet of those pads that old ladies put in their pants in case they wee themselves. Like I said, pretty weird, huh?'

'We're going to need to see the feed covering the concourse for the same time, Chloe.' Maitland turned to Bernard. 'We should be able to get a reg. number.'

'No.' Chloe shook her head, and they looked at her in surprise. 'He wasn't in a car. He was on foot.'

'On foot?' asked Maitland. 'Are there houses nearby?'

'There's a row of farm cottages round the back of here, but other than that, nothing. I thought maybe his car broke down or something?'

'Could be. Did you notice which way he went when he left the shop?'

'He went in the direction of the cottages, so,' she turned herself so she was facing the front of the shop and thought for a moment. 'Left.' The buzzer sounded, indicating another customer. 'Excuse me.'

'We need to go.' Maitland got to his feet.

'What about the feed?' said Bernard. 'We can't just leave it. It's important evidence.'

Maitland hesitated. 'Fair point. How do we copy it?'

'I guess we download it onto a USB.'

His colleague nodded towards the laptop. 'On you go then.'

'I don't have one with me.'

Maitland sighed. 'That's the kind of nerdish thing you're supposed to be good for.'

'I'm not responsible for ... you know, never mind. I'll see if Chloe sells them.'

'Don't bother. Let's make this someone else's problem, while we follow up this lead. Who do we call?'

'HET/CID Liaison, I suppose.' Bernard's heart sank. 'You can make the call. They both hate me.'

'Can't say I blame them.' He pulled out his phone. 'Leave it to me.'

Bernard watched as Maitland scrolled through the numbers on his phone before pressing on one of them. He wondered whether they would have to wait for the liaison officers to turn up or whether they could leave them to it. He very much did not want to see Ian Jacobsen again if he could possibly avoid it. Also, to his surprise, he realised he was really keen to go and check out these cottages. Maitland's enthusiasm for investigation seemed to be rubbing off on him. Although if the activists were still in the cottages, he would definitely be suggesting they phoned the police rather than tackling anything themselves.

'No answer,' said Maitland, letting Bernard listen to the phone ring.

'Leave a message on their voicemail, then at least we have tried to tell somebody.'

Maitland left as brief a description as he could of what was going on, but still managed to get cut off before he had finished explaining. In fairness, it was a complicated situation. He hoped that when CID finally picked it up, they could make some sense of it.

'Should we try to phone Paterson?' asked Bernard. 'Or maybe Hunter?'

'Let's try them from the car.'

They got some directions to the cottages from Chloe before leaving, nodding profuse thanks to her on their way out.

'What do you think is going on?' asked Maitland, as he put the car into gear.

'My guess is that one of them wasn't as careful as he should have been when it came to trying to set fire to himself. I reckon one of them has got burned.'

Maitland grimaced. 'Could be, although I'd have thought most of the would-be fire starters would be in police custody.' He thought for a moment. 'It would definitely explain the need for bandages. Although his urgent need for female hygiene products suggest that they need something that's a bit more absorbent. Either way, they don't sound like the most professional of operations, do they?'

'So, what's the plans when we get there?' asked Bernard. 'You're not going to attempt to do anything that is really the responsibility of the police, are you, Maitland, like trying to kick down the front door or something?'

'No,' he said, grinning. 'But I do think we need to scope out the lie of the land – knock on a few doors and things.'

'I'm really not sure that's a good idea,' said Bernard, his earlier enthusiasm waning rapidly as the reality of the situation set in.

'Bernie, don't be such a— *woah*.'

Maitland brought the car to an abrupt halt, shooting Bernard forward in his seat. 'What are you playing at?' He rubbed his neck where the seatbelt had caught him.

'What if he didn't walk to the petrol station from the cottages? What if the lorry was parked not very far away?' He pointed at something. Bernard followed his finger and found himself staring at a large metal sign. *Industrial Unit For Sale.*

'Wouldn't be a bad place to stash a stolen lorry would it, Bernie? With or without the owner's knowledge that it's there.'

Bernard looked down the isolated country lane. 'I strongly think this is the point where we phone this one in and get some police officers to accompany us.'

'Your suggestion is noted,' said Maitland and turned the car in the direction of the units.

Bernard twisted round in his seat, looking at the hedgerows going past. 'It really is very dark down here, Maitland, and if there is anyone is hiding out in the building, they're going to hear our car coming from a mile off. They could have guns or anything.'

'Guns? They didn't even have a first aid kit. I think we'll be OK.' He pulled into the yard outside the industrial unit, which to Bernard's relief looked completely deserted.

'Right, I'm going in for a look. Are you with me?'

'I suppose so.' Accompanying Maitland was marginally less scary than sitting there in the dark, waiting to be ambushed.

His colleague bounded enthusiastically in the direction of the unit. 'Door's locked.'

Bernard's feeling of relief was short-lived as Maitland started rattling all the other doors that he could find on the building. 'This one's open,' he said, triumphantly.

'Maitland, I'm really not sure we should be—'

His colleague disappeared into the darkness of the building without a backward glance. Bernard stood for a moment, eyeing his surroundings. There was no-one to be seen and nothing to be heard, beyond the distant hum of traffic on the main road. That wasn't to say that there wouldn't be anyone in the building. After a further moment weighing up the possibilities he reluctantly followed Maitland inside.

'Lights don't seem to be working.' Maitland pulled out his phone and turn the torch function on. 'And there she is.'

Illuminated by the cold blue light of Maitland's phone was a white lorry, parked in the middle of the room. It was smaller than Bernard had been expecting; it reminded him of the little vans he saw pootling about doing supermarket home deliveries, except instead of Tesco branding, there was a large green WCH logo on the side. The rear door of the vehicle was slightly ajar.

'Bloody hell.' They'd actually found it. In spite of his misgivings, Bernard found his excitement rising. He had to give Maitland some credit here – he'd done a great job. He also pulled out his phone and shone it around the building, still keen to reassure himself that there was no-one else hiding in the dark extremities of the unit.

'I'm going in for a better look,' said Maitland. 'Cover my back in case we're not alone.'

'Ehm, OK.' What exactly Maitland was expecting him to do if there was anybody else there, he wasn't quite sure.

'Looks like it's open.' Maitland pulled the back door of the lorry wide and climbed up on the back step for a better view. 'And the food's all gone, which I have to say I'm not too surprised about. There are a couple of boxes . . .' He tailed off.

'What?' asked Bernard, still busy shining his torch around the room. 'What can you see?'

'I'm not sure. There are a few boxes still at the back of the lorry but I think there's something else in the—Jesus!' He nearly fell off his perch and grabbed at the lorry's door to right himself. 'Is that what I think it is?'

Bernard climbed up beside his colleague, eager to see what had spooked him. His torch light snaked back into the lorry, confirming that it was nearly empty, save for a couple of rows of cardboard boxes stacked high at the far end. 'I don't see anything.'

'You need to shine the light down towards the floor of the lorry.'

He leaned forward, angling his phone as instructed, and after a second realised what Maitland was concerned about. There was a dark substance pooled on the lorry's floor, starting from about halfway back, and fanning out in the direction of the remaining boxes. He let his light follow the liquid, and found it shining off a single white trainer, poking out of the end of a denim-clad leg. 'That's a body, isn't it? There's an actual dead person on this lorry.'

'Calm down,' said Maitland and heaved himself up and into the vehicle. He crouched down beside the corpse, using his phone to illuminate it from a number of different angles. 'Been dead a while, I'd say. And I tell you this, Bernie, whatever's happened here, it would have taken more than a couple of packets of *Tenalady* to sort it out.'

7

Paterson listened impassively as Mona updated him on the events of the past few hours. When she finished her edited highlights, he sat back in his chair and stared up at her. 'That poor woman has been in the job less than twenty-four hours, and she's already got herself into a job-threatening situation. Did you really think that I was going to glory in her mistake?'

'Actually, Guv, yes I did.'

'How well you know me, Mona.' He rubbed his hands together, gleefully. 'I can't believe that she's messed up so much, so fast. Not a team player, that's her problem.'

Paterson was definitely inside a greenhouse chucking pebbles on this one. If any one of the North Edinburgh HET had been a team player, they wouldn't have ended up there in the first place.

'Did you know that SHEP staff couldn't sign off on Health Checks, Guv?'

'Can't say I'd given it a lot of thought, but I suppose I assumed they would be able to. It makes sense that they can't – they're supposed to be strategic, while we do the operational stuff. So, I'm not saying that this isn't a "there but for the grace of God" situation, but whichever way you look at it, she cocked up, we didn't, so allow me a small moment of pleasure.' He let out a tiny sigh of theatrical happiness.

'This has got to undermine Carlotta's position when it comes to light, hasn't it? Hunter was her appointment.'

'Maybe.' He shrugged. 'But her popularity is riding pretty high after today's announcement.'

'What announcement?' She felt a sudden stab of anxiety.

'Have you not seen the news today?' He swivelled his screen round so she could see the BBC Scotland headlines. 'Look at this.'

She read the headline in dismay. *Minister in Experimental Vaccine Tests: Carlotta Carmichael, Minister for Virus Policy, allowed herself and family members to be tested as part of a highly experimental vaccine programme.*

'Oh God.'

'Not how I remember the situation playing out, but she's coming out of it well. Look at that bit.' He jabbed at the screen. '"I couldn't ask others to put themselves at risk without being willing to do so myself." I seem to remember her not going anywhere near the vaccine until they were damn sure it wasn't dangerous, then buying off any members of staff who found out what she was up to, including that young lassie that we ended up supporting, what was her name? Catriona something?'

'Catriona McBride.' said Mona, her head in her hands. She sat back up, and saw Paterson was eyeing her suspiciously.

'Why are you so bothered? Carlotta does this kind of stuff all the time. She's Teflon-coated.' He frowned. 'This wasn't part of the master plan with Stuttle was it? He wasn't planning to leak this to the press?' His frown deepened. 'And please tell me your part in this wasn't to get Catriona McBride onside?'

'No, of course not,' she lied. 'I'm just thinking that it makes Stuttle's attempts to get his job back less likely to succeed if Carlotta's coming across as one of the good guys.'

'I hate to say it, Mona, but I don't think Stuttle will be coming back. We need to start making nice with Hunter. It looks like we're stuck with her. If you want my advice—'

His phone rang, and she never got to find out what his unsolicited suggestion was going to be. It seemed to be Bernard on the phone from what she could make out. She stood up, but didn't leave, listening in on the conversation.

'Right, Bernard, slow down. I can't make out what you're saying. Did you say you found *the lorry*, or *a body*?' He gestured to her to sit back down, which she did, intrigued by the one-sided dialogue. 'What do you mean you found both?'

'It's in there.' Bernard ran towards the car. 'And we can't get hold of either of the CID Liaison Officers, although maybe that's because Ian Jacobsen is harbouring a grudge against me and won't take my calls or—'

Paterson strode past Bernard. 'Maitland, what the hell's going on here? Why's Bernard being hysterical?'

'I'm not being hysterical, there's a—'

'This is the missing lorry.' Maitland gestured over his shoulder, looking considerably calmer than his colleague. 'Door was half closed but not locked, so we opened it up and climbed in and found her.'

'Her?'

Maitland nodded. 'I checked for a pulse, though judging by the amount of blood in there it was unlikely she was going to still be alive. Then I got us out of there sharpish, seeing as it's a crime scene, and I didn't want Bernard to barf over it.'

'Good point,' said Paterson.

Bernard shot an exasperated look in Mona's direction. She tried to look sympathetic, but she couldn't help noticing that he was still a bit green about the gills.

'Mona.' Paterson turned to her. 'There's a pair of gloves in the car. Chuck them over. And you pair.' He waved a hand in the direction of Bernard and Maitland. 'Take a large step away from the crime scene.'

'What are you going to do, Guv?' asked Maitland.

'Take a look at the crime scene, obviously.' He put on the gloves that Mona had offered him, and opened the doors of the lorry again.

'Are you sure you should be doing this, Guv?' asked Mona, in a low voice.

'Do you want to know what's going on here or not?' asked Paterson. He walked towards the lorry.

She was torn. 'Yeah, but—'

'I'm not getting into the lorry, I'm just taking a look.' He hauled himself up on to the back step. 'I can't see a bloody thing. Mona, get over here with a torch.'

She hurried over, and after a moment's indecision, pulled her sleeve over her hand and pulled herself up beside him. She lit up the torch on her phone and moved it slowly over the van.

'Where's all the food?' asked Paterson.

'There are still a few boxes there.' She let the light linger on them.

'Nowhere near a full lorry's worth though.'

She let the light shine over the floor of the lorry and saw the body lying there.

'You weren't wrong about the blood, Maitland,' said Paterson.

She angled her phone to get a better look. The body was definitely female, her long blonde hair lying in the blood which had pooled round the body. She was wearing jeans and a waterproof jacket. Mona couldn't see her face.

'What do you think, Guv?'

'Well, she could have been here on her own, fallen on something sharp, and been unable to save herself.'

'She'd have phoned someone, surely?'

He made a non-committal noise. 'Maybe you can't get phone reception inside one of these things?'

'I reckon she was stabbed, Guv.' Maitland shouted over his opinion.

'Thank you for that, Maitland. That was the next possibility I was looking at.'

Mona shone the torch around the lorry again. 'Funny how all the boxes have been removed right up until where she is, but they've left the ones behind her.'

'I'm sensing something went wrong here. Someone, or more likely a group of people, decide to help themselves to the contents on the lorry, get taken by surprise when they find her on board, there's a struggle and she comes off worst.'

Mona wondered if the girl had been hidden there, frightened and panicking as the boxes were removed all around her. 'Do you think she's one of Boucher's crowd?'

'Could be. Although if Marcus's intel is correct, she's probably not Ana Procházková , as her colouring is all wrong. Ana's dark haired and dark eyed, and that poor girl a blue-eyed blonde. Soon as we get through here I'll get Marcus searching Bryce's records, see if we can identify her. I'll tell you one thing though, she didn't nick this lorry all by herself. She's not going to have convinced West Coast Hauliers that she was Adam Stone. So, where's our missing driver?' He jumped back down. 'Time to phone this one in.'

'Who to?'

He sighed. 'I suppose I'd better ring the new boss.'

'Do you think Ms Hunter will be happy we've found her lorry?' asked Maitland. 'She should be in a good mood with us; after all, we've done what she asked.'

Paterson looked at him in disbelief. 'Are you kidding me? What she wanted was us to find her a lorry full of food, and a driver she could have either prosecuted or deported as suited Carlotta Carmichael. Instead, we're presenting her with this ...' He searched for a word. 'Fiasco. She's not going to be happy, she's going to be furious and looking for someone to blame.'

'I can't believe that Maitland and I risked life and limb to retrieve this lorry, and now you're saying we could be in trouble for doing so?' Bernard was looking even greener than before.

'Life and limb is overstating it a bit, Guv, but it was a pretty good bit of detective work, if I say so myself. Anyway, it was Mr Mauchline who told us to look for the lorry.'

'He told you to look for the lorry *driver*.'

'This is better!' Maitland looked outraged. 'We've saved Carlotta the embarrassment of someone else finding it.'

'Except, genius, all the food is gone. It's the worst of all possible worlds. No driver, no food and a dead body.'

'But on the plus side, Guv,' said Mona. 'At least we don't have to give her a Health Check.'

8

Carrie had been on the phone for twenty minutes now, talking non-stop about pregnancy, the potential impact of hyper-tension, what the doctors were suggesting that she do about it, and how she felt about their suggestions. Bernard's attention had wandered some time back, reflecting over the events of the day.

He'd not seen the body himself, having turned back as soon as he'd spotted the foot sticking out from the boxes. Maitland's description had been plenty enough for him, and he could have lived without the hour his colleagues had spent speculating about how she had met her end while they waited for Hunter and the police to arrive. He leaned towards Maitland's theory that the body was one of Boucher's fellow activists, although he'd tuned out of the more graphic imagining of the circumstances of her death.

To his mind, his colleagues were focussing on the wrong angle. The woman's death was part of a much bigger unanswered question. Why was the lorry there in the first place, and how had anyone known how to find it? The tracking device had been disabled, so it was unlikely the driver had been followed. The outside chance remained that the lorry had been spotted and someone, some people, had taken it upon themselves to investigate and got lucky. Well, lucky right up until they'd found the girl on board and it had all gone south.

One other possibility was that someone had told the thieves the lorry was there. Yet the fact that the thieves had fled without taking the remaining boxes suggested a certain panic had set in. The girl obviously hadn't been part of the plan. Bernard wondered why she was in the lorry in the first place. Appraising the contents, starting to unload it, hiding there in panic? And where, oh, where was the fake Adam Stone?

Bernard's phone made the beeping sound that indicated someone else was trying to call him. It was the second time that had happened in the course of the conversation. He glanced up at the living room clock. It was exactly the time of evening that he usually spoke to Lucy. When he phoned her back, he should really make a clean breast of what was going on. Lucy was a lovely and compassionate woman, who would understand the bond between him and Carrie. Although Lucy had never actually been married, so it might be harder for her to understand the loyalty that develops over the course of a long relationship.

He muttered a few supportive noises in response to Carrie's latest concern, and his mind drifted back to the lorry. He'd given as full a statement as he could to Police Scotland, a process that had been made slightly more nerve-wracking with both Hunter and Mauchline hovering in the background hanging on his every word. There had been some discussion of their impact on the crime scene, and he had an appointment for the following day to give police colleagues his fingerprints and shoes 'for elimination purposes'. Everything else that he needed to know he'd find out tomorrow morning at the briefing Hunter had called, at *'9am sharp, not whenever the members of the North Edinburgh HET bother to roll in.'*

'So, Bernard, I know it's a big ask, but I have an appointment at the Royal on Thursday which I'm really nervous about. Is there any chance that you could come with me?'

He snapped back to the conversation. 'Ehm, I don't know. I should be at work. Can you text me the details and I'll see if I can get time off?'

'That would be brilliant. It's so good that I can rely on you to be there for me.'

'Yeah, about that—'

'Because with all the health issues attached to this pregnancy, I'm so scared I'm going to lose this baby. I couldn't bear that, Bernard.' There was a catch in her voice. 'I think it would literally kill me too.'

Bernard felt his stomach do a small flip. This didn't feel like a good time to be introducing new information about who was dating who, but at this rate Carrie's baby would have started school by the time he got round to telling her he now had a girlfriend. The silence stretched out and he realised that he had to say something. 'Yeah, well, OK, text me.'

He hung up, and almost immediately his phone rang again. 'Hi, Lucy.'

'Hello. You were on a very long call there. Is everything all right?'

'Yeah, yeah.' He stared up at the ceiling. 'It was just my mum. She likes to talk.'

'Oh, OK.'

There might have been the tiniest hint of disbelief in Lucy's voice, which Bernard tried very hard not to acknowledge. He was going to see Carrie through her next couple of appointments, then ease out of her life and focus one hundred and ten per cent on being the best boyfriend in the world. Everything was going to be OK. Probably.

9

Stuttle looked remarkably chipper given the complete and utter failure of his plan. He kept up a cheery monologue as they climbed the stairs at the Masonic Hall, and Mona wondered if this was evidence that he'd already identified a workable Plan B. Her optimistic frame of mind continued right up until she walked into the function room and saw the look on Mauchline's face. His expression was a mixture of frustration, mild irritation, and something else that she couldn't quite name, but might possibly have been embarrassment.

'So, this is a setback, I'll not deny it.'

'It's a bit more than a setback, Cam,' said Mauchline. 'Carmichael has never been more secure.'

'She got lucky—'

'More than luck! There's a double spread in the *Mail* today highlighting the sacrifice she's made on behalf of the country.'

Stuttle shrugged. 'That's just one paper. Twitter's being a lot more sceptical on the issue.'

'Twitter's default setting is scepticism,' Mona said. 'It's not exactly a balanced reflection of society. I think Carlotta's outplayed us on this one.'

'On this one, perhaps, she's come off best, but it's by no means our only line of attack.' Stuttle turned in her direction. 'Mona, anything going on at the HET that we can capitalise on? How's Hunter getting on? Any cock-ups yet that might reflect badly on Carlotta?'

She looked at Mauchline who was staring up at the roof. Either he was admiring the ornateness of the wooden carving, or he didn't want to catch her eye. If he had chosen not to pass on today's events, she didn't see why she should bring it up. 'Ms Hunter seems pretty efficient, Mr Stuttle.'

He looked disappointed. 'Well, that's rather unfortunate. I have to admit, I was hoping she'd be out of her depth.' He stood up. 'I'll get a round of drinks sent up, and we can have a further brainstorm.'

They watched in silence as Stuttle ran back down the stairs. The silence stretched on while Mona tried to work out how to broach the subject. She decided that there wasn't a tactful way to do it, so dived right in. 'I couldn't help but notice that you didn't mention Ms Hunter's difficulties today.'

Mauchline stared back at her. 'I couldn't help but notice that you didn't mention it either.'

'I was taking my lead from you, as the senior officer.'

He sighed. 'Fair enough, I suppose. I think we share the same problem, Mona. Carlotta's one step ahead of us in guessing what we might do. She's outplayed us on this one, and whatever genius idea Stuttle comes up with next, there's a good chance she'll have thought of it too. I hate to say it, but I think we could be stuck with Hunter. She's in, and barring a miracle, Stuttle's out.'

'Where does this leave us?'

'Personally speaking, it leaves me keeping my head down for the next few months while I see if I can get a transfer back to the police.'

'Will they let you do that?'

He nodded. 'It's only the front-line HET staff that can't leave.'

Mona pondered the unfairness of this. She hoped Carole never became party to this information.

'Anyway, Mona, you're here for the long haul. I suggest you think very carefully about which way you jump.'

'So, we just abandon Mr Stuttle?'

'I don't feel great about it.' He picked up a glass, and realising it was empty put it back with the others. 'But unless you've got a masterplan, I think we need to accept the reality of the situation.'

They heard footsteps and turned in Stuttle's direction. He met their gaze with a broad grin. 'I forgot to ask your order, Mona. I assumed that you weren't a real ale drinker, so I took a guess and got you a white wine.'

'Good guess, sir.'

'So ...' Stuttle looked round at them. 'Who's got a good idea?'

The silence was deafening.

WEDNESDAY

STEAK AND PRAWNS

I

'You're too late.'

Mona cursed her sleepless night. As was always the case when she woke up at 5am with her mind racing, she'd fallen into a sound asleep just before seven, and had crawled out of bed groggy and miserable when the alarm went off. She had planned to be up and out early, into the office and well prepared for Ms Hunter's meeting with them, but her befuddled state required a couple of cups of proper coffee before she was ready to face the day.

She hadn't intended to stop for a paper, but the headline on the board outside the newsagents was just too tempting. *HET staff are 'slaves' claims officer*. Cassandra Doom had been working her poison and Mona was desperate to read what she'd said. Unfortunately, it wasn't proving easy.

'Most of our papers are gone by 8am.' Mrs Patel was behind the counter, phone in hand. 'And today the *Citizen* is particularly popular. You work for the HET don't you?' She looked down at her phone again, then stared up at her. Mona assumed she was keeping track of the story online.

'Yeah.' Like Mrs Patel, she'd have to read it on their website.

'Bernard has a copy.' She smiled. 'He's a lovely lad. So polite. Usually he picks up a *Guardian*, but he saw the

headline, and said he'd better take the *Citizen* instead.'
Mrs Patel reached over and patted her hand. 'I'm very
sorry for you both. The HET does not sound like a good
place to work.'

Mona muttered a thank you and sprinted the remaining
few metres to the Cathcart Building. She had to read the
article before the morning briefing. She looked at her
phone. She had ten minutes until Hunter arrived,
assuming she was there sharp at nine, and Mona felt safe
in the assumption that Jennifer Hunter was a punctual
kind of person. She pressed her Green Card against the
box, pushed open the door and hurried in the direction of
the stairs, before stopping and retracing her steps.
Marguerite was sitting behind the reception desk,
engrossed in a copy of the *Citizen*.

'Can I borrow that?'

Marguerite folded the newspaper up and laid it on the
desk in front of her. 'Borrow?'

'I don't have any change, Marg. Come on, do me a
favour and I'll pop back for tickets later.'

'I'd like to believe you, Mona, but I've been burned by
that kind of promise before. Anyway, these are at a
premium. I got the last one in the shop, so I'm thinking
that the price of this is— hoi!'

Mona snatched the paper and bolted for her office,
Marguerite's curses following her as she ran.

'Bernard, have you seen the ... oh.'

Carole was seated behind her desk, a pair of scissors in
her hand and a small pile of *Citizen*s in front of her.
Bernard was hopping anxiously from foot to foot.

'You're back then, Carole.'

'I was never away, Mona.'

'It's just that you weren't in work yesterday, and ...
anyway, never mind. Ehm, what are you doing?'

Carole waved her scissors in Mona's direction. 'I'm pretty sure you can guess what I'm planning.' She dropped a packet of Blu Tack onto her desk. 'I'm cutting out Cassandra Doom's column from all of these papers, and I'm going to wallpaper Paterson's office with them.'

Out of the corner of her eye Mona could see Bernard checking the time on his phone. She shared his anxiety.

'You do know that our new boss is going to be here any minute?'

Carole smiled. 'Bernard told me. Saves me the trouble of posting her a copy.'

'Are you really sure you want to—' Mona broke off at the sound of voices in the corridor.

Paterson flung open the door and did a double take at the sight of Carole. 'Ah you're here, Carole.' His eyes drifted to the pile of papers. He didn't look surprised to see them, which led Mona to believe he was aware of their contents. She wondered if anyone would notice if she flicked through her paper to pick up the gist of the lies that Cassandra had told. Or worse, the truths.

'You must be Carole.' Jennifer Hunter smiled in Carole's direction, a gesture which was not reciprocated. 'Star of this morning's Cassandra Doom column.'

'As I'm sure you'll see, *Jennifer*, the paper refers to an anonymous source. It could have been anyone. God knows there's enough disgruntled members of staff in the Health Enforcement Teams across Scotland.'

Hunter nodded. 'True, true. Although there were some strong specifics here, including reference to court proceedings, which led me to believe that it was either you or your colleague in Forth Valley who is currently attempting to sue us. Anyway, we can come back to that later.' She spun round to face Paterson. 'Is your IT person here? I specifically asked for him to attend.'

There was a look of guilt on Paterson's face that led Mona to believe that inviting Marcus had been left off Paterson's 'to do' list. He quickly recovered. 'He's clearly running late. I'll go and get him.'

He nearly collided with Maitland who had appeared in the doorway. 'Morning all.'

Hunter gave a pointed look at her expensive watch.

Maitland shrugged. 'Traffic.' He looked at the pile of *Citizen*s. 'What's with all the papers, Carole?'

'Here he is.' Paterson ushered Marcus and his laptop into the room. 'He was just on his way to join us.'

Marcus looked outraged. 'Actually, Ms Hunter, I—'

'Please just get on with it.' Hunter's expensive watch got another airing. 'I have other places to be.'

Marcus gave an extended sigh and placed his laptop down on Mona's desk. 'This is where I've got to with Bryce's files.' He spent several minutes pulling different files up on screen, while Paterson and Hunter both watched him in irritation. 'I think you're going to find this very interesting.'

'Please just get on with it,' Hunter snapped.

'I've been through all the files that were set up by Bryce, well, the ones that I can actually access on our system at least. And given that he used passwords he knew I could guess, and the fact the files were stored on our system and not on some top-secret server of his own, I think we can assume that he is happy for me, and by extension you guys, to see them. So, we have the files here, in date order—' he gestured to the screen '—starting with the earliest file and moving on to—'

Paterson couldn't stand it any longer. 'For God's sake,

Marcus, just tell us if you have any information that could identify our dead girl.'

'Yes, Mr Paterson, I'm getting to it, it's just that the information itself is somewhat—'

'Please just precis what you've found.' Hunter looked as if she might explode if Marcus didn't get to the point soon. For once, Mona found herself in sympathy with her boss.

'I think I found the girl you're looking for.' He tapped at the keyboard again. 'There's a fourth member of the cell that Florian Boucher is part of, a woman by the name of, and pardon my pronunciation here, Natálie Svobodová. Aged twenty-four, blonde, and like the others, no evidence of a recent valid Health Check, which does lead to some questions about how they managed to access the country—'

'Right, Marcus. If you could email that information over to me as soon as possible.' Hunter picked up her bag and turned to leave.

'Not even a thank you?' asked Carole.

'I beg your pardon?' Hunter slowly turned back.

'Marcus has clearly worked his butt off looking through all these files, and has produced some information that's going to be really useful for your investigations, and all you say is email it to me? No "thank you"? No "well done"?'

The heightened colour in Hunter's cheeks suggested that Carole may have struck a nerve.

'And what about the massive result that Maitland and Bernard pulled off? Half of the police in the South of Scotland were looking for that lorry without success, yet they managed to find it with the limited resources that the HET has. Have you even said well done to them?'

Hunter's eyes flashed in the direction of Maitland and Bernard. Maitland grinned expectantly, then looked confused when Hunter turned her back on them and advanced in Carole's direction. 'I find it interesting, and a little bit ironic, that you of all people are lecturing me on staff motivation. Aren't you the woman who's been undermining the work of her colleagues at every turn? Aren't you the one who nearly got a colleague killed by leaving him in a burning building? And God only knows what you're planning to do with these?' She knocked the pile of *Citizen*s onto the floor. 'Cassandra Doom spouts filth week in, week out. You choose to ally yourself with the likes of her, then you lecture me on ethics? How dare you!'

Carole smirked and leaned forward to pick up her papers. Having retrieved them she got to her feet. 'If anyone wants me, I'll be in the cafeteria.'

Hunter stepped in front of her. 'I strongly suggest that you stay here and do some work.'

'Noted.' Carole stepped round her and kept moving.

'Have you spoken to your lawyer today, Carole?'

Carole paused with her hand on the doorknob.

'Because I had a very interesting conversation with SHEP's lawyers last night. The judges in the Forth Valley case made a ruling yesterday evening.'

Carole stood very still.

'It was behind closed doors, of course, so word might not have reached your lawyers yet, but a little bird told me they found in favour of SHEP.'

Carole spun round, fury written on her face. 'Excuse me if I don't believe you until I hear it for myself, but even if that is true you can't make me work here. You can insist that I turn up here every day, but you can't make me do anything. If you can't sack me, what exactly are you going to do to me?'

Hunter smiled. 'I'm glad you asked. We haven't really had a chance to get to know each other yet, but let me fill you in a little on my previous work history. Before I was seconded into this position, I worked on a number of projects that the Minister for Virus Policy was keen to see progressed. One of the most important ones was a re-examination of the legislation relating to misconduct in public office.'

Carole shot a questioning look in Bernard's direction. He helped out. 'It's the legislation they use to prosecute people for things like corruption.'

'Yes, Bernard,' said Hunter. 'It does usually relate to corruption, but it also covers reckless behaviour by public officials. It's an area of the law that can be a bit frustratingly vague to be honest, so Ms Carmichael had me carry out a review of how the law might affect, say, HET officers who were unhappy in their position and expressing that unhappiness through potentially harmful workplace behaviour. My finding was that we need one or more test cases to come to court to really establish legal thinking on this.' She grinned. 'Would you like to be the person to set a precedent in this area?'

'You can't—' Carole looked at Bernard again, who shrugged. 'This is just so BLOODY UNFAIR!'

'Unfair?' Hunter looked furious. 'There's a pandemic happening. Over a million people have died, and you are complaining because the worst thing that's happened to you is that you're being made to work in a well-paid white-collar job. You should be grateful that you're able to help.'

'There's more to my situation than that, as you well know.'

Hunter picked up her bag. 'John, please find Carole something useful to do today. Mona, you're with me.'

'You can't take a member of my staff again, Ms Hunter.' Paterson joined the list of HET staff who were currently furious with Jennifer Hunter. 'I need Mona here.'

'I'm sure you will cope. Come on, Mona.'

Mona shot an apologetic look at her boss, then followed Hunter out of the room. As the door closed behind them she heard Marcus speak. 'But I didn't even get a chance to tell her what the interesting bit was.'

2

There was absolute silence in the HET office. Bernard assumed that this was very much a temporary state, as Carole had stormed out of the room to phone her lawyer and Paterson had stormed into his office with a copy of the *Citizen*, so it was only a matter of time before one or both of them reappeared and the shouting began.

Marcus was still sitting at Mona's desk, tapping away at his laptop. His continued presence seemed to be annoying Maitland. 'Shouldn't you be back in your own room now, Marcus?'

He sighed. 'Just enjoying the companionship. I won't underplay his appalling behaviour, but I have to say that I do miss Bryce's company. It's a long day when you're sitting in a room all by yourself.' He looked round their office. 'I wonder if it would be possible to fit another desk into this room?'

'It wouldn't,' said Maitland, firmly.

Marcus looked at Bernard, a mute plea for support in his eyes. However, much as Bernard liked Marcus, the thought of listening to him discuss fantasy novels and progressive rock for eight hours every day was less than appealing. He played his trump card. 'You really want to spend all day within shouting distance of Mr Paterson?' he asked, his voice low to avoid the man in question hearing them.

'A very good point, Bernard.' Marcus mulled this over. 'That can't be easy. Maybe we could persuade Mr Paterson that you should move into my room?'

'Excellent idea!' Maitland spun round on his chair. 'Contain all the geeks in one area so no-one else has to be bothered by them.'

'This is a bloody disgrace!' Paterson loomed in their direction, the now-read copy of the *Citizen* being brandished like a weapon. 'Listen to this: "The Health Enforcement Teams provide nothing more than a retirement home for fat, second-rate coppers to see out the twilight of their careers." That's me she's having a go at, isn't it?'

'You're not fat, Guv, you're sturdy.' Maitland said, as if imparting a great truth.

'It's not necessarily about you, Mr Paterson,' said Marcus. 'Statistically speaking across Scotland a lot of the HET Team Leaders are ex-police officers, generally in their forties or fifties, and considering that a very high percentage of over-forties are also overweight, that would imply—'

'Why are you still here, Marcus? Don't you have an office of your own?'

'He gets lonely, Guv. Maybe Bernard could join him?'

'Actually, Mr Paterson, I'm still here because I've got something important to tell you.' Marcus stopped, doubt appearing on his face. 'Or maybe it's something I'm supposed to tell Ms Hunter?'

'Any information relevant to HET cases comes to me,' said Paterson, firmly. 'I can decide if it merits her knowing about it.'

'OK.' Marcus looked pleased that someone was, at last, listening to his revelations. 'I was trying to explain this earlier, but everyone seemed to be in too much of a hurry to listen.'

Paterson sighed. 'That's because you start every discussion with so much back story that we've lost the will to live by the time you get to the useful part. We didn't need to know about the files being listed in date order and—'

'But you did need to know that, Mr Paterson. Dates and times are of key importance here.'

Paterson gave up trying to hurry proceedings along and sat down in Carole's chair.

'OK, now, as you know I first attempted to look for information about Florian Boucher and his colleagues in Bryce's files on Monday, with pretty limited success. I found one file that had reference to him and Dieter Lange and Ana P?'

Bernard nodded. 'Yes, and you found another file today that indicated there was a fourth activist.'

'Yes, and the interesting part of all this is HOW I found that additional information. See.' He gestured them to look at his screen. Bernard rolled his chair closer to the laptop, and found he was looking at a list of files.

'Marcus, I have no idea what I'm looking at.' Paterson was looking particularly fed up. 'Please just spell it out and do it quickly.'

'When I first looked for these files, their encryption status was set to restricted access only. Look at them now.'

'They're all set to open,' said Bernard. 'Who changed them?'

'I don't know,' said Marcus. 'But when I noticed that, I went back into the files and I was able to open them right up.'

'But if Bryce is dead, who would have the ability to do that?' asked Maitland.

'Someone he'd trained up to do it, I assume,' said Marcus.

'Could Blair Taylor have done this?' asked Maitland.

Marcus shrugged. 'Possibly. He was an engineering student, so probably would be able to grasp this kind of thing, and Bryce could have talked him through it.'

At the talk of Blair Taylor, Bernard could feel a sickness rising within him. They'd start looking for Blair and who knew where that would lead.

'OK, so we can work out that Bryce could get this done from beyond the grave,' said Paterson. 'But the big question is, why? What's in those files that someone is keen for us to know? And who are they?'

'Guv, we ought to talk to Blair Taylor's parents, let them know that he might still be alive.'

Paterson shook his head. 'Not on this evidence. It's all too tenuous to get their hopes up. How many new files have been released?'

'About 500.'

There was a collective sigh of dismay from the room. 'And how many have you read so far?'

'About thirty.'

'Right, get this pair onto the case. The three of you ought to get through them in no time. I'll let Hunter know. And, if you bastards are still bugging this office,' his voice was louder now, and he spun slowly round as he spoke. 'We're looking into these files, just as I assume you want us to. Feel free to give us a clue what's actually going on here.'

There was a moment's silence when he finished. Bernard half expected to hear someone knock three times in response, but the silence continued.

Paterson turned on his heel and made for his office, then doubled-back to pick up the copy of the *Citizen* he'd discarded. 'Twilight of my career, my arse. We'll show Cassandra Doom some proper police work.'

3

Jennifer Hunter did not appear to be a fan of small talk. They'd been stuck in traffic on North Bridge for ten minutes due to a set of temporary traffic lights that appeared to be allowing only two cars at a time to proceed. Mona had attempted a couple of conversational openings which had been quickly shut down, so she'd taken the hint and kept quiet.

Another two cars passed through the set of lights before they turned red.

'This is infuriating!' Hunter let out a short but forceful sigh. 'We're going to be here all day.'

'I think we'll make it through on the next turn, Ma'am, I mean Ms Hunter.'

'I hope so. I was hoping this wasn't going to take all day.'

'Where are we going?' Mona was curious. After the way she had parted from Ms Hunter after their previous meeting she was struggling to identify why, of all people, Ms Hunter would want her around.

'Drylaw. I need to reinterview Boucher, and you'll have to accompany me.'

'Me? Surely that's something that CID should be doing?'

'You are a former CID officer so I'm sure you have the requisite skills.'

'Yes, but ...' Mona still didn't see why she was being co-opted. 'There are plenty of actual CID officers who could assist you.'

The lights changed, and Hunter accelerated, hugging the bumper of the car in front until she was safely through. 'Finally. And actually, no there aren't a lot of CID officers who could assist. Our two HET/CID Liaison Officers have been diverted onto working on some other project, which no-one consulted me about.'

'But someone else could assist surely?'

'Apparently not. Boucher is still refusing to participate in a Health Check—'

'A second Health Check?'

'Yes, Mona, after the unfortunate confusion of the first one he is now refusing to do it again. I think he's hoping that the misunderstanding with the first Health Check might play in his favour.'

Mona wondered if he was correct about that. She wondered if it was a situation that had ever arisen before, or did Hunter have the honour of inventing a whole new category of cock-up?

'Anyway,' continued Hunter, 'I am informed that the police are not allowed to interview suspects without an up-to-date Health Check so I either wait for a court order that allows us to take Boucher's blood against his will, or I look for another method.'

'But there must be police officers who've already had the Virus and are now immune. Couldn't one of them help?'

'You would think so, wouldn't you? It's almost like they're all sticking to the letter of the law because they don't like being asked to do something by someone who isn't a serving police officer.'

And who has just taken over from a former police officer who everyone knows is getting the boot for political reasons.

'And I assume, Mona, seeing as your whole job involves working with people who have missed a Health Check, you won't have any qualms about assisting me here.'

Did she have any qualms? She might not be too popular with her police colleagues if she helped out, and one of these days she was going to return to active police work. However, if Mauchline was right and Stuttle was definitively out of the picture, it would be a good opportunity to get in Hunter's good books. Although the way Hunter had handled things so far Mona wasn't entirely convinced she's be around for long. Either way, if she was going to say no, she needed to think of a watertight reason why she couldn't do it, and her brain wasn't coming up with anything. 'I suppose it will be OK, so long as I'm not breaking any regulations by doing so.'

'Well, if you are, I'm sure you'll just blame me.'

There was a short silence, and Mona decided to use the fact that Hunter was now speaking to her to ask another question that was on her mind. 'Is SHEP really going to be pursuing misconduct cases against HET officers?'

'Yes.'

Mona felt a twinge of anxiety about how her previous conduct might be considered. The North Edinburgh HET had made a few questionable moves in the past, usually for the right reasons. If any of it came to light, were they about to be publicly shamed? Without Stuttle around to protect them they were undeniably vulnerable.

'I'm not keen to do it, obviously.' Hunter looked over at her. 'It's not good for anyone, but we do need all the HET officers pulling their weight. At some point there will be test case about inappropriate behaviour by HET officers who are keen to leave the service. Is Carole a friend of yours?'

'Yes, I suppose so.'

'Then talk to her. Don't let her be the person we need to take to court. I've got no personal grudge against her, even in spite of that awful Cassandra Doom article, and I know that she has problems at home, with her son being a drug addict—'

'Her son isn't a drug addict.'

'Well, got caught dealing drugs.'

'He was never into drugs. Her fifteen-year-old was set up by the brother of a Health Defaulter we were chasing in an attempt to blackmail the HET into doing what he wanted. The man doing the blackmailing is a nasty bit of work, a hardcore drug dealer – the kind of person you wouldn't want near your kids in a million years. So Carole was terrified of what might happen to her son and decided she had to get her boy out of Scotland. Her entire family apart from her now lives in the North of England, so I think she's got reason to be upset. If she didn't work for the HET, none of that would have happened.'

Hunter turned the car into the driveway of Drylaw Police Station. She pulled up in a parking space and turned the engine off, but remained sitting. 'I don't remember any of this being on Carole's staff file.'

'Did it say her son was a drug addict?'

'No, I was told that by—' She stopped herself and opened the door of the car. 'We need to get on with this, Mona. Let's hope Mr Boucher is a little more cooperative today.'

'How are you planning to handle this, Ms Hunter?'

'I want to see how he reacts when we tell him that we have the lorry, and that one of his colleagues has been found dead on it. Hopefully that will shake him up a bit and make him a bit more cooperative.'

Mona thought this unlikely. Boucher had been willing to set himself on fire to further his cause. He and his colleagues clearly accepted that death might be part of their campaign; he wasn't going to break down and confess everything that had happened in an outpouring of grief.

'Do we have anything to directly connect Boucher to the lorry? Any fingerprints or anything?'

Hunter shook her head.

'Ah.'

Her boss looked irritated. 'What does "ah" mean?'

'I'm not trying to be rude, Ms Hunter, but that's a pretty delicate line of questioning. It would really benefit from an actual police officer leading on—'

'And that's not going to happen, is it? Not with the militant branch of the Police Association in there standing on their rights. We've got no evidence linking him to the lorry, and this situation with his Health Check means that it could be months before anyone can actually get him interviewed about his breach of the peace, and all the time he'll have some lefty lawyer working to get him off on some technicality, and the Minister for Virus Policy is very keen to see a speedy resolution to all this, so if you have a better idea, I'm very keen to hear it.'

Mona stared out the window and decided which way to jump. *Stuttle or Hunter*. 'Actually, Ms Hunter, I think I do have an idea.'

Hunter had Boucher installed in an interview room, with a police officer stationed outside the door. As before, he looked relaxed, smiling up at them when they walked into the room.

'Mr Boucher.' Hunter smiled in return. 'How are you?'

'I am hungry. I have asked repeatedly for vegan food but they keep giving me vegetarian.'

'Well, we can't have that. I'll have a word with them. Now, I think we'll make a start.' She pressed the button to start recording. 'Interview with Florian Boucher commenced—'

'You can't interview me.' Boucher looked concerned at the turn of events. 'You are not police.'

Hunter grinned. 'Oh, I'm sorry, you are not being interviewed on a police matter, this is an interview under Health Enforcement legislation. Interview with Florian Boucher commenced 10.15am, in the room are Jennifer Hunter, Scottish Health Enforcement Partnership and Mona Whyte, North Edinburgh Health Enforcement Team. Health Enforcement Officer Whyte has some questions.'

Mona put her plan into action. 'Mr Boucher, the Scottish Health Enforcement Act gives us the power to require individuals to give us information about other individuals who have defaulted on their monthly Health Check.'

Boucher's grey eyes were fixed on her face, alert and wary about where she was going.

'We are currently seeking two individuals who have recently entered the country who are in default of the Health Check arrangements in their home countries, Dieter Lange and Ana Procházková. We believe both of these people are known to you.'

Boucher sat back on his chair, a look of exasperation on his face.

'Please give us all the information you have on the likely whereabouts of these two individuals.'

He stared silently back at them.

'You may not be familiar with Scottish legislation on this matter, but we have indefinite powers of detention where we suspect that an individual is deliberately obstructing our attempts to locate a Health Defaulter.'

He was still silent, but his colour was rising. Mona decided to put some pressure on. 'We believe that both these Health Defaulters were instrumental in the recent hijacking of a lorry.'

He shifted in his seat. 'I do not see how that is the business of the Health Enforcement Team.'

'Finding two missing Health Defaulters is entirely our business.' She stared at him, but he was looking into the distance, obviously recalculating how he needed to handle the situation. 'There was a third Defaulter that we are seeking, Mr Boucher, one Natálie Svobodová. The only thing is, and there's no easy way to say this, we think she might no longer be with us. When the lorry was recovered, there was the body of a young woman on board. Do you know anything about that, Mr Boucher?'

There was a moment's pause, then Boucher shot to his feet, whipping his arm behind him to grab his chair. Mona caught hold of a leg as he swung it, and found herself thrown to the wall. Despite his laid-back appearance, Boucher was strong and easily able to defend himself. Hunter must have pressed the panic alarm as a siren sounded, and two police officers burst in the door. Mona was glad that their hostility to Hunter hadn't stopped them responding promptly. Between them they got Boucher cuffed, and the police officers led him down the corridor to the cells, one on either side of him, Boucher keeping up an angry monologue in French as they walked. Mona couldn't remember enough of her school language studies to understand it, but she'd been yelled at plenty by unhappy Health Defaulters so she could make a good guess at what he was saying. Chances are it involved her being a fascist, tool of the state, and probably a stupid bitch as well.

'Are you OK?' Hunter appeared at her side.

'Yeah, fine.' She did a few stretches to make sure. 'Totally fine.'

Hunter smiled. 'That must have been like being back in your old police days – having to deal with someone turning violent.'

Mona looked at her in disbelief. 'We get faced with violence day in, day out. How do you think people are going to react when we turn up unannounced and tell them off for missing a Health Check?' Hunter stared at her in confusion, and she wondered if their new boss actually knew anything about the realities of the organisation she was managing. 'You've got people seconded to the HET who worked in health promotion, who are now faced with irate members of the public who try to punch them, or in some case stab them, and it's only a matter of time before—'

'Ma'am?' The desk sergeant was heading towards them. Hunter looked relieved at the distraction. 'You asked me to let you know as soon as any of the lab reports were back.' He handed over an envelope.

'Thank you.' She began slitting the envelope. 'And while you are here, Mr Boucher was complaining about not getting vegan food. He says you keep giving him vegetarian food and he is apparently starving.'

The sergeant rolled his eyes. 'I'll see what we can do. But I tell you this, he's not starving. He's eaten everything that we've given him, so he can't be that strict in his beliefs.'

'OK, thanks.' Hunter was distracted, caught up in the paperwork. She looked up and Mona could see she was debating whether to tell her something.

'News, Ms Hunter?'

She gave a small smile. 'It seems like a strict adherence to vegan principles wasn't the only thing that Mr Boucher has been faking. I think the self-immolation attempt was just a stunt.'

'My HET colleagues seemed to think it was pretty real. He was covered in petrol.'

'Yes, he was. He was definitely covered in something highly flammable. However, the lab analysed the lighter he was carrying. The liquid in it was water.' She shot a thoughtful look in the direction that Boucher had just gone. 'I think Boucher is a fake. The question is, why is he faking?'

Mona followed her gaze. 'And if he is faking, who is he really?'

4

'Anybody found anything useful?'

'I'm not sure I'd know if I had, Guv.' Maitland leaned back with his hands tucked behind his head. 'All I've read so far is file after file about people SHEP has been keeping tabs on. Although why SHEP is holding files on people is beyond me. I'd have thought it would be more Police Scotland's thing.'

'There's always the possibility that this was a little side project for Bryce,' said Marcus, 'rather than something he was pursuing in an official capacity.'

'That does seem more likely,' said Bernard. 'If it's one of Bryce's friends that has made these files public, what do you think he or she is expecting us to do with them? Do they want us to publish them?'

Maitland frowned. 'But we don't know who these people are or what they're supposed to have done, so how could we do anything with the info?'

'Well, we'll have to put our discussion on the subject on hold. I need you to take a break from trawling the files and come with me.'

'Where are we going, Guv?'

'A food bank. I got a call from my son's girlfriend—'

'Your son who's a police officer?' asked Bernard.

'Both his sons are police officers, loser.' Maitland joined in. 'Is it the one that's in Glasgow or the one in the Met, Guv?'

144

'Will the pair of you shut up with the questions! My son who's in the Met is in town and his girlfriend is volunteering at a food bank today, and apparently they recently had a large donation of goods which Liz thinks came from our lorry.'

'How could she possibly know that?' Maitland looked sceptical.

'Because they opened one of the boxes and it was full of after dinner chocolates wrapped in special labels celebrating their attendance at the V8 Supper.' He grinned. 'No wonder Carlotta's keen to get them back. What a bloody waste of taxpayers' money. So, let's grab a couple of the pool cars and pick up the boxes before anyone tips off the *Citizen* and Cassandra Doom gets her mitts on this story.'

'Ehm, Mr Paterson, when you said you needed everyone to come with you, were you meaning me as well?' Marcus looked hopeful.

'Can you carry a box without arsing it up, Marcus?'

'I think so, Mr Paterson.'

'Then come on.'

Marcus grinned. 'Many hands make light work.'

'He's not going to be quoting the Bible the whole time he's with us, is he, Guv?'

'Ah, Maitland, that's a common error. It's not actually a biblical quote, it's a proverb—'

'Bernard.' Paterson had suddenly swung round in his direction, making him jump.

'Yes, Mr Paterson?'

'Marcus is in your car.'

'I have to say, Bernard, that food banks do wonderful work.' Giddy with the excitement of being liberated from the office, Marcus had not stopped talking since they got into the car. 'With food prices the way they are, there's a whole section of society who wouldn't be sure where their next meal was coming from if it wasn't for these kinds of operations. I have to say I feel a little bit of shame when I think about them.'

'Shame?'

He nodded. 'There was a time when I never went into a supermarket without picking up a couple of cans for the local food bank. But then food prices went crazy, and now you're only allowed to buy a certain amount of everything, and I've stopped buying for them. Don't hate me.'

'I don't hate you.' It had been a long, long, time since he'd dropped any tins into the food bank donation trolley at his local Asda. 'And I feel anger when I think about food banks, or soup kitchens, or care vans.'

'Anger?' Marcus turned to stare at him. 'Surely not. How could such laudable institutions incur your wrath?'

'I don't feel angry at them, Marcus, I feel angry that they're needed. We're one of the richest countries on earth – why do we need to rely on charity to make sure that our children get fed? It's like we've returned to the Victorian age.'

'Oh, I see.' Marcus rambled on, but Bernard did his best to block him out. Much as he loved a debate about food politics, at the present moment his number one priority was keeping up with Paterson's car. Despite his feelings about the existence of food banks, he had the greatest respect for the people who staffed them, and the last thing he wanted was a bunch of volunteers being bawled out by his boss over their inadvertent handling of stolen property.

Unfortunately, his urban driving skills couldn't

compare with Paterson's, and he found himself confounded by the traffic lights on Newington Road. By the time he pulled up in the car park at the Southside Food Bank he could already hear his boss's voice blaring out. When they entered the building he could see Paterson and Maitland were surrounded by a group of volunteers. A woman with an Australian or New Zealand accent was doing her best to mediate between them.

'John, they weren't to know these goods were stolen.'

'I'm sorry, Liz, but the monogrammed chocolate should have given them some idea.'

'We get all kinds of odd donations here.' A small grey-haired woman in a green apron spoke up, her accent cut-glass. 'Things that haven't sold, or leftover food from weddings or events. We couldn't have known. We're desperate for donations since rationing started.'

Paterson stared down at her. Even he seemed to be struggling to shout at a seventy-year-old community activist. 'OK, well, who took the delivery?'

'That would be me. Mrs Rosemary Martin, I can provide my home address and telephone number should you require it.'

Paterson looked slightly mollified. 'OK, well let's find somewhere we can discuss this a bit more privately. Liz, can you show this pair where the "donated" food is?' He pointed at Maitland and Marcus. 'Bernard, you're with me.' He let Mrs Martin lead the way, then put a hand on Bernard's shoulder. 'If she starts to cry when I question her, it's over to you.'

'OK.' Bernard didn't think there was any danger of Mrs Rosemary Martin being intimidated by his boss, but he did think that there was a very good chance that she might be close friends with one or more councillors, police chiefs, or assorted other people who could make the HET's life difficult.

Mrs Martin showed them into a small office. 'I really am very sorry about this. We had no idea the food was stolen.'

'We understand,' said Bernard. He perched on top of a stack of boxes, leaving the two chairs in the room to the others.

She peered out of the office window. 'I hope the volunteers all come back tomorrow. We have a lot of men who have had run-ins with the police in the past, and it doesn't take much to spook them.'

'Interesting.' Paterson also stared out. 'I thought I recognised a couple of them.'

She looked at him sharply. 'None of our volunteers was responsible for this mistake.'

'We know that,' said Bernard hastily. 'We just want to know more about the people who donated the food. Could you describe them?'

She nodded. 'There were two of them, a man and a woman. Well, I would have said a girl really, but when you get to my age everyone looks so young. I suppose she was actually in her twenties. He was older, thirties I would say, balding, solidly built, and dressed quite scruffily, you know, several layers of baggy jumper and an old sports jacket on top. The girl had long dark hair and dark eyes, very pretty in my opinion. She was a bit more sensibly dressed, jeans and a waterproof. And they both had accents. European, I'd say, possibly Polish or something like that.'

'That's quite a full description.' Paterson looked almost impressed.

'Yes, they were here for a little while. I couldn't persuade them to have their picture taken for our Twitter feed though. We generally like to post something positive when we get a particularly big donation.'

'Your Twitter feed?' Paterson looked surprised.

'Oh yes, everyone needs a social media presence these days. Is your team on social media?'

Bernard stifled a grin. Hell would freeze over before Paterson would engage with Twitter.

Maitland knocked on the office window. 'That's us, Guv. Got it all.'

They filed back out into the hall. Marcus tapped Bernard on his shoulder. 'I thought I might ...' He showed Bernard the ten pound note he was holding in his hand.

'Oh, good idea.' Bernard dug into his pockets and also pulled out a note.

Maitland appeared. 'What are you two doing?'

'We're going to make a donation.'

'Really? We're here on work business.'

'Even so, look at this place. They're doing good work.'

Maitland sighed but pulled out a ten-pound note which he added to the pile. Paterson caught sight of them, and without a word pulled out a note which he added to the pile. 'Liz?'

She came over. Paterson picked up the notes and passed them over. 'From the HET. But don't tell Greg. I don't want him thinking I'm going soft in my old age.'

She smiled. 'Your secret's safe with me.'

They said their goodbyes and headed out to the car park.

'I thought you would be longer shifting the boxes,' said Paterson.

'Me too, Guv, but there was only about twenty of them.'

Paterson looked thoughtful. 'That's not a full lorry load. Bernard, how many food banks do you think there are in Edinburgh?'

He shrugged. 'I don't know. Maybe a dozen?'

'Well, get a list pulled up on your phone. I think we've got a few more visits to make.'

5

She'd been hanging around Drylaw for nearly two hours now, waiting for Boucher to agree to another interview. According to the sergeant she'd met on the front desk earlier, Boucher was refusing to leave his cell. 'He's standing on his rights. Says he doesn't have to comply.'

Hunter looked furious. 'What rights?'

Sergeant McGarry shrugged his shoulders. 'Don't know, Ma'am, but you know how it is with these types. They always feel hard done to. Can always get a lawyer to back them up, too.'

Mona felt that this last comment might have been more about putting the wind up SHEP's new boss than anything else.

'Well, can't you go and drag him into the interview room?'

The sergeant turned to Mona. 'I understand he's now being interviewed in a Health Defaulter case, not about the breach of the peace?'

She nodded.

'Well, then.' He threw his arms up in a manner that suggested that the issue was all self-explanatory.

'Well, then, what?' said Hunter, irritably.

'It's delicate, isn't it? The law isn't too clear on the support that the police should be giving to a Health Defaulter interview. We usually rely on the HET/CID Liaison guys for advice on this, and no-one—'

'No-one can get hold of them, yes, I know.' Hunter was looking more furious by the minute.

'And, of course, there's the issue of his uncertain health status. Not sure that we can really be laying hands on him, unless there's an immediate threat to life and limb.'

'OK, Sergeant McGarry, thank you for your ...' Hunter paused, presumably searching for a word that wasn't *help*. 'Your input on this issue. Mona and I can take it from here.' She waited until Sergeant McGarry had gone back upstairs then turned to her. 'Do you have any bright ideas?'

'We ask him nicely?'

'Seriously?' Hunter rolled her eyes.

'He doesn't want to be here either. At the moment he's in danger of being detained indefinitely, until he has his Health Check. I suggest that we send Sergeant McGarry in to say that we think we have a solution to our current stalemate, that could see him released by the end of the day.'

'That's not true, is it?'

'Well, it's not a complete lie. It's just that the solution involves him agreeing to a second Health Check and admitting to a breach of the peace. He's not going to like it, but it is technically possible.'

Hunter rolled her eyes for a second time, but set off to find the sergeant.

To everyone's surprise, not least Mona's, the plan worked. Boucher loped into the interview room and shot them both a smile. 'Ladies, so good to see you.' His eyes lingered on her. 'Mona Whyte, again a pleasure.'

Something about his accent sounded familiar, touching a memory that she couldn't quite rouse. Had they met before?

Hunter kicked off the proceedings. 'Interview with Florian Boucher commenced 11.55am. In the room are Jennifer Hunter, Scottish Health Enforcement Partnership and Mona Whyte, North Edinburgh Health Enforcement Team.'

Boucher was still smiling at her. 'How can I assist?'

'We were thinking a second Health Check, some information about your friends who are also in default on their Health Checks, admission of your part in a breach of the peace, some intelligence about your involvement in international terrorism, that kind of thing.'

He laughed. 'I don't think so.'

'OK, let's start small then. Where are Dieter Lange and Ana Procházková?'

He shrugged. 'I'm not sure how much assistance I can be to you. We were all active in our protests but I didn't know them well.'

'Really?' Hunter looked sceptical. 'You were both part of the same cell.'

'Cell?' Boucher shook his head. 'You watch too many spy films, Ms Hunter. We are just a bunch of people who share a common goal.'

'Which is?'

'That everyone in the world should have access to affordable food. This is not a particularly offensive view, is it? I don't think it makes me a terrorist, does it?'

'No, threatening to set fire to yourself in a public place and putting a whole load of people in fear of their lives is what makes you a terrorist.' Mona stared him in the eye. 'Wouldn't you say?'

'OK, Boucher.' Hunter sounded impatient. Mona hoped that she wasn't going to dive in with her questions. Boucher was smart; he was not going to give them a direct answer. The only hope was to trip him up. 'Who are you working for?'

Mona sighed, silently. Boucher leaned back on his chair his arms folded, and the irritating little grin on his face. 'We've met, you know.'

Mona had a brief moment thinking that she had been correct in her earlier assumption, before she realised that Boucher was talking to Hunter.

'I don't think so.'

Mona could sense the interview slipping away from Hunter and stepped in. 'Nobody is interested in your nonsense, Boucher. Just answer the question.'

Boucher's eyes were still locked on Hunter's. 'The Women and Virus Business Forum. Ms Carlotta Carmichael booked a very nice meeting room.'

'You weren't at that meeting. You couldn't have been,' Hunter said, looking decidedly uncomfortable.

'But I was! You, and Ms Carmichael, and all the other pleasant young ladies, all focused on where your careers might go next. And me, invisible to all of you. This is what happens, Mona Whyte, isn't it?' She ignored him, but he kept staring at her. 'You put on a white shirt and a black bowtie, and you hold a tray of drinks and everyone ignores you. I get to mingle with all these very important people, and you know why? Because this capitalist society won't invest in workers. They don't want to employ people full-time for years and years, building up a good, trusting relationship with their staff. No. They want to pick them up and drop them again, as cheaply as possible. Hotels use agency staff. *Haulage companies* use agency staff. We could be anyone.'

Mona could see Hunter's mind dealing with this information. 'There were no staff in the room while our discussions were taking place.'

He smiled. 'I'm not saying I came away with any state secrets. But I was this close,' he held his hands up, six inches apart, 'to your Minister for Virus Policy, and several key civil servants. And what was that word you used to describe me? Oh, yes, "terrorist". How big a security breach is it to have a terrorist in such close proximity to your Virus team?'

Hunter stood up. 'Interview terminated.'

Boucher winked at her as she passed him. Once the door closed behind them, Hunter grabbed her arm. 'Not a word to Paterson, or anyone else about what he just said,' she hissed, before running up the stairs.

'Was any of it true?' Mona asked to Hunter's retreating back but didn't receive an answer. She sighed and started back in the direction of the main entrance. *The Masons. The Women and Virus Business Forum.* If she was going to have any kind of career at all, she definitely needed to start networking.

6

Mona flung open the door to the HET office, only to have it bounce back on her. She pushed it open a little more cautiously and found that the cause of the obstruction was a pile of cardboard boxes. She manoeuvred cautiously into the room and saw that behind another stack of boxes, Carole was sitting at her desk.

'What's all this?'

'It's the contents of that lorry that you were looking for.'

'Really?' She pulled open the lid of the nearest box, and found it was full of pats labelled *Finest Scottish Butter*. 'Where was it?'

'According to Bernard, it had been distributed to food banks across the city. I don't know why they've brought it here, though. It's all going to go off.' She looked round the room. 'I wonder what Cassandra Doom would make of all this?'

'You're not going to speak to her about it?' Mona sat down more heavily than she'd intended, caught up in her horror at the thought of Cassandra Doom seeing their office in its current state.

She shook her head. 'Our new boss put the wind up me this morning. I spoke to my lawyer and Hunter was absolutely right, in the Forth Valley court case they found in favour of SHEP.'

'So where does that leave you?'

'Well, my solicitor said that it is a precedent, but that doesn't rule out us continuing. She thinks that the judges will take the view that every case needs to be treated on its own merits, and that SHEP can't get away with having a blanket policy that nobody can resign under any circumstances.'

'That sounds positive. You've got really strong personal reasons why you need to leave.'

'That's what my solicitor said. But she also said that the precedent is important, and that we'd have to go back to court and plead the specifics of our case. I'm not sure that we can afford a court case, and I'm really, really, sure that I don't want to have the whole world know what Michael did.' She sighed. 'Whichever way I dress it up, he did procure illegal drugs. It wouldn't be fair to him to broadcast his stupidest mistake to the whole world.'

'I'm sorry, Carole. It looks like you're stuck here.' Mona sat down at her desk. 'You know, the last round of vaccine trials looks really promising. If they do manage to get something that works, they're probably not going to need a HET, or at least not on the scale that we have now. You could be out of here sooner than you think.'

'It's a nice thought, but in the meantime if I don't want to end up in court as our new boss's test case, I have to pretend to do some work.' She sighed. 'You'd better give me something to do.'

'I'm not entirely sure what we're supposed to be doing.'

Someone attempted to fling open the office door, only for it to bounce off the boxes and slam shut. A moment later it reopened and Maitland stuck his head round and slid into the room. 'I've just had to give Marcus a lift back to the office. Does he ever shut up?'

'In my experience, no. Where are the others?'

'Paterson's been summoned to Carlotta Carmichael's office for a meeting with her and Hunter. He insisted that Bernard went with him as moral support.'

'What are we supposed to do with this food?' asked Carole. 'I'm sitting next to a crate of finest Scottish prawns, and the ice around them is starting to melt.'

'I know. I carried multiple boxes of Aberdeen Angus steaks up the stairs. I'm not sure that they'll still be edible. What a waste! If anyone finds out about this, Carlotta is going to get sacked.' He turned to Carole. 'You're not intending to, you know ...' He did a little mime of Carole making a phone call.

She shook her head. 'Do you think we ought to ring Fettes and see if they're able to accommodate it in their kitchen?'

It was a good idea; the police HQ had a sizeable cafeteria. Yet she was reluctant to do so. 'I'm not sure what Ms Carmichael would want us to do. The more people that we involve in this, the more chance there is of someone leaking it to the press.'

Maitland snorted. 'I think the horse has well and truly bolted on that one. There are twelve food banks each with a stack of volunteers who've been rifling through the contents of these boxes. A couple of them had already started distributing the food. There will be bairns across Edinburgh tucking into monogrammed chocolate bars even as we speak.'

'So, what do we do now?' asked Mona.

'I think we have to sit on this lot until we get further instructions, but before that, you need to phone Mauchline.'

'Why?'

Maitland grinned. 'The Guv's parting words to me were somebody get on the phone to SHEP and find out if we're chasing the missing activists or what. There was a bit more swearing in his version.'

'So, "somebody" means me?'

He shrugged. 'I can toss you for it if you like?' He produced a coin which he spun up in the air, and failed to catch. It hit the floor and disappeared between two of the boxes. 'Bugger.'

'No, you're all right, I'll do it.'

Mauchline answered on the first ring. 'Mona. What's up?'

He sounded busy, so she leapt right in. 'Mr Paterson asked me to ring you for a steer on whether we are to pursue Dieter Lange and Ana Procházková to get them Health Checks.'

'Does Paterson not make his own phone calls to me these days?'

'He was summoned into a meeting with Carlotta Carmichael.'

'What?' Mauchline sounded furious. 'That's not how things are done. If Ms Carmichael wants to speak to front-line HET staff, she comes through us.'

'Ehm . . .'

He picked up on her hesitation. 'Jen Hunter knows about this, doesn't she?'

'She's attending the meeting.'

A long and irritated sigh came through her phone. 'Fine. I'll speak to you later.'

'Sir,' she said, alarmed that he was about to hang up. 'I phoned you about the missing activists?'

'Sorry, I was a bit distracted there. I thought you were all busy looking for the missing food?'

'We found it.'

'Really?'

'You sound surprised, sir.'

'I am. No reflection on your team's detection abilities, I just assumed it was all sitting in the back room of a shop somewhere, about to be sold under the counter. Where was it?'

'At several food banks across the city.'

'Seriously?' He laughed, loudly and heartily. Mona held the phone away from her ear. 'Ms Carmichael might struggle to keep a lid on all this. Does this mean that these are genuine do-gooders that we're dealing with?'

'Certainly looks like some of them are.' She thought about Boucher. 'Maybe not all of them though. So, should we be looking for them, sir?'

'Usually I wouldn't hesitate to set you looking for them, because the police aren't going to be able to talk to them until you've done your bit.'

'Why are you hesitating, sir?'

'Because *usually* we'd have police support from our HET/CID liaisons, but they've been reassigned. I'm slightly reluctant to send HET officers solo into a situation where we don't really know what's happening.'

'But like you say, sir, we need to do our bit.' There was no way she was stepping away from this if she could avoid it.

There was a moment's silence while Mauchline thought it over. 'OK. The sooner we have this pair found, the better. I'll generate the paperwork. And one thing you need to know, the Czech Republic got back in record quick time with dental records for Natálie Svobodová, and they're a perfect match for the body on the lorry.'

'One mystery solved, sir. We'll start work looking for the other two.'

'Just before you go, Mona,' he lowered his voice. 'Stuttle's been in touch, asking for a meeting tonight.'

'What did you say?'

'I haven't said anything yet, but I'm thinking I put him off until we've got something of use to discuss.' There was a brief pause.' Have you got any good ideas?'

It was her turn to pause. 'Absolutely none, sir.'

'I'll put him off. I'll say we're working on something.'

Mona thought that perhaps they should be honest with Stuttle about his prospects but decided to keep that to herself.

'OK, Mona, I'll let you go, but I can't stress this enough, be cautious. We've already had one fatality linked to these activists, I don't want any HET officers added to the list of casualties.'

7

'I'm just not sure why I need to be at this meeting.' Bernard's anxiety was working overtime. He had no desire to be anywhere near Carlotta Carmichael. He would be perfectly happy if Ms Carmichael had no idea who he was or what he did.

'You don't *need* to be at this meeting, Bernard. I can't imagine that you're going to say anything useful, and there's the ever-present danger that you say something really stupid that drops us in it with Carmichael.'

'So, why—?'

'Because I *want* you there. I want a witness to whatever it is that Carmichael is going to say to me. I don't want her instructing us to do something, then changing her mind, and Jennifer Hunter backing her up saying I got it wrong.'

'But Ms Carmichael can't instruct us to do something. She doesn't have the power to instruct the day-to-day running of the HET; that's Ms Hunter's job. She can tell Ms Hunter to do things, but not us.'

'And your encyclopaedic knowledge of procedure is the reason I brought you and not Maitland. I don't seem to be able to instruct you, or Marcus for that matter, to tie your shoelaces without you both quoting me chapter and verse on why I can't ask you to do that, because I haven't risk-assessed the impact of bending down, and the shoelaces that you've been given aren't ethically Fair-Traded cotton—'

'I don't think that's a fair interpretation of my approach, Mr Paterson. I just like to be aware of my rights.'

'Well, that's the kind of out-of-the-box thinking I might need.'

'It's not so much out of the box, Mr Paterson, as how normal people behave in any job that isn't based on an unthinking willingness to obey orders, no matter how ridiculous they are.'

Paterson sighed. 'I'm beginning to think I should have brought Marcus. Anyway, we're here. Now, keep it buttoned unless I give you the nod.'

Bernard submitted to the Parliament's security searches and tried not to sulk.

Jennifer Hunter was sitting alone in a small meeting room, with a tray full of refreshments in front of her. She looked surprised to see Bernard.

'I thought it might be useful for Bernard to be in attendance due to his key role in locating the food.'

Hunter looked worried. 'I'm not sure that the Minister will be happy about that.'

Paterson exerted pressure on Bernard's left shoulder, and he found himself shoved down onto a chair. He thought about offering to leave, but that would be just storing up trouble for his return to the office. Hunter and Paterson could fight it out between themselves.

'Ah, tea.' Paterson pounced on the refreshments. 'Shall I be mother?'

Bernard found himself the recipient of an unwanted cup of brown liquid. Did Paterson really think that Carlotta wouldn't throw him out because he was halfway through a cuppa?

'Where's Ms Carmichael?' Paterson asked.

'She's been delayed, but I'm sure she'll be here soon.'

Right on cue, they heard the sound of voices in the hallway. Bernard struggled to hear who Carlotta was talking to. It seemed to be one other person, a man, whose voice sounded quite familiar. *Oh no.*

The door opened, and Ian Jacobsen stood there. Once upon a time Jacobsen had been, if not exactly a handsome man, then certainly one who could have passed with a shove. Bernard's self-defence with a window pole had left Jacobsen some distance from any future modelling engagements, with scarring to the side of his head, and one eye that was decidedly smaller than the other.

'Bernard.' Jacobsen smiled at him, a frosty baring of his teeth. 'I didn't know you were coming to this meeting.'

'I can go.' He tried to stand up, only to find that someone had a very strong grip on his knee. He looked at Paterson, who was staring straight ahead, and gave up. Maybe it would be better not to leave the meeting on his own, anyway. Mona had left a meeting on her own with Jacobsen at the City Chambers and had 'fallen' head first down a flight of stairs. He'd stick close to Paterson.

'Can we get on with this, please?' Carlotta bustled into the meeting. She didn't so much as glance in his direction, and Bernard wondered if she was even remotely interested in who was there. 'So, you've found all the missing food?'

'We think so, Minister.' Jen Hunter stepped up. 'We have recovered a substantial amount of goods from food banks across Edinburgh.'

'Well, that's something. We can at least begin to deal with this cock-up.' She glared round the table, and Bernard waited for someone to point out to the Minister that the cock-up was not the fault of any of the people in the room, but nobody spoke.

'All the food is now sitting in the HET office in the Cathcart Building, Minister,' said Hunter. 'What will happen to it?'

Carlotta waved a dismissive hand in her direction. 'Get it destroyed. We can't be sure that any of it is safe to eat.'

'I see, Minister, but the removal of it isn't really the responsibility of SHEP or the local HET staff. Is there someone else that could—'

'Oh, for goodness sake! Can you please just make it happen?'

At this point in the meeting, back in the days when Carlotta had a competent and experienced Parliamentary Assistant, Paul Shore would have leaned in with a discreet comment to the Minster, and after the meeting would have dialled one of the numbers in his little black book to sort out the whole rotting foodstuff problem. But Paul was dead, and his absence left a huge hole.

'Minister.' Jacobsen spoke. 'Jen and I will have a conversation about this after the meeting. We'll get it sorted.'

Bernard watched the vacuum left by Paul's death being less than subtly filled by the HET/CID Liaison Officer. Paul had been apolitical, and as fair and transparent as it was possible to be in his kind of job. Jacobsen was none of these things.

Carlotta smiled. 'It's so good to have you back, Ian.'

'Yes, it was unfortunate that my work had to be diverted into pursuing what turned out to be a wild goose chase.' His head turned in Bernard's direction, and Bernard wondered if he could make a bolt for the door, and not stop running until he reached somewhere safe, like, say, Antarctica.

'But, Minister,' Jacobsen lowered his voice slightly, 'there is the other matter about Boucher.'

'Ah, yes, Ian. Perhaps you could update everyone with your intelligence.'

'Now that I'm back concentrating on these matters, I put in a few calls about Boucher and his friends, and what they've been up to. From what I can make out, we have three genuine activists, and in Boucher, a grade A chancer, who sees the protest movement as a good way to get laid and make himself a few quid on the side. Apparently, he's been in discussions with some of the less savoury businessmen on the East Coast about how much they would be willing to pay for a lorry-load of hijacked food.'

'Did his fellow activists know about this?' asked Hunter.

'I'm guessing not. Their plan to hijack the lorry was bloody brilliant, in my opinion.'

'Not quite how I would describe it, Ian.' Carlotta looked put out.

'Apologies, Minister. What I should have said was, the activists accurately identified a weak spot in the preparations for the V8. They knew that they'd never get near any of the visiting dignitaries, or the buildings where the summit was taking place, due to our security. But stealing the dignitaries' food? Who'd think to protect that?'

'So, this was going to be some kind of propaganda thing?' asked Hunter. 'Once they'd delivered all the food to the food banks they'd go on the internet and say what they'd done?'

'Yes.' He nodded. 'Until Boucher spotted an opportunity to make some money.'

'I'm guessing the other activists weren't aware of this,' said Paterson.

'That's our guess too. One or both sides got taken by surprise, and that poor girl got caught in the middle.'

'So, what happens to Boucher now?' asked Hunter. 'Will you be prosecuting him?'

'We've considered the options.' Carlotta leapt in. 'Our view is that it isn't in the public interest.'

Paterson, Hunter and Bernard stared at her in surprise.

'We think it would be a distraction from the good work undertaken at the V8 so far.' She looked round impatiently at the three of them, all of whom were still staring at her. 'Anyway, that's what will be happening.'

'So, you're just going to release Boucher, without charge?' asked Paterson.

'Yes.'

Paterson turned in Jacobsen's direction. 'This boy has taken money off of Edinburgh gangsters on the promise of a lorryload of top-quality grub. Now that he's not delivered on it, they're going to be looking for him. We release him onto the streets they're going to kill him.'

Jacobsen shrugged. 'Not our problem.'

'Not our problem?' Paterson looked apoplectic. 'Have we completely stopped trying to prevent crime?'

'We can't release him,' said Bernard. Everyone ignored him. He tried again. 'We can't release him because he hasn't had a Health Check.'

'Still?' Carlotta's voice was only decibels away from being a screech. 'How is that possible?'

Hunter's face was bright red. 'There were some issues, misunderstanding . . .' She tailed off.

Bernard could sense Paterson's head turning in his direction. He needn't have bothered. Bernard got the point that this was one of the 'dropping people in it' moments that was why he wasn't usually invited to meetings.

'Nobody knows that except the people in this room and their colleagues,' said Jacobsen.

There was a brief silence, then Paterson got to his feet. 'But we do know it. Excuse me, Minister, but Bernard and I have HET work to be getting on with.'

Bernard scurried after his boss. As he passed Jacobsen, his arm shot out and he stopped him. 'Later, Bernard.'

Antarctica wouldn't be far enough.

8

'What's everyone working on?' Mona looked round at her colleagues. Both Maitland and Carole had their heads down over the keyboards, a position that neither of them usually adopted without significant cajoling. Marcus had also taken the opportunity to join them, confident that Paterson was not in the building. He seemed particularly absorbed by his task, his nose only inches away from the screen of his laptop.

Maitland looked up in surprise. 'Oh, yeah, I forgot you weren't here when Marcus was giving us his revelation.'

'Do you want me to explain?' Marcus looked up.

'No, she doesn't because you'll take all day.'

Marcus looked put out. Mona tried not to smile, and felt a certain gratitude that Maitland had stepped in. No matter how hard he tried, Marcus was incapable of a brief summary. Or even a long summary.

'Marcus identified that a whole load of files which previously had restricted access have now mysteriously been made open to all.' Maitland turned him. 'That's it in a nutshell, isn't it?'

The IT officer inclined his head in a way that acknowledged that this may have been an approximation of what he would have said. 'Although the timing is also important. The files regarding Florian Boucher and friends were made public first, then the other ones.'

Mona felt a rising sense of excitement. 'So, what's in them? Anything relevant to our investigation?'

'Who knows?' Maitland shrugged. 'All I've read is file after file about people I've never heard of.'

'Files? Like HR files?'

Maitland shook his head. 'No. More like surveillance files. Names of people. Suspected aliases. Names of their family members and known associates. Where they live. What bars they frequent. That kind of stuff.'

'Why would SHEP have surveillance files?' Mona frowned. 'It doesn't make sense.'

'I suppose the only legitimate reason would be if they were concerned about them being Health Defaulters,' said Maitland. 'Although it does seem overkill.'

'Has anyone cross-referenced it with the Green Card database?'

There was a brief silence. 'We would have got round to that.' Maitland's tone was on the defensive side. 'We've been kind of busy.'

'Give me some names and I'll start checking them.'

Marcus gave her a printout. 'Here's the first twenty I looked at. Maybe they're all Defaulters?'

'Maybe.' She worked her way through the list, ticking them off as she went. Every single one of them was bang up to date with their monthly Health Checks. Whatever reason SHEP had for spying on the people, it wasn't because they were playing fast and loose with the current public health regime. She was about to announce it to the office, when a thought struck her, and she went back through the list. 'Now that is interesting.'

'Are they all in default?' asked Carole.

'No, they are all fine upstanding citizens as far as Health Checks go. The interesting part is the fact that every one of their aliases also has a Green Card and a flawless record of attending Health Checks.' She looked round at her colleagues. 'Why are we giving Green Cards to imaginary people?'

9

The Professor's street was deserted. All the villas were locked up tight for the night, and each and every car lining the road was empty. She knew this because she'd checked them all, walking up one side of the street, then down the other. It wasn't subtle, but if the surveillance team noticed her, so what? She'd deal with the consequences, whatever they were. There was a part of her that would almost welcome a confrontation. If the dark haired 'neighbour' she'd spoken to last time reappeared, she had a few questions she'd like to put to her.

Mona moved her scrutiny on to the houses opposite the Professor's. There was a possibility that the observation had been embedded further, and that the operatives had installed themselves in the front bedroom of one of his neighbours. It seemed unlikely; they'd have needed to give the householder an explanation of what was going on, which would involve a huge leap of faith that details of their spying weren't going to be shared over a G&T at the next local bridge club meeting. However, depending on how keen they were to keep tabs on the Professor they might have deemed it a risk worth taking. Happily, none of the curtains so much as twitched, despite her staring.

She pushed open the gate and walked up the path. Something snagged her ankle and she looked down to see that a plant from an overgrown flower bed had snaked its way out and onto the concrete. She suspected the garden had not seen much in the way of attention from the Professor at the best of times. Without much hope of a response, she hammered on the door and listened to the sound echo through the hall. A quick glance through the letter box identified that the pile of mail seemed much the same, but neither had anyone been round to pick it up. Where was the Professor? She sat on the doorstep and tried Theresa Kilsyth's number again, but no-one picked up.

What was she trying to achieve here? She wanted, no, *needed*, to talk to him about Bryce's theory. The Professor was the only person she knew who could put her mind at rest about the Virus being manmade – or possibly confirm her worst suspicion. She wanted to tell him what Bryce had said about him having spotted something significant and not being aware of it. But first and foremost, she wanted to know that he was OK. His sudden flight had alarmed her.

She had strong protective feelings towards the Professor. He was a decent man through and through. His honesty didn't stop him being the target of threats; in fact, his honesty might well have been the problem. There was a fine line between a commitment to openness, and naivety about how the world actually worked. The Professor believed in science, he believed in truth, and he did not believe that an academic should have to take steps to protect himself, however controversial his field of study. Still, if he'd actually listened to Mrs Kilsyth's nagging and taken greater care of himself, she would probably never have met him.

She'd first encountered Bircham-Fowler several months earlier when he had gone inexplicably AWOL, causing the management of SHEP to have conniptions at the possibility of Scotland's leading virologist missing a Health Check. Stuttle had despatched her and Paterson to retrieve him and get him health checked PDQ. It was fair to say the operation had not been a resounding success. The malevolent forces that Mrs Kilsyth was so aware of were quite happy to see the Professor dead rather than make his Health Check, in an attempt, she assumed, to discredit the whole Health Check regime. Mona and the Professor had ended up running for their lives into the forest at the back of a motorway service station. The Professor had tried to protect her with his life when they'd been shot at. *When they'd been shot at.*

Now she knew where she'd heard Boucher's voice before, that studied neutral accent. She'd heard him shouting to her through the trees as he'd stalked them like wildlife, shooting at them as they cowered in the pines. She leaned her head back against the Professor's front door. Was that possible? The Florian Boucher she'd met was a mass of contradictions, several different personas inhabiting one body. He was Liz's ladies' man, all style and no real substance. Then he was the seasoned activist, who knew how to run rings round his interrogators in an interview. And now he was a ... She didn't know what he was, but she did know he was someone who was happy to kill. She needed more information on him; Marcus hadn't identified anything so far. Bryce would have known, but he was dead, and probably wouldn't have shared the information anyway. She racked her brains for anyone else who could help her. The scent of the roses wafted over to her, and the cogs in her head fell into place. There was someone who could help.

Could – but would she?

*

173

Mona hammered hard on the woodwork of a main door flat in Marchmont. After a moment's delay it opened.

'You left this in our office.' Mona waved the William Morris diary at Elaine. 'I thought I should return it.'

'Now?' Elaine raised a quizzical eyebrow. '11 o'clock at night? To my home address?'

Mona shrugged, shoving the book back in her bag. 'I thought it might be important. Who knows what a gutter journalist keeps in her diary?'

'Gutter journalist? You come all the way to my door just to insult me?' She didn't look particularly upset. 'And I'll let you into a little secret, darling. That's not my real diary. It's the one that I accidentally forget, whoops, silly me, in the hope that people will seek me out to return it.' She winked. 'Works every time. Are you coming in then? Or are you just going to stand on the doorstep and be rude to me?'

Mona followed her in, intrigued in spite of herself to see Elaine's flat. It was homely, the walls painted red and ochre, and the floorboards stripped back and polished. There were books everywhere; overflowing from bookcases, piled on the floor, chairs, and mantle-pieces. Mona perched on an armchair and noticed a thin layer of dust on the ground, and a couple of dead plants. Elaine's housekeeping appeared to be no better than her own.

Elaine was watching her from the sofa, her legs tucked under her. 'Tea, darling?' She pointed to an oversized stripy mug on the coffee table. 'I was just having a peppermint brew. Or, if you're planning to stay a while, I could crack open a bottle of something?'

'I don't want a drink.' Then remembering her manners she added, 'Thank you. Actually, I need some information.'

'Really?' Elaine looked amused. 'And there was me thinking this was a booty call.' She laughed at the expression on Mona's face. 'I should have known better than to think Mona Whyte would lower herself to such depths. What *do* you do for sex, Mona?'

'That's none of your business.' She sat back in the chair and pulled her bag on to her lap.

Elaine laughed. 'OK, I give up. Why are you here?'

'Do you have any information about Florian Boucher?'

'What makes you think I would?'

'Because I'm sure Carole told you all about him. That must have piqued your interest, and I bet you dug around to see if there was a story.'

'How well you know me.' Elaine stretched out on the sofa. 'That's pretty much exactly what happened. And I should thank Carole for her help, because it's a great story.'

'So, what did you find out about him?'

'Why should I tell you anything, Mona?' For the first time since Mona had arrived, Elaine stopped smiling. 'You never get in touch except when you want something. You're rude to me. When I have given you information in the past, it hasn't led to anything for me either personally or professionally. I'm not helping you out again unless you can give me something first.'

'Like what?'

'Well, you must hear interesting things at the HET that would be of interest to a "gutter journo" such as myself. Any "anonymous source" stuff you could tell me?'

Mona thought for a moment. 'Professor Bircham-Fowler's home is under surveillance.'

She shrugged. 'That's not news. I'd be amazed if it wasn't.'

'Why?' Mona was surprised. 'He's been forced out of his job. What threat is he to anyone?'

'There's a legion of folk on social media who still think he's the messiah when it comes to the Virus. If he went on telly and made a series of criticisms about Virus policy, there are plenty of people who'd rally to his side. If I was Carlotta, I'd want to know what he was up to. Anyway, the Prof isn't at home.'

'I know that – but where is he?'

'Yet more information, Mona? The price is going up.'

Mona was reminded of Marguerite with her raffle tickets. If only she could just throw a few quid at Elaine for the information; she had a feeling the cost here wasn't going to be measured in notes and coins. How had she got into this position where everything she wanted involved her giving away a little bit of herself? Was it the Virus, or was this what life did to you, eroded your principles with every passing year?

She thought for a moment, trying to locate a piece of information that would be intriguing enough for Elaine to help her, but also innocuous enough that Cassandra Doom couldn't do any real damage with it. She caught Elaine's expression, mocking her. 'Spoiled for choice? So many HET cock-ups you can't decide which one to tell me about?'

Mona sighed. 'The work of the HETs is hard enough—'

'Without the likes of me sniffing around, I know, Mona. We have this conversation every time we meet.'

'And yet you never listen.'

'And I never will. Anyway, to save us both the embarrassment of you attempting to make something up, why don't you answer a question for me?' She carried on without waiting for Mona to agree. 'Why was someone matching the description of John Paterson shouting at a bunch of food bank volunteers?'

So, Elaine was onto the missing lorry. It wouldn't take her long to get the whole story, and while Mona would rather the HET's involvement in it didn't come to light, it definitely wasn't their cock-up, so all in all, she felt that she could happily drop Carlotta in it. 'I'm saying nothing, except that there are some very revealing monogrammed chocolate bars out there that you might want to get your hands on.'

Elaine swung her feet onto the floor, and sat upright. 'This is to do with the V8, isn't it? Has someone buggered off with Carlotta Carmichael's food? Because if that is true, Cassie is going to be beside herself with joy.'

'Will you stop talking about Cassandra Doom as if she was a different person, instead of just the name you use when you're busy destroying the lives and careers of hard-working public servants?'

'That's a very harsh way to describe her. I prefer to think of her just as my naughty side. And on that note, are you sure you don't want a glass of wine?'

'No, I don't.' This was a lie. She could really have done with a large glass of white, but drinking with Elaine fell into the 'supping with the devil' category of dining. 'Now it's your turn. Florian Boucher. Spill. Is he really an activist?'

'What else would he be?' she smiled.

'I don't know. Police? A spy? He's way more clued up than your average environmental activist.'

'Ah, Mona, always so suspicious. Well, you've got him all wrong. He's a schoolteacher.'

'A teacher?'

Elaine nodded solemnly. 'English and French to lycée pupils in Antwerp.'

'You can't honestly believe that he's just an ordinary teacher who does a bit of environmental protesting on the side?'

'I don't. At least, I don't think he is any more. But he did start his career teaching in Antwerp, which he did for a couple of years, then he took up an overseas post in Africa. The Democratic Republic of Africa, to be precise. Known to both of us as where Carlotta Carmichael sends her civil servants when they've been very naughty.'

'That can't be a coincidence. What happened to him? Was he radicalised?'

She shrugged. 'Perhaps. But it's equally possible that he met some people who made him a very lucrative offer to infiltrate local activist groups and create as much trouble as possible.'

'But who would make him that offer, and why?'

'If I knew the answer to that Mona, I'd be on the front page of not only the *Citizen* but all the broadsheets too.'

Mona sat in silence, processing this information. 'I should go.'

'I'll show you out.'

Mona let herself be ushered along the narrow corridor to the front door.

'Well, this was fun.' Elaine looked rueful. 'We must do it again sometime, maybe next time the HET is completely out of ideas on how to solve one of its cases?'

'Ehm, yeah, thanks for your help.' Elaine was standing close enough that she felt herself being enveloped by the faint smell of Chanel No 5.

'You need to give the door a strong pull. It sticks sometimes.'

Mona stared at the door. All she had to do was reach out for the handle, yet for some reason her hand was still at her side. She turned back to Elaine, who sensed her indecision and smiled. She reached her hands up to Mona's face.

'Ah, Mona. Why do I let you do this to me?'

She kissed her hard on the lips.

THURSDAY

PAYING THE BILL

I

Her phone was ringing. Mona woke in confusion and grabbed for it, only to find that it wasn't there. Her bedside table had vanished, in fact her whole room had gone. She looked round in confusion at her surroundings. In the lamplight, she could see books everywhere and piles of clothes draped on the furniture. The floor was covered in a clutter of high heeled shoes and boots. Her memory came back. She'd stayed the night at Elaine's.

The phone had stopped ringing, and Elaine was no longer in the bed. She pushed back the duvet and climbed out. She debated stopping to put some clothes on, but she was too eager to hear what the journalist might be talking about. She stood silently beside the door to the living room and listened in to Elaine's half of the conversation.

'So, you haven't seen a body?'

Pause.

'You don't even know where the body is?'

Pause.

'Mm, mm, yeah I agree, but if we haven't seen a body, it could all just be a big hoax. Leave it with me.'

With that she hung up, and the door to the living room opened before Mona could dive for cover. At some point during the past couple of hours, Elaine had taken the time to put on a pair of pyjamas. She looked her up and down and grinned. 'Mona Whyte naked in my hallway. I can't tell you the number of times I've had that dream. Do you want to pinch me to check I'm awake?'

'Shut up. What was all that about?'

'All these questions. What are you – a police officer? Oh, that's right, not any more.'

Mona followed Elaine through to the bedroom where she was opening the drawer on her dressing table.

'You were talking about a body being found? Because that is something that you should be reporting to the police right away.'

'Hey, Nancy Drew, if you're going to eavesdrop, at least do it properly.' She slammed the drawer shut, having retrieved a pair of pants that were both large and lacy. 'I didn't say a body had been found, in fact, the whole issue is that we don't have a body.' She picked up Mona's T-shirt from the floor. 'You need to put these on.'

'You're going out?'

'Yep, and you're coming with me.'

Mona didn't move. 'Why is it that any woman that has anything at all to do with an investigation gets called Nancy Drew? The books were written decades ago.'

Elaine smiled. 'OK, then, I don't know – Jane Tennison? Vera? Can't say I'm really up to date on famous female detectives.'

Mona still didn't move. 'I'm not going anywhere until I get some background on what is actually going on here.'

'OK.' Elaine sighed. 'I am respectfully requesting your assistance. I want the two of us to work together.'

'Work together?' said Mona. 'That's not something that would go down well in my office.'

Elaine sighed. 'Mona, we think there has been a death that is related to your investigation. Do you want in or don't you?'

She still couldn't shake her feeling that something wasn't

right here. 'Why are you offering this up on a plate? What happened to all the "It'll cost you" stuff from last night?'

Elaine laughed. 'I think we can both safely say there's been a lot of water under the bridge since then, hasn't there?' Her eyes flicked up and down Mona's still naked figure. Mona grabbed the proffered T-shirt and pulled it over her head. 'Although my willingness to share is nothing to do with that. I need your help.'

'Seriously?' Mona struggled to think what Elaine was after. She was pretty capable of finding things out for herself. 'You said someone has died?'

'So, you're in then?'

'Probably. Maybe.'

'Dieter Lange is dead.'

Mona raced through the possibilities. 'Who killed him? Is it related to Florian Boucher?'

'Nope, you're barking up completely the wrong tree. One of my colleagues phoned me to say I'd been sent a suicide note from someone called Dieter Lange. Said that he couldn't go on, not with everything that happened, and that he was going to find a "sturdy tree" and hang himself from it.'

Mona thought this over. 'And of all the journalists in Scotland he just happened to send this to you?'

Elaine smiled. 'There may have been some prior contact between us. We were attempting to track down Boucher's known associates. It would have been a great story for my readers. Everything they worry about in one paragraph – Health Defaulters entering the country illegally and trying to bring down the Government.'

'So, you harassed him? That probably contributed to his feelings of despair.'

Elaine's eyes flicked away to the side. 'There may have been some comment to that effect in his suicide note.

Anyway, in the course of our investigations I discovered the name that Dieter Lange used when he illegally entered the country.'

'And you're going to share that with me?' This seemed too good to be true.

'Of course! I'm delighted to be able to help the HET.' She smiled, and pulled Mona closer to her. She whispered into her ear, her breath soft on Mona's skin. 'Just one tiny condition, darling. You have to use your little HET database thingy to tell me where his Green Card was last used.'

Mona pulled away. 'Is that where you think his body will be?'

'Well, there or thereabouts I'm hoping. We don't have much else in the way of clues.'

'It's a bit of a long shot,' said Mona. 'Don't you have anything else to go on? What did the suicide note say?'

'I'll tell you, but can we head in the direction of your laptop while we do that?'

The streets were deserted. They were in the few hours that existed between people going home from clubs, and early risers getting up to go to work. Elaine reached for her hand, and she didn't pull away.

'OK, darling, this is the story so far. As I said, the *Citizen* has just been emailed an apparent suicide note from your friend and mine, Dieter Lange. In the note he says that he was responsible for the death of Natálie Svobodová, he's overcome with guilt, and therefore he has taken his own life.'

'Quite convenient for a number of people, I would assume, to have all this neatly tied up.'

'Indeed. And my nasty suspicious mind had my colleague reread the letter to me. It was in absolutely flawless English. So here we have a Czech citizen, not a native English speaker, at one of the most stressful points of his life, yet doesn't make a single spelling mistake or grammar error.'

'You'd make a good detective,' said Mona.

'I make an even better gutter journalist, darling. How far is it to your flat from here?'

'We're not going to my flat. The only place I can access that information is at the office.'

'Two visits to your office in one week. Here's hoping that John Paterson hasn't decided to come in early.'

Amen to that. 'You do realise that as soon as I look up this name on the system I'll have to report it to the police?'

Elaine looked horrified. 'You can't do that! If the police are there, I'll not get near the crime scene. I need a photo of the body, preferably still hanging.'

Mona winced. 'Really? A man's last, horrible moments on earth are going to be splashed across the front page of the *Citizen*?'

'That is how journalism works, Mona.' She stopped walking. 'You can't involve the police until after I've been there.'

'There's a digital footprint from me accessing the information. How do I explain me suddenly deciding to access this guy's details, then him turning up in the papers tomorrow?'

'We could ...' She frowned, deep in concentration. 'Actually, I've got no idea.'

They walked on, and Mona outlined what was going to happen. 'OK, we go to the office, find out where this guy has been, I let the police know, and I keep you in the loop about what they find. I mean, you still have the suicide note, don't you? That's quite a scoop?'

Elaine grunted. 'Let's just find out where the guy has been.'

They walked the last few streets to the office in silence. Mona ran up the steps and unlocked the door, holding it open for Elaine to enter. With a last look up and down the street, she closed the door behind her, and pressed her Green Card against the reader.

'Probably best I don't use my mine,' said Elaine.

'God, no. You were never here.'

Mona hurried up the stairs, keen to get Elaine off the premises as quickly as possible; it would be just her luck for Bernard or Marcus to have a sleepless night and decide they were better off at work. She turned on her computer and sat down, Elaine pulling up a chair beside her.

'So, what name am I looking for?'

'John Smith.'

'Seriously?'

'Yes. John Smith. Why is that a problem?'

'Because it's going to pull up shedloads of potential people. See.' She entered the name and a pop-up informed them that due to a large number of returns it was only showing them the first 100.

'What am I looking at here?' asked Elaine.

'It's a list of all the people with Green Cards called John Smith, whose last card usage was in Edinburgh. I think we can assume that Dieter Lange committed suicide somewhere local?'

'I guess so,' said Elaine. 'There doesn't seem to be much info on each of them.'

'Once we identify the correct person I can go into their file and look at them in more detail – we can download a list of all the places that they've been.'

Elaine stared dejectedly at the screen. 'Are there really that many John Smiths in Edinburgh?'

'Looks like it. Although it also brings up near spellings

as well. There's probably a few Smythes and Smithsons in there as well.'

'Hmm.' Elaine pondered this. 'Can we narrow it down?'

'We can. Does John Smith have a middle name?'

'He does.' Elaine thought for a moment. 'Darryl with a y.'

She retyped John Darryl Smith. Her search brought up two entries, plus a host of other near spellings.

'Two possibles.' Mona grinned. 'This is more like it. I'll print both of these and send them over to Police Scotland.' She sent them to print, and bounded over to pick them up. When she turned back, Elaine was sat in front of her computer screen.

'You can memorise the locations all you want, but the police are going to get there before you do.'

'I can't beg you to give me a head start, not even after last night?' Elaine reached for her hand. Was it her imagination or had she undone one or more of the buttons on her shirt since Mona had last looked? She kept her eyes on Elaine's face.

''Fraid not.'

With a sigh, the journalist got to her feet. 'Then I'm going to get back to the office and start writing this up.'

'The police will need the suicide note.'

'Don't worry. I'll scan them a copy.'

Mona sensed an eagerness in Elaine to get away and start work on her story. It would be good to have her off the premises before she made the call to Police Scotland. She hurried after Elaine, chasing her down the stairs.

'You'll need me to let you out.'

On the doorstep, Elaine pulled her close, and kissed her. 'I'll be in touch.'

And with that she was off. Mona locked the door behind her and felt a pang at her leaving. Was this thing with Elaine going to go anywhere? It'd be difficult, not least because she wouldn't be able to tell any of her colleagues. Then there was the small matter of the Cassandra Doom columns, but then maybe she could be a good influence on her, maybe she could ...

Her daydreaming was interrupted by her phone beeping. Cassandra Doom flashed up on the screen. It was a one-word message.

Sorry.

What was Elaine apologising for? Running out on her? Or something else?

2

The car park behind Canonmills Tesco was large and dark.

After several long and rather bad-tempered discussions with Police Scotland, Mona had come to realise that she may have overstated their willingness to get involved to Elaine. Apparently their manpower did not stretch to a search of the areas surrounding the last known whereabouts of the two John D. Smiths. She had had a horrible feeling that perhaps Elaine hadn't shared her faith in the police, and was busy taking tasteless photographs of Dieter Lange's corpse, which had led to her borrowing a pool car and driving rather faster than she should have to the first of the supermarkets on the list.

Now that she was here, she sincerely hoped that if Dieter Lange was anywhere in the vicinity, it was in the car park, because she was struggling to see how she could narrow the search area down if he wasn't. If he'd ended his life outdoors, he could be in one of the children's playparks nearby, somewhere on Edinburgh's winding cycle paths which passed by the supermarket, or hidden on the small industrial estate a couple of streets away. And that was assuming that he had actually found a *sturdy tree* from which to hang himself. If he'd changed his mind and downed a packet of pills, he could be anywhere. His last known Green Card check-in wasn't proving to be much help, but it was all they'd got.

The car park stretched back a good distance from the supermarket, its upper level open to the elements with a dark concrete bunker underneath. She walked briskly round the perimeter, checking the undergrowth that surrounded it, to no avail. She jogged back to the building, and after a moment's indecision took the stairs down to the lower level. As she'd suspected, there was nothing there, neither person nor car. Her phone rang.

'I've found Dieter Lange.' Elaine sounded slightly breathless. 'Took a bit of hunting but I've got him. And he is unequivocally dead.'

She'd been right. Elaine had gone straight out looking for him. 'I assume you're at Lidl's in Granton then? You couldn't wait for the police?'

'The police were never going to prioritise this, Mona.'

'Well, furious as I am, I also have to say that you are, you know, amazing.'

'Yeah, hold that thought. I—'

'No, seriously, Elaine, that was some fantastic detective work. I really didn't think it would be—'

'Mona.' Elaine cut across her. 'There's something I need to tell you. Dieter Lange wasn't using the name John Darryl Smith; he was using the name John *Darryn* Smith.'

Mona's brain struggled with the significance of what she was being told.

'So, when you got up to get the paperwork for John Darryl Smith off the printer, I sneaked a good look at the last whereabouts of Scotland's only J. Darryn Smith, which is where I currently am.'

'But—' Mona's brain was trying hard to deny what was going on.

'I'm in Inverleith Park. Lange's swinging from a tree near the duck pond. I've got my photo and I'll be out of here by the time you get here.'

Mona's brain snapped into gear at last. 'Have you any idea what you have just done to me? And how much trouble I could be in if you publish that picture and I'm found to have been looking at his Green Card data? I thought you liked me?'

'I do! Very much. But, you know,' she sighed. 'A story is a story. You have to do what it takes. Anyway, it's not the end of the world. Tell Paterson you got a tip-off from me, and popped into the office to check it out before phoning him.'

Mona thought this over. The timings would be a bit out but it would probably work.

'Send one of your plods over to the office if you want to pick up the suicide note. Do you want to meet up later?'

'Meet up later? You have got to be—' But Elaine had gone, taking with her several of Mona's hopes and dreams, along with the last of her faith in the decency of other human beings.

By the time she'd driven to the park she'd calmed down slightly. On reflection, Elaine's suggestion worked fine. She wondered if she had worked out in advance that accessing the database could be done without getting her into trouble, or if she'd been thinking on her feet after the act. She was leaning heavily towards the latter, but either way, she was never, ever, sleeping with Cassandra Bloody Doom again.

Her phone's Satnav told her to turn right, then confirmed she was at her destination. She pulled her car up at the side of the road and looked round. The street was deserted, the park dark and devoid even of dog-walkers. She felt relieved at this. She didn't want to attract the attention of any members of the public, or even worse, have them stumble across Lange's body before she did.

Her mobile had beeped several times on the drive over. Now that she had a chance to look at the messages she could see Elaine had sent further directions of where to go, although she hadn't felt it necessary to offer any further apologies. She grabbed a torch from the glove compartment and set off into the dark reading Elaine's directions as she went. *Follow your way round the pond. Exit the park and find the small path that leads to Stockbridge. Walk forward fifteen paces and look to your left.* It was like the world's worst treasure hunt. She followed the directions, and as instructed, shone her torch to the left. *X marks the spot.* The body of Dieter Lange was hanging motionless from a tree, his feet dangling less than a metre from the ground. She stood where she was, and methodically shone her beam of light all over the tree and the surrounding area. Satisfied that she'd seen all there was to see, she texted Elaine.

Did you remove anything from the crime scene?

Almost immediately there was a reply. *Absolutely not.*

A second later there was a follow up. *And why are you calling it a crime scene?*

She didn't reply. She was pretty sure that when Elaine had a good look at her photographs she would come to the same conclusion. In order to hang yourself, you needed a rope, or similar, something sturdy to attach the rope to, and something to step off. She could see a rope, she could see the tree, but nowhere in the surrounding area could she see what Lange had jumped from.

She pulled out her phone. The protocol, as far as she understood it, was to call the HET/CID Liaison Team, but there was no way on God's earth that she was phoning either Ian Jacobsen or Bob Ellis. She thought for a moment, then pressed another number.

'So, Cassandra Doom just happens to phone you to say that she's found a body?' Paterson's eyes narrowed as he stared at her.

'It wasn't a random choice, Guv. You know that we had some engagement with her in the past.'

'Is she a friend of yours?' Hunter looked horrified.

'No, definitely not.' Mona could say that without lying.

'You didn't contribute to that article she wrote about the HET treating their staff as slaves, did you?' Hunter was now also eyeing her with suspicion.

'No, that was all ...' She was about to say Carole but checked herself. 'An anonymous source. I think Cassandra Doom trusts me.'

'We should charge her.'

'What with, Guv?'

'I don't know.' He stared at the Scene of Crime team, who were swarming all over the site. 'Withholding evidence.'

'Except she alerted us to the body and passed on the suicide note.'

He grunted. 'What do you make of this, anyway?'

'Don't think it's a suicide.'

'You think it's murder?' Hunter looked horrified. 'That's not something the HET should be dealing with. I think we need to step back and leave this to the police.'

'We would if we could, Ma'am,' said Paterson. 'However, this situation has an impact on our search for Ana P. We still need to get her in for a Health Check. If she's seen what's happened to her comrades, she's going to be terrified, which will have driven her further underground.'

'She might have left the country, Guv?'

Paterson frowned. 'Unlikely. Her picture has been circulated to all the airports and ports. I say she's still here and freaking out.'

Hunter was looking more and more uncomfortable. Suddenly her face brightened. 'Ian.' Mona turned to see Jacobsen walking towards them. 'You can straighten this all out.'

'I certainly hope so, Jen.' He eyed Mona malevolently. 'What mess has the HET created this time?'

'Absolutely nothing to do with us, Jacobsen,' said Paterson. 'We're just picking up the pieces.'

'What are your thoughts, John?' Ian stepped between her and Paterson, effectively signalling that there was nothing that he wanted to hear from her.

'Looks like a piss-poor attempt at faking a suicide to me.'

He nodded. 'I'm inclined to agree. Any thoughts on who or why?'

'Well, we can rule out Boucher, as he was in custody. My money is on whoever Boucher was delivering the food to. They probably took umbrage when they found their purchase had been distributed to the food banks of Edinburgh.'

Ian looked round the scene. 'I can't believe Cassandra Doom found him. How did she know he was here?'

Mona wandered away from them. She'd been wondering the same. Even with the help that she had given to Elaine, it had still been a long shot that she would have been able to find him. She pulled out her phone.

'Darling—'

'How did you find Lange?'

'Your very helpful database said he last used his Green Card at the Coop on Stockbridge High Street, so when it came to sourcing a sturdy tree the park was the obvious choice. It took me about fifteen minutes stumbling round the darker corners of it, but when I found the path he was right by it.'

'That was amazingly convenient.'

'Wasn't it? Can't help but think we were supposed to find him. I think someone is sending out a message.'

'Who to?'

'I don't know – his fellow conspirators? SHEP? You're the detective. Have the police turned up anything else?'

'As if I would tell you if they had.'

'Don't be like that, Mona. Let's meet up later and compare notes.'

'You've got to be kidding.' She hung up.

3

Many, many, terrifying things had happened to Bernard in his time at the North Edinburgh HET. He thought that by now he ought to have exhausted all the awful things that could happen to someone in their workplace, and yet here he was, nerves tingling, as he contemplated his biggest challenge yet. He had to phone John Paterson and tell him he was taking the day off sick.

At least with most of the horrifying scenarios that arose at the HET they tended to sneak up on him, without him having time to worry about them in advance. But this time, ever since Carrie had said that her appointment was at 11.30am he'd known that he'd have to make this call.

And why shouldn't he be sick for a day? He'd never been ill in his time there, aside from the days off he'd had after getting beaten up while on official HET business. They owed him.

There was, of course, a little voice at the back of his head telling him he could just tell the truth. Honesty was his default setting, at least it had been until he'd joined the HET where he found himself lying, prevaricating, and generally avoiding the truth on a daily basis. But telling the truth would lead to a lot of questions, and inevitably unsolicited advice. While he could happily ignore unsolicited advice when it came from Maitland, if Mona or Carole said the same thing it would just be that bit harder to disregard.

So, lying to his line manager it had to be. He'd double-checked the Staff Handbook which clearly stated that if a HET officer was sick, they had to let their manager know by 10am. There was nothing in the document that said you couldn't phone before 9am and leave a message on said manager's landline answerphone, thus avoiding having to speak to him at all. He took a deep breath and dialled. To his horror, the phone was picked up.

'John Paterson's phone.' A woman's voice.

'Is that Carole?'

'Hi, Bernard. Yes, I'm the only one in.'

He looked at his clock. He wasn't sure what was more surprising – Carole being in the office early, or Mona not being in. Although maybe Mona had had a late night.

'OK, right, well, could you just tell Mr Paterson that I'm off sick today.'

'Off sick?' She sounded surprised. 'He's not going to like that.'

For a second Bernard considered changing his plans. The second passed. 'Well, he'll have to put up with it. Can you relay the message?'

'OK. What shall I say is wrong with you?'

'I've got a cold.'

'You don't sound like you have a cold. Bernard, is everything OK? Has something happened?'

'No, I'm fine. Well, I'm not fine, I'm poorly. Will you let Paterson know?'

'Yes, I will but—'

Bernard hung up, and went into the kitchen, opening the fridge and pulling out a box of eggs, and half a ripe avocado. If Paterson was going to kill him tomorrow, at least today he could have a really nice breakfast.

4

Mona cautiously pushed open the office door, and found it was an even tighter squeeze than the previous day. She flattened herself against the wall and slid round the door. There was a pungent smell coming from some of the boxes. 'That's unpleasant.'

'I know,' said Carole. 'Even with the window open we can't disguise the smell. Do you think we should dump it in the bin outside?'

'Paterson said Hunter was dealing with it, but she's got other things on her mind at the moment. We had a bit of excitement last night.'

'Did it involve your girlfriend Cassandra Doom?' Maitland's head appeared round the side of a stack of boxes.

For a horrible moment, Mona thought that Maitland knew about her sleeping with Elaine, then she realised he was just being his usual annoying self. 'She's not my girl-friend, and why do you ask?'

'Because the lead article on the *Citizen* website is about finding a body in a case that the North Edinburgh HET has "failed to crack, despite the resources at their disposal".'

So, Elaine hadn't pulled any punches. No easing up on her poison pen campaign against the HET just because she'd screwed over one of the team. What had she been thinking when she slept with her?

'Not sure exactly what resources Cassandra Doom thinks we're sitting on,' continued Maitland. 'Do you think any of this is true?'

'Unfortunately, yes I do.' She updated them on the events of that morning.

'Wow.' Maitland thought it over. 'Do you think he genuinely committed suicide? I mean it all ties it up a bit neatly, doesn't it?'

'My thoughts exactly,' said Mona. 'Also, the scene didn't look right for a suicide. The forensics will tell us one way or another, if CID bother to share their findings with us.'

'So ...' Carole looked thoughtful. 'Out of the four activists involved in the theft of the lorry, one is in police custody, one was murdered, and one committed suicide. Where's the fourth one?'

'That's a very good question,' said Mona. 'And I hope we manage to find her before something equally bad happens to her.'

The door to the office opened a crack, hit a box, and slammed shut. It opened again, more tentatively, and stopped at six inches wide. An irate female voice asked, 'What's going on? Why can't I get in?'

Maitland grinned. 'Sorry, Marg, the office is full of stuff.'

'It stinks as well. What have you got in there?'

'Tell you what, Marg, why don't I buy a couple of raffle tickets and you go away?' Mona reached for her purse.

'You can't. We did the draw last night. Bernard won something. Is he there?'

'No,' said Maitland. 'But you can leave it with us and I'll pass it on.' He lowered his voice. 'If it's alcohol I'm keeping it and not telling him.'

'I'm having the spa voucher. The amount of money I've given her over the past couple of days I—'

Mona broke off as Marguerite squeezed a large pink teddy bear round the corner of the door. They stared at it in surprise, then Mona caught Maitland's eye, and felt an uncontrollable desire to laugh. All the tensions of the past few days were washed away on a tide of hysteria.

'What are you all laughing at?' Even from the other side of a wooden door they could hear the indignation in Marguerite's voice. 'It's a lovely prize. I thought Bernard could give it to his girlfriend, now he's finally got one.'

'Good idea.' Mona managed to squeeze the words out.

'It's not just a teddy bear, you know. It's got a zip at the back so you can keep your pyjamas in it.'

This was too much for Maitland, and he fell from the chair onto his knees, doubled over with laughter. 'Stop, Marg, please!'

Carole retrieved the bear. 'Thanks, Marguerite, we'll definitely make sure he gets it.'

Marguerite didn't respond but they could hear her high heels clicking down the corridor outside. The admin team was going to be hearing all about this.

Maitland resumed his seat. 'Where is Bernard anyway?'

'He phoned in sick,' said Carole, shoving the bear onto Bernard's empty seat.

'Sick?' Paterson's face appeared in the crack of the door. 'Who's sick? And get those boxes moved so I can actually get in.'

Maitland and Mona edged a couple of the boxes away from the door, and with a bit of grunting Paterson made it in.

'Bernard's off sick,' said Carole.

'What's wrong with him?'

'Well, when I spoke to him he said he had a cold, but he didn't sound like he did. I'm actually a bit worried about him.'

Paterson looked over at Bernard's desk.

'And the teddy bear is—' began Mona.

'Something to do with Marguerite, I'm guessing, from the mouthful I just got about you lot when I saw her in the corridor. OK, well, we'll follow up with Bernard later on. There's a couple of things we must do first. Number one, do something about the smell in here.'

'Can we just dump everything, Guv?' asked Mona.

'Not sure,' said Paterson, frowning. 'But', he wandered round the room, stopping to sniff at the different boxes, 'I think we should lose the prawns as a matter of urgency.'

'Shall we dump them in the bin in the kitchen next to the admin office?' asked Maitland.

Paterson grinned. 'That would be fun, but not exactly discreet. Get them parcelled up and into the outside bin round the back of the building. Mona, you're with me.'

'OK, Guv.' She pulled on her coat. 'Where are we going?'

'I need your help to kidnap someone.'

'All in a day's work, Guv.'

5

Bernard had eaten what felt like the entire contents of his kitchen, but he still felt hungry. He suspected this was some kind of reaction to stress. He made a mental note that he needed to pace himself, foodwise, so he could eat a hearty meal at Lucy's birthday celebration. Yet the smell from the hospital café was delicious, some kind of cake or cookie aroma that suggested they were still warm.

'Shall we head up then?' asked Carrie.

'Yes. Are you sure you're feeling OK?' Carrie hadn't been looking great when he'd picked her up at her home, and she seemed to be even paler now. This had to go well. If things didn't go smoothly, there was no way that his wife's fragile mental health would cope. She'd go back to the way she had been after the death of their son, unable to function, staying in bed, and relying on— A thought struck him.

'Carrie, you aren't still drinking, are you?'

She looked horrified. 'Of course not. I haven't drunk alcohol since I became pregnant. Actually, since well before then.'

Bernard's train of thought moved on to the next station. 'Did you stop drinking because you were planning to get pregnant?'

There was the briefest of pauses. 'No, I stopped drinking because I knew it was getting out of hand. I didn't want to go on the way that I was.'

'But maybe you thought the way to feel better was to put all your efforts into getting pregnant.' He couldn't quite catch her eye. 'One way or another.'

She looked at her phone. 'We should go up. I don't want to be late.'

'Carrie, we do need to talk about this baby.'

She had already set off, moving remarkably fast for a pregnant woman. He gave up and followed her through the white corridors of the hospital.

'We're here for an appointment with Dr Blake? I'm Carrie McDonald.'

The receptionist looked at him. 'And I'm Bernard McDonald.'

'OK, if Mummy and Daddy could take a seat in the waiting room, it shouldn't be long.'

'Mummy and Daddy.' Bernard spoke to Carrie in a low voice. 'Is that how you would describe us?'

She nodded at the other couple sitting in the waiting room. 'Not now, Bernard. We can discuss this later.'

'When will that be?'

'Caroline McDonald?' Dr Blake appeared in the doorway of his consulting room, and Carrie heaved herself back upright and headed into the room. Bernard sighed and followed her.

'Hello, Mr and Mrs McDonald, please take a seat.'

Bernard sat, slightly uneasy that Dr Blake didn't know that he didn't have a happily married couple before him, but he couldn't think of a way to broach the subject.

'Mr McDonald, I don't think you've made any of the previous appointments, so if there are any questions that you haven't had a chance to raise, please don't hesitate to ask them now.'

'Just for clarity, I haven't made any of the previous appointments because—'

'My husband is very busy with his work,' Carrie broke in, while shooting him a look that clearly communicated that *Dr Blake does not need to know our business*. This was not a point of view he shared, but he held his tongue.

'My main concern is for Carrie's health.' He gave the doctor a weak smile and received some emphatic nodding in response.

'Yes, as you are aware Mrs McDonald's blood pressure is on the high side, which we are monitoring. It may be that we need to take her into hospital well in advance of her due date if there is any danger of pre-eclampsia.'

Bernard looked at Carrie, who was, if anything, even paler.

'The most important thing,' continued Dr Blake, 'is that Mrs McDonald has as much rest as possible. I know at our last meeting, Mrs McDonald said that her mother wasn't fit enough to help out much, and I know that you are busy with your work but—'

'Your mother?' Bernard interrupted the doctor. 'What's wrong with your mother?'

'Can we talk about this later, Bernard?' Carrie was staring at her nails.

'No, can we talk about it now? What does your mother think about you being pregnant? Does she think I'm the world's worst husband, or is she a bit more in the loop than I am?'

'Ehm', Dr Blake was looking confused, 'do you two need a moment?'

'Is your mother, perhaps, a bit peed off with your pregnancy; therefore not too willing to run round after you?'

'She's delighted for me.' The positivity of this statement was undermined slightly by Carrie starting to cry.

Bernard edged forward on his seat, and launched into the question that had consumed most of his waking hours recently. 'Is the baby mine, Carrie? I'm going to know soon anyway, amn't I?'

Dr Blake was looking more and more embarrassed. 'I'm just going to give you two—'

'Please don't go anywhere, Dr Blake,' said Bernard. 'I think we all need a definitive answer to that question. Carrie?'

Carrie shook her head.

'The baby's not mine?' Bernard felt a sudden flood of emotions, the chief of which, to his surprise, was disappointment.

'No. I'm so sorry, Bernard, but I thought I could do this on my own, but then I've been so tired and stressed, and you were being so nice to me, I thought . . .' She tailed off.

Dr Blake was intently studying the case notes on his computer, in a manner that suggested he would quite happily climb into the PC rather than listen to one more word of this conversation.

'And I know you didn't want another child, Bernard, but I thought that once I was pregnant you might come round to the idea, even though it wasn't yours, and we could get back to where we were before.'

Bernard slumped back in his seat and tried to work out what his emotions were telling him. He was disappointed, but what did that mean? Deep down did he really want to be with Carrie, picking up where they'd left off when Jamie died? But then there was Lucy.

'Carrie, my life has moved on. I have a girlfriend now.'

She looked up at him. 'You have a girlfriend? You've never mentioned her?' There was an accusatory tone to her voice, undercut with an implication of betrayal.

'I know, I'm sorry.' He stopped, trying to work out how Carrie could have strung him along about this baby, let him pay for the mortgage, refuse to tell him if he was the father or not, and yet somehow put him on the defensive, apologising as if he had an equal part in this mess. He got decisively to his feet, and pulled a £20 note from his pocket, which he put on the table in front of Carrie. 'I need to go, please get a taxi home.'

'Ehm.' Dr Blake's face was bright red. 'It sounds like you both have a lot to talk about but before you go, I just wanted to reiterate my earlier point. Due to the complications of Mrs McDonald's blood pressure, she really should be having complete bed rest at this point. Stress and exertion could be dangerous both to her and the baby.'

He looked back at the doctor, who quickly looked away. He looked at Carrie who had her head buried in her hands, crying to herself. He had enough medical training to know that pre-eclampsia could be fatal. He reached forward and picked up the £20 note and sat back down. 'What do I need to do?'

6

'Are you sure about this, Guv?' Mona looked out of the car window and hoped that no-one from Drylaw Police Station had clocked them sitting there. This wasn't one of Paterson's better ideas.

'Do we need to speak to Boucher as part of our search for Ana P, who is currently in default of the Health Check regime in both this country and her homeland?'

'Yes, but—'

'Is Boucher about to be illegally released from custody, due to the fact he has not had a legitimate Health Check undertaken while under the care of Police Scotland, thus making him a walking affront to public health?'

'Yes, but—'

'For both these reasons, is it not perfectly acceptable that he is, therefore, taken into the custody of the North Edinburgh Health Enforcement Team?'

'Yes, but—'

'So, is the fact that you are sitting there with your face tripping you more to do with your concerns about your future promotion prospects than to do with the righteousness of our actions?'

'Stop, Guv!' She glared at him. 'I totally get what you're saying but I just think that if Hunter, who is actually our ultimate boss, wanted the HET to do this, she would have mentioned it.'

'And is Hunter not a jumped-up Carlotta Carmichael clone

who is head of SHEP more because of who she has brown-nosed than any actual experience or aptitude for the job?'

'I'm not sure if that's entirely fair.' Although it was a pretty accurate description of the situation. 'Why are you doing this, Guv?'

'Because despite what you might think of me, Mona, I do actually have a conscience. We've already got two dead people connected to our investigation, and I don't fancy Pretty Boy Boucher's chances on the streets if he's left to his own devices. He can't leave the country, his bank account is frozen, I don't know if he's got any money or any friends in Scotland, and there are some very dangerous people looking for him. And *you* know that, *I* know that, and our friends in Police Scotland and SHEP know that, yet they're quite happy to let him walk out of there because it would probably quite suit them if Boucher ended up disappearing. Who knows – maybe they'll even tip off his disappointed customers that he's at large? Is that the kind of world you want to live in Mona? Is that why you joined the police?'

She sighed. 'Maybe Hunter and Jacobsen have arranged some kind of protection for him? They could be tailing him, seeing who he meets up with?'

'Do you really believe that?'

She thought it over. 'No, not really.'

'Well, time to pick a side, Mona, because there he is.'

She watched as Boucher walked out of the car park at the police station. He stood for a moment looking anxiously up and down the road.

'Are you in or out, Mona?'

'In, Guv. For better or worse.'

'Monsieur Boucher, I presume?'

Boucher's head whipped in the direction of Paterson's

voice. He looked confused, and not a little nervous, until he caught sight of Mona, and his expression changed to one of exasperation.

'I have been released without charge. I am free to go.'

'You've been released by Police Scotland, Mr Boucher,' said Paterson. 'Yet my understanding is that you have not yet participated in a Health Check.'

'I did.' He looked at Mona. 'You know that I did, against my will. The fact that it was not done in accordance with the bureaucracy in your country is not my problem.'

'Well, we wouldn't want to burden you with our problems. But there is the other issue that we are currently searching for one Ana Procházková who is also in breach of Health Check regulations in this country, and we happen to think that you are our best lead in finding out where she is.'

'You are looking for Ana?' his eyes flicked between them both, suspicion still written all over his face. Mona steeled herself in case he made a break for it.

'You may not be aware of this, Mr Boucher, but we have powers of detention that are very similar to the arrest powers of Police Scotland. If you don't agree to assist us willingly, we can compel you to accompany us to ...' There was a slight hesitation while Paterson obviously remembered that they were supposed to take the unwilling Health Defaulter witness to a police station ' ... our office, where you will remain until you give us the information you need.'

Mona hoped to God that the prawns were now gone. Boucher still hadn't moved.

'Come on, Boucher, it's not like you've got lots of options.' Paterson frowned. 'Where are you planning to go? Have you got any money that you can access now that your bank account is frozen? Any friends who can help you out? Because whoever it was that you were supposed to deliver that food to is going to be mightily pissed off, and probably looking for you. Helping us with our enquiries might not be such a bad option.'

Boucher looked thoughtful. '"Helping with our enquiries" is a euphemism, isn't it? You usually say that about people who are under arrest.'

'You wouldn't be under arrest, you would be legally detained.'

'But the outcome is the same. You are legally obliged to keep me detained while I assist, which, as you say, may not be a bad thing for me at the moment.' He smiled. 'But, let me clarify, you are legally obliged to keep me detained *until* I assist you?'

'Yes.' Paterson nodded emphatically.

'So, if I do help you, you might let me go?'

'Well, possibly—'

'Please, take me to your office.' He grinned. 'But I think it might take me a very long time to remember anything about where Ana is.'

'Whatever.' He looked over at the police station. 'Let's just get out of here before anyone comes out to join us.'

7

Bernard paced around his living room, furious with Carrie, Dr Blake, and, mainly, himself. He should have kept walking, despite the doctor reminding him of the severity of the situation. He should have gone as far as the hospital's reception, then phoned Carrie's mum and made it all her problem. The only thing that had stopped him taking that course of action was his lingering fondness for his mother-in-law. It didn't seem fair to leave her to provide the sole support for what was turning out to be a difficult pregnancy. At some point he would make contact with her, just to put his side of the story. He wouldn't put it past his wife to have dropped some hints to her mother that the baby was, in fact, his.

With a sigh he flung himself onto the sofa, and wondered what to do with the rest of the day. He could go to the gym, but he was supposed to be poorly and he didn't want to bump into anyone related to the HET when he was meant to be home in bed. Also, he really couldn't be bothered. He checked the time on his phone. He could go into work, tell them that he was feeling better, but again, apathy had a strong hold on him, and he couldn't face dealing with Paterson and Maitland, not today.

However, the alternative of sitting there brooding was particularly unappealing. He really didn't want to dwell on the morning's events, so he was going to have to come up with some kind of task to keep his brain busy. It occurred to him that he could actually do some work without going near his colleagues. He grabbed his rucksack and pulled out a folder of printouts that he had brought home with him. The reluctance of the HET to invest in laptops for them all continued to frustrate him. If he wanted to look anything up, he had to go into the office. He'd taken to smuggling bits of paperwork out in his bag, which probably contravened all kinds of data protection issues but he didn't really care any more.

He emptied the folder onto the coffee table and spread the sheets out next to each other. It was a summary that Marcus had produced of the 500 files he had discovered. Five hundred names, each of which was under surveillance, probably by SHEP, not that that made any sense. All SHEP was interested in was making sure that people complied with the Health Check regime. What possible need there was to spy on people who weren't actually in default of the system was beyond him.

His eyes scanned up and down the names, looking for people he might know, or patterns. There wasn't anyone who immediately seemed familiar, either through personal contact or because they were a famous name. Bernard couldn't claim to be strong on celebrities, but he knew his politicians. If there had been a smattering of MSPs or MPs in amongst the names, he was pretty sure he'd have spotted them.

Marcus had helpfully included a date of birth against each name, although the spread of dates gave no particular clue. All adults, none younger than thirty, none older that sixty-five. So, working age, probably in a relatively senior job. Against each name, there was a slightly cryptic code, a V with either a 1, 2, or 3 next to it. V for Virus? Or V for Vaccine? Vaccine Version 1, 2, or 3? Had they all had the experimental vaccine, and were being monitored to see any side effects? Yet, if that were the case, they'd have a stack of health information in the files, instead of information about who their friends were, and what pubs they visited on a Saturday night.

He read them through again, and a thought occurred to him. It wasn't as strong as identifying a pattern, but there was, potentially, a slight link in the aliases that were listed. To his eye, the names all seemed a little on the old-fashioned side. *Ernest, Arthur, Stanley* for the men. *Joan, Doreen, Shirley* for the women. He knew that names went in cycles; one year's old lady moniker suddenly became an on-trend baby name. But these names weren't fashionable. Why a thirty-year-old had been given the alias Mildred escaped him.

Placing his finger at the top of the list of aliases, he went slowly down them, considering each in turn. Halfway down the second sheet his finger stopped abruptly at a name. It couldn't be, could it? And if it was, surely there would be a matching one? He looked up and down the list, looking for something to confirm his suspicion, but the other name wasn't to be found.

He leaned back into the cushions and wondered what to do with this information.

8

'What are we going to do with him, Guv?' She glanced at Boucher in her rear-view mirror. The one advantage of being in a pool car was that it had a soundproof panel between the front and rear seat so that they could converse with privacy. 'We should be taking him to a police station so he can be detained securely.'

'Not sure that's the way to go really, seeing as Police Scotland have just booted him out of Drylaw.'

'We could stand on our rights, Guv, insist that they do what it says in the legislation.'

'Yes, but one call to the Head of SHEP and he'll be booted out again. God, I miss Stuttle.'

Mona was surprised. 'You think he would be doing this differently?'

'Maybe not, but at least I could tell him what I thought of him and it would make me feel better.'

Her mind turned to the practicalities. 'Where are we going to put him? The Facilities Manager will have a fit if he knows we're detaining someone on the premises.'

Paterson slowed down and turned into the car park of the Cathcart Building. 'Third floor conference room? It's out of the way. With a bit of luck no-one will even know he's there. You get the key sorted out. I'll park up and meet you both there.'

*

'I need a key.'

Marguerite focused on shuffling the papers on her desk with an intensity of focus that was never present when she was actually working.

'The key for the third-floor conference room.'

The silence indicated that Marguerite had in no way forgiven them for their reaction to her raffle prize. Mona was torn between exploding with irritation or apologising again just so she could get moving.

'We are very sorry to disturb you,' said Boucher.

Marguerite looked up in surprise, and after a second staring at the Belgian, smiled flirtatiously. 'Oh, it's no problem.' She jumped off her seat and hurried over to retrieve the key from the rack on the wall. She placed it on the counter in front of her. 'So, who are you then? Are you going to be working here?'

Boucher leaned over the counter, his hand reaching for the key.

'I'll take that, thank you.' Mona picked it up and stuck it in her pocket.

'Are you from SHEP, then?' Marguerite was twirling her hair while staring up at Boucher, who was, inexplicably, still leaning on the reception counter.

'Sadly, no.'

'Can we get a move on, please?' Mona swept her arm in the direction of the stairs, in the hope Boucher would get moving.

'I have to go.' Boucher shot Marguerite a smile that expressed a sincere regret that he was being dragged away from her company. Mona was pretty sure that this was not a look that Marguerite routinely got from people.

'Mr Boucher, please.'

He loped up the stairs behind her, singing softly to himself. Was he even slightly worried about his situation? He'd pissed off some pretty dangerous people; in his position, she'd have been jumping at the sight of her own shadow. But then this was a man who had tried to kill the Professor. The man who would happily have shot her as well, if she'd got in the way. He wasn't likely to suffer from nerves.

'We're in here.' She shepherded him into the conference room then heard the distinctive thump of Paterson taking the stairs two at a time.

'Right, Boucher, time to start talking. Where can we find Ana Procházková?'

Boucher took his time settling into a chair. 'It is cold in here. Also, I am hungry. Our friends at Police Scotland did not offer me lunch before they asked me to leave.'

'Tell us what we need to know, and we'll be happy to arrange for you to be fed.'

The Belgian made a show of looking round at his surroundings. 'Are you really supposed to keep people detained in a room like this? Are you sure I should not be in a police cell, or maybe a prison?'

'We can detain you here, or you can take your chances wandering the streets of Edinburgh. Exactly how much money do you have in your pocket?'

Boucher smiled. 'You make a very good point, Mr Paterson. I am very grateful to you for your protection.'

'I expect you'd have had plenty cash if your friends hadn't decided to donate all the lorry's contents to a food bank.' Paterson leaned forward. 'Where exactly does selling the contents of the lorry come into it? I can see distributing the food to food banks makes a pretty strong political point, but selling it to Edinburgh lowlife gangster scum? Isn't that just you making a few quid? What happened to your principles?'

'I don't know what you mean by that. No-one is saying that the food was sold. But,' Boucher smiled, 'for the sake of argument, it could be said that as well as making a political point it did present an opportunity to raise much-needed funds for our activities.'

'Not for personal gain, then?' asked Mona.

He shook his head, still smiling. 'I am an activist through and through.'

'How did your fellow activists feel about this hypothetical sales arrangement?'

'Hypothetically, there may have been a breakdown in communication.'

'Which ended up with one poor lassie dead.' Paterson hit the table, and both Boucher and Mona jumped. 'Is that on your conscience?'

He shrugged. 'We are all aware that there are dangers involved in our activism.'

'Dieter Lange is also dead.'

Boucher stopped smiling, and for the first time in the conversation looked interested in what they were saying. 'What happened to him?'

'Suicide. Apparently he was responsible for the death of Natálie Svobodová and was overcome with remorse.'

'He was always very sensitive,' said Boucher, looking thoughtful.

'Really? Because I don't think anyone is buying this suicide theory.'

'Aren't they?' Boucher's grin was back, the momentary disruption to his equilibrium gone. 'In my experience when the police and politicians are offered an explanation that gives them a ready solution to a problem they are generally quite happy to take it. Are you both sure that your police colleagues have been so quick to dismiss this?'

'Just tell us where Ana is.' Paterson was clearly running out of patience.

'I don't know – why would I? She's not a close friend of mine – it's you who keep telling me that we were working together as a cell.'

'OK.' Mona decided on another approach. 'When you came to Scotland where were you staying? Were you in a flat, hostel, whatever?'

'A flat. Owned by a friend of a friend of a friend.'

'And the address of the flat, and the name of this friend?'

'I don't know. It was a very informal arrangement.'

'You stayed there!' Paterson's patience had completely gone. 'You must have some idea of where you were.'

Boucher shrugged.

'We've gone out on a limb here to protect you, Mr Boucher. If you don't want to help us, we might as well just let you go.'

He smiled. 'Ah, now you are confusing me. One moment, you are the good guys who must follow the rules to keep the public's health safe, and now you are telling me you will throw me back out there to take my chances.'

'Yeah, well, what can I say?' said Paterson. 'I'm complicated. Now give us an address.'

'Leopold Street. Maybe number 2?'

'Right.' Paterson opened the door. 'You better not be messing us around.'

'I am still hungry. Please bring me something to eat. It must be vegan.'

Paterson ushered Mona out, then slammed and locked the door behind them, ignoring Boucher who was still shouting his menu instructions. 'Right, get hold of Maitland and check out this address. I'm not putting too much faith in it though – he's probably stringing us along.'

When she walked in Maitland jerked his head in the direction of Bernard's desk. For a moment Mona thought Bernard had returned to work, then she realised the figure sitting there was Marcus.

'Marcus. You're here.'

He beamed at her. 'Yes, when I heard poor Bernard was off sick today, I thought it was a perfect opportunity to have a desk and some company today.'

'Yeah, we're delighted to have Marcus entertaining us.' Maitland glared at the IT officer, who remained oblivious.

'What have you done to the boxes?' Paterson looked round the room. The containers had been stacked more neatly around the fringes of the room, allowing people to access their desks.

'We separated them out into perishables and non-perishables.' Carole spoke up. 'I don't think we can have the perishables here much longer. The steaks are beginning to smell.'

'I'll have a word with Hunter. Maitland, you and Mona need to check out a place where Boucher may have been staying, see if Ana P is there, or if anyone knows where she might be. And don't let these hippies fob you off – if they're not helpful, feel free to bring them back here.'

'Oh no,' said Marcus. 'Just when I get some company, everyone starts leaving. Oh well, at least I've still got Carole and Mr Paterson.'

Paterson stopped dead in the doorway to his room, then slowly turned back to face everyone. 'Yeah, actually, Marcus, I'm getting a bit worried about Bernard. It's not like him to be off sick, so I'd really like someone to check on him. Could you do us a favour and pop by his flat?'

'Now?'

Paterson nodded. 'We take the safety of our operatives very seriously. I need you to recce the situation and then report back.'

Marcus got hurriedly to his feet. 'Out in the field again. Delighted to assist.'

'Take the bear.' Carole handed him the pink teddy.

'I'm sure this will cheer him up no end.' Marcus hugged the bear close to him and set off on his mission.

9

'Catch me up on all of this.' Maitland was frowning as he tried to make sense of it all. 'We're going to this flat because?'

'Because Boucher stayed there, or says that he stayed there, at least. He's told so many lies I wouldn't be surprised if when we get there it's a little old lady who owns it who has never heard of him.'

'But if he's telling the truth, you think Ana might be there?'

She frowned. 'I think it's unlikely, because she'll know that Boucher is in custody and might tell us about the flat. She's probably moved on and is hiding somewhere else. I'm just hopeful that we can put a bit of pressure on her flatmates and they'll tell us where she's gone.'

'Say we do manage to find her – what do we do with her?'

'Well, obviously, she's going to need an Emergency Health Check.'

'Obviously.'

'Then we'll have to find somewhere safe to put her in case some of the less-than-legitimate business people Boucher's been dealing with want to hold her responsible for him not delivering the goods.'

'The office?'

'Tricky, with Boucher already being there. And then there's the small matter that Police Scotland are probably also looking for her, as after all, she did help to hijack a lorry.'

'We should probably phone Ian Jacobsen.'

'Probably, but we can worry about that later. We're here.'

The door was opened by a young man with short brown hair. He was topless and carrying a towel, leading Mona to surmise they'd interrupted him in the middle of his ablutions.

'Sorry to call at a bad time.'

'No, it's fine, I'm just getting ready for work.' He continued patting himself down with the towel. 'How can I help you?'

'We were informed that Florian Boucher has been staying here.'

The man abruptly stopped rubbing his hair with the towel. 'Who told you that?'

'Florian Boucher.'

'He's not in.'

'We know.'

The man was looking more uncomfortable by the minute. 'Who are you anyway?'

'Mona Whyte from the Health Enforcement Team.' She flashed her ID. 'And what's your name?'

'Ryan Wilson. So, are you like the police, then?'

'We work closely with them.' She was picking up on a lot of anxiety on Ryan's part. Whatever had been going on here, he may not have been a willing participant. 'Can we come in, sir?'

Ryan searched for a reason to say no and failed to find it. Maitland stepped in to the flat. 'Living room through here is it, sir?'

'Yes, but, do we have to—'

'We do, sir.' She closed the front door behind her. Ryan Wilson was looking like a trapped animal, his gaze firmly on the door behind her. Worried that he might be about to attempt to flee, she tried to move things on. 'Shall we go through?'

He moved reluctantly down the hallway. She followed him into the living room, and found Maitland standing in the centre of it, looking confused. After a brief look round the room she realised why. There was an eclectic mixture of furniture, but absolutely nothing you could sit on.

Ryan looked slightly embarrassed. 'I'd ask you to take a seat but,' he shrugged, 'no chairs.'

'Yeah, we can see that. It's fine. We can stand.'

He seemed to feel the need to explain further. 'I split up with my girlfriend, and she came round when I was out and took half the furniture.'

'OK—'

'Was it her furniture?' Maitland interrupted.

Ryan shrugged again. 'That's debatable.'

'Anyway,' Mona leapt in, firmly, before Maitland started commiserating with their potential witness about the shortcomings of ex-girlfriends. 'Boucher. He was here?'

'This is about the car, isn't it?'

Mona had no idea what he was talking about but gave a professional little smile that indicated to Ryan that he might just have hit the nail on the head. 'Do you want to tell us about it?'

'It was the flood.' He shook his head. 'None of this would have happened if it wasn't for that.'

'Where was this flood, sir?' asked Maitland. He didn't seem to have any more understanding of what was going on here than she did.

'The *Rose Bowl*. I work behind the bar there. One of the downstairs bogs, I think, anyway, the whole place

223

was underwater when we opened up, so we all got sent home.'

Mona closed her eyes. Ryan seemed to be going a particularly scenic route with his storytelling. 'Maybe we could go back a bit, Mr Wilson, and start with why Boucher was staying here?'

'Yeah, OK. Claudine, my ex, is part of a climate challenge group at the university – she's a student there – and they were asked if they could host some people who were coming to Scotland to take part in the V8 protests. So, she says someone can stay here, without even asking me, which I was pretty pissed off about because, you know, it's my name on the lease if anything goes wrong?' He appealed to Maitland who nodded empathetically. 'I'd no idea what she was signing us up for.'

'So, Boucher was staying here?'

'Yup. He was assigned to us. Soon as he walked through the door I knew he was sketchy, but Claudine thought the sun shone out of his arse, she really did. Giving it all that,' he made a little snapping gesture with his hand, 'going on about all the protests that he'd been part of, and how he was prepared to die in the pursuit of a better world. And Claudine, who is an intelligent woman, is sitting there lapping all this up, taking it all at face value. I dropped out of uni in second year, but even I've got the brains to see the guy's a twat. But Claudine,' he shook his head, 'she's doing a Phd for God's sake, but doesn't have the critical faculties to spot a wanker when she sees one.'

Judging by Ryan's strength of feeling towards Boucher, Mona was beginning to speculate how he'd come to split up with his furniture-stealing ex. 'So, you came home early from work.'

He leaned against the table, eyes shut, his fingers pinching the top of his nose. Mona was momentarily concerned he was about to cry, but his eyes snapped open and he let out a string of clearly cathartic curses, before continuing with his story. 'Clothes all over the living room floor. Her clothes, his clothes, all over the place.' He looked round the room, as if mentally remembering what he'd seen. 'There was no sign of the pair of them, but I could hear music playing really loudly from our room.'

Maitland looked enthralled. 'So, did you burst in there?'

'Naw. Probably should have done, but I didn't really want to get an eyeful of, well, you know . . .'

'Good point,' said Maitland. 'I'd have been just the same.'

'So, I was going to head out, and come back and confront her about it later, but when I opened the front door, there were a couple of people standing there, a man and a woman.'

'Did you recognise them?' asked Mona.

He shook his head. 'But I knew right away they were looking for Boucher. They were foreign, and the guy absolutely stank of weed. I mean, I like a puff, don't get me wrong, but this guy was reeking.'

'What did they want?'

'They demanded to see Boucher, and I said you can't because he's busy right now shagging my girlfriend, which probably wasn't the best thing to say but I was pretty annoyed—'

'Understandably.' Maitland nodded.

'But then the girl looked really upset, and I thought whoops, bet he was knobbing her as well, and the bloke put his arm around her, but she wasn't having any of that and kind of shook him off. Then she said, "We still need to speak to him. We need his keys."'

'Keys?'

'Yep. So, I said, well his trousers are hanging off a chair in the living room, so feel free to help yourself.' He looked sheepish. 'Did I do the wrong thing? Have they nicked his car or something? I only let them take it because I was annoyed about Claudine.'

'Not a great move,' said Mona, sternly.

Ryan looked worried. 'Am I going to be prosecuted?'

'For theft?' It would be a long time before anyone got round to prosecuting Ryan for standing idly by while one set of people stole the keys to a lorry from another set of people who had already removed it from its rightful owner. However, it wouldn't hurt to keep Ryan on his toes if they were going to get information out of him.

'I think the best thing you can do is be very helpful with our enquiries. Now, do you have any idea where the people who picked up the keys were staying?'

He shook his head. 'That is literally all the conversation I had with them. They went into the living room, picked up the keys, then legged it.'

'How did Boucher react when he found his keys were missing?' asked Maitland.

'Don't know.' Ryan shrugged. 'I went round to one of my mates, got wasted, and didn't get back to the flat until the next day. Next time I saw Boucher he was on the news, threatening to set fire to himself.' He shook his head. 'Arsehole.'

She looked up at Maitland, and he nodded in the direction of the door. They'd probably got as much as they were going to out of Ryan.

'Thanks for your time, sir. We might have to come back and talk to you again—'

'So, I'm not under arrest?' Ryan interrupted.

'Police Scotland might also want to talk to you.'

He looked miserable, and she felt sorry for him. 'I would imagine they'll be more interested in talking to you as part of their ongoing investigation into Boucher than pursuing any charges against you. Just be helpful with their enquiries.'

He brightened at the thought. 'I'm very happy to tell them all I know about Boucher. Hope they lock the dickhead up.'

They took their leave and headed back outside.

'Do you think there's still an ongoing enquiry into Boucher, Mona?'

'I don't know. I think they're trying to pretend the lorry hijack never happened.'

He snorted. 'Pretty difficult with all the dead bodies.'

'Yeah, but they can be spun as a murder/suicide, lover's tiff or whatever. If the Guv hadn't scooped Boucher off the streets, his unhappy customers would probably have done for him. The police don't know we've got him.'

'But your mate Cassandra Doom knows that there's something going on. She's not going to let it go, is she?'

'It would be unlikely.' Elaine would die in the attempt to get this story out, but she didn't want to think about her. She changed the subject. 'You know how you said back there that you wouldn't have burst into the bedroom and confronted the pair of them either, is that true? It doesn't sound like you.'

He laughed. 'I was trying to be sympathetic, but honestly, what a wuss! I'd have been straight in there to sort him out. Not that my Kate would ever do something like that.'

'Yup, I think you got the last decent woman out there. Let's get back to the office.'

He didn't answer, his attention taken up entirely by his phone.

'Maitland?'

'Sorry. Just going to pop by the uni on the way back.'

'Why?'

'Because the last decent woman out there should be in between lectures at the moment and I want to surprise her.'

Mona felt a small pang of jealousy that everyone on the HET seemed to be in a fully functioning relationship except her. 'Well, don't be long. You don't want Paterson finding out you're skiving.'

He winked. 'Tell him I'm following up a red-hot lead.'

'Whatever.'

10

Bernard lay on his bed staring at the ceiling. He was wearing a suit he hadn't had on since his graduation day, which was now slightly tight around the waist. He'd had a brief moment of doubt that he'd actually be able to eat anything tonight without it bursting back open, but he wanted to look smart for his evening with Lucy's parents, so he'd just have to cope.

He let out a small sigh. He'd been busy since he finished looking at the surveillance files. He'd tidied up, not that the flat had been untidy. He'd cleaned the kitchen, not that it had been particularly dirty. He'd had a long shower, shaved, and removed some extraneous nose hairs. He'd put on the suit, dabbed a small amount of gentleman's cologne on his neck, and, when he really couldn't put it off any longer, he'd lain down on the bed to reflect on the day's events and his complicated emotional response to them.

He had truly loved Carrie. If the Virus hadn't come along, if their son hadn't died, they'd have been together forever, he was sure of it, enjoying a long and happy married life. When they'd split, he'd been left with a deep affection for her, the kind of connection that could only exist between two people who had shared a life. The kind of connection that could only exist between two people who had lost a child. But now, he was head over heels in love with Lucy. The one thing that had been clarified by all this was quite how deep his feelings were for her. If all worked out, maybe he'd be sharing the rest of his life with her, and maybe, just maybe, once the Virus had run its course, children would feature in that.

Swinging his legs round carefully so he didn't crumple the suit, he sat up and sighed again, longer and more deeply. Daydreaming about theoretical children was all very well, but there was a very real child who was going to be arriving in a couple of months' time, and whether he wanted to or not, he was going to be involved in its life. He'd promised Dr Blake that he'd keep an eye on Carrie, make sure that she wasn't overexerting herself, and if there was any sign that Carrie was unwell, he'd sworn he'd get medical help, quick smart.

He was going to have to explain all this to Lucy. He couldn't keep sneaking around like he had been. He'd just have to give her the full story, and hope to God that once the baby was born, Carrie could cope with the challenges of motherhood, and he could gently ease himself out of the picture. Pulling back his cuff, he checked his watch. It was time to go. The restaurant was ten minutes' walk away, but he'd left himself fifteen minutes so that he could be there early, though not too early, and make a good impression.

He was reaching for his keys when the flat's buzzer sounded. He checked his watch again. Whoever this was, he needed to get rid of them and be on his way.

'Hello?'

'Bernard, it's me, Marcus.'

His heart sank.

'And I'm with, sorry, what was your name again?'

He heard a female voice. Marcus didn't know any women, and rarely had any reason to interact with females who were not in some way linked to the HET. Under other circumstances Bernard would be intrigued at what was going on, but right now he couldn't care less. There was no woman on earth who was going to make him late for his meal tonight.

'I'm with Anna Porca, Porcha, Procha-something. She says you're looking for her?'

Except possibly this woman.

'Marcus, are you telling me that you brought a Health Defaulter, who is wanted by the police with regards to theft of a lorry, and possibly terrorism charges, *to my home address*?'

There was a pause while he thought this over. 'Yes, that is correct.'

Somewhere, there was hopefully a mad scientist working on a potion that would allow sarcasm to be rendered audible to anyone who heard it. He would be first in line to buy a bucketful and inject it into his colleague. Bernard slammed the door entry phone back on its hook, and picked up his keys, a box of chocolates, and the bunch of flowers that were in a vase. He shook the water off the stems and popped them in a bag. He might be late, but he wouldn't be empty handed.

Ana Procházková was standing on the pavement looking rather bedraggled. Marcus was looking anxious, hopping from foot to foot, his hands raised, almost as if he was preparing to rugby tackle the woman if she tried to run off.

'Bernard, I'm so glad you were in. I really wasn't sure what to do, but I knew that you would have a plan.'

Marcus looked expectantly at him. Exasperated, Bernard had a sudden realisation of how Mona must feel every time he indicated that he maybe perhaps wasn't a hundred per cent sure what he should be doing.

'Ms Procházková, there are a lot of people looking for you.'

She nodded, looking at him pleadingly. 'I am very scared. You must please take me to Florian Boucher. I know he is in your office.'

'Do you? We'll come to that in a minute.' He turned his back on her, and grabbed Marcus's arm, pulling him a little way down the street. 'Marcus what the you-know-what is actually going on?'

'I don't know! I think she followed me when I left the office, and then somewhere around The Pleasance she jumped me and tried to steal my keys.'

'Did she get them?'

'No, I'd actually left them in the office. So, after I'd, you know, fought her off, I asked her what she was up to and she burst into tears and said she needed to see Boucher, who is apparently in our office.' He stopped and looked at Bernard. 'Why are you wearing a suit?'

'I'm going out for a meal.'

'At 5.45?'

'It's a pre-theatre—' He stopped himself. 'That's not important. Why did you bring her to my home?'

'I was on my way to visit you, and I was nearly here when she jumped me, and I didn't really know what to, you know, do.'

Ana appeared beside them. 'Please.' She touched his arm. 'I am very scared. People, they are looking for me. We have made big mistake. I could die.'

'Great.' Bernard looked round the street. There didn't appear to be anyone who was following her. 'Right, let's get you to the office. Mr Paterson can sort this out.'

'Shouldn't we be heading in the other direction?'

'I need to make a small stop first.'

11

Mona hurried back in the direction of the office. She was keen to check on Boucher, and discuss with Paterson what his game plan actually was. Were they really going to keep him in the building overnight?

Her phone buzzed as she approached the door of the Cathcart Building.

hyntr in office chek butcher

She deciphered that in amongst the predictive text errors and the spelling mistakes, Paterson was trying to tell her that Hunter had arrived unexpectedly.

Bugger. They had a perfect right to be interviewing Boucher, and nobody could deny he was their best, possibly only, link to finding the other missing Health Defaulters. Yet she couldn't help feeling that if Hunter stumbled across Boucher on the premises, it would still lead to some awkward discussions about why he was here rather than in a police cell and why no-one had thought to keep the Head of SHEP in the loop.

Marguerite was pottering about behind the front desk, doing something with a can of polish and a duster. Mona hurried past, but not quite quickly enough.

'Who was that guy you brought in earlier?' Marguerite leaned across the desk and shouted after her. 'Is he still here? I didn't see him leave.'

That explained why Marguerite was still at her post, half an hour after the other admin staff had clocked off.

Mona glanced up the stairs, weighing up the merits of stopping to chat or just running on past. Making a break for it was very appealing, but with Hunter loose in the building she couldn't risk a Marguerite indiscretion; previous experience told her that when Marguerite dropped you in the shit there was quite a splash. The Admin Officer wouldn't have moved from her desk for even a second if she was waiting for the handsome Belgian to return, so she was struggling to come up with a plausible scenario she might buy. The only other ways out were the fire exit or jumping out of a window; neither of these things were unknown at the HET but they would require some explanation. She opted for a diversionary tactic. 'I think he liked you, you know.'

Marguerite patted her hair. 'I thought that too. Will he be in again tomorrow?'

'Yes.'

'Maybe he'll want my phone number.'

'I thought you had a boyfriend?'

'I do.' She smiled and picked up her handbag. 'But he doesn't look like that.'

Heaving a sigh of relief that her loud-mouthed colleague had finally started packing up her things to go home, she ran up the steps to the conference room. Boucher was lolling back on one of the chairs, his feet up on another. He peered round the side of her. 'You are on your own?'

'My colleague will be joining us shortly. Here.' She dug into her bag. She'd made a pitstop at a Sainsbury's Local on her way back and picked up a sandwich that seemed to contain a layer of grey mush and some brightly coloured peppers. It didn't look appealing, but it did have a sticker proclaiming its vegan credentials. She placed it on the table, along with a bottle of water. 'I'm sure you're hungry.'

'I am.' He didn't pick them up. 'Was my information useful? Did you track down the naughty Health Check-avoiding Ana Procházková?'

'Not yet.' She sat down. 'You didn't mention she was a girlfriend of yours.'

He grinned. 'You didn't ask.'

Mona stared at him. 'Aren't you worried about her?'

He laughed, long and hard. 'Poor little Ana, all alone and friendless.'

'Well, isn't she?'

'No, no, no, no.' He shook his head. 'Ana is very resourceful. She's been trained to be that.'

'Trained? Who by?' He shrugged, infuriating her. 'You must know. We were right about you being a cell, weren't we? Have you all been trained together? Learning your lessons on how to be a good little terrorist?'

'Terrorist.' Boucher snorted. 'A ridiculous description of citizens whose only concern is for the planet. Anyway, if you have any questions for Ana, you can ask her directly. She's on her way here.'

Mona was confused. How would he know where Ana P was? 'Coming here? To hand herself in?'

He laughed again. 'No. She is planning to kill me.'

'To kill you?' Her confusion was deepening. She wished Hunter wasn't in the building so she could phone Paterson and get him to listen to this nonsense too.

Boucher nodded, slowly. 'She called me to say that was her intention.'

'She couldn't have phoned you. We took your mobile.'

He grinned. 'You took *one* of my mobiles.'

Mona closed her eyes. This was turning into a shit-storm. As far as she'd been aware Ana was a well-meaning, if misguided, young activist, who had Robin Hooded some food. The idea that she was on her way here with murder on her mind sounded like bullshit.

Boucher laughed at her confusion. 'Ah, Mona Whyte, I can see I have perplexed you.'

'How about you start dealing with my confusion? How about telling me what you're really up to, because I'm not buying this activist bullshit?'

'I'm sorry you doubt my sincerity.'

She felt anger bubbling up within her. 'Are you? I must apologise for that, it's just that I have this really strong sensation that a few months ago you nearly killed me.'

He stared back at her, his expression giving nothing away.

'It was you, wasn't it? It was your strange, accentless Eurotones I heard that night.' Boucher looked away from her gaze. 'You shot at us, me and the Professor. You followed us halfway across the country, then tried to—' She stopped at the feeling of something cold and sharp against her throat.

'I was there, Mona Whyte. I wondered if you would recognise me. My apologies for attempting to kill you, well, attempting to kill your friend Professor Bircham-Fowler; I was never actually aiming at you. This time, if I do have to kill you, at least you can take comfort from the fact that you are my target.' He put more pressure on the blade. She felt it sting, and a slow trickle of blood run down her neck. 'The very helpful young woman who we met earlier, was kind enough to leave her letter-opener lying on the front desk. Please thank her for letting me use it.'

She was going to throttle Marguerite.

'Put your hands out in front of you, flat on the table.'

She reluctantly complied. With his free hand he produced a set of laces from his pocket and tied them tightly round her wrists. She could feel them cutting into her skin.

'You should have taken me to a police station. They would have searched me properly and removed my shoe-laces.' He grinned. 'Perhaps you shouldn't be so keen to help people in future. Stand please.'

He pushed her over to the window and used his other lace to tie her hands to its handle. The laces were thin, and she could be out of them in five minutes, but that was still longer than it would take Boucher to get out of the building. She contemplated yelling for help, but there were no offices based on this floor, and she ran the risk of him deciding to silence her permanently if she called out. Even worse, if someone did hear her and came to her aid, she ran the risk of getting them killed instead. The only useful thing she could do was try and get more information about what was happening.

'Why does Ana Procházková want you dead?'

'Because she's a fanatic.' He gave a little tug on the laces, to check his handiwork had held. Pain shot through her wrists. 'Remember that hypothetical cell you mentioned? Let's pretend that it really did exist, and it was a mixture of well-meaning climate activists and a couple of people like myself with, you know, *other aims*. So, we all get trained to allow us to undertake the little, ehm, pranks that we did.'

'But all that stuff around the V8 *was* just pranks, publicity stunts. Why do you want to get involved in this nonsense?'

'It suits my employers for there to be a little bit of chaos going on.'

'Your employers?'

'Oh, Mona, I'm not going to share that information. Please move your elbow a little.' He hoisted her arm up onto the window ledge. 'We like the food movement. It provides us with a great cover. Gives us a legitimate reason to get people out on the street, stirring up trouble for your government. These climate activists, they're young, idealistic, they'll let us take a lead. Mostly.' He sighed. 'But not always. Ana wasn't just a student trying to make a point. She's the real thing, totally fanatical. My employers actually thought she had a lot of potential. I gave her a little bit of mentoring, taught her a few tricks that allowed her to do a little bit more than just a university prank. Ana would die to further her climate aims, or as it turns out, she'd kill.'

'Ana killed Natálie Svobodová?'

He nodded, slowly. 'Ana was very upset when she found out that we weren't using the lorry to make a political point, it was just about generating some dirty old cash for my employers. Ana made my life very difficult by stealing my keys, then helping herself to the food – *my* food – that I had promised to some men who will in all likelihood have me tortured when I can't deliver. To say nothing of how my employers will react to the failure of my mission.'

'I'm so sorry for your predicament.'

Boucher tugged hard on the laces round her wrists. She let out a little yelp of pain and he laughed. 'Natálie took very unkindly to the discovery that Ana and Dieter had taken things into their own hands. Of the three of them she was the only one who really understood the concept of following orders. She was the only one who understood that there would be consequences if they didn't do as I said. I suspect she was scared enough of my wrath to put up quite a struggle to protect the food, but as we know, she didn't win that particular fight.'

'Was it an accident?'

He shrugged. 'I haven't given it a moment's thought. Intentional or accidental, the end result is the same. I'm more concerned about the death of Lange. It suggests that my employers are aware that the situation has become, ehm, *unfortunate*, and that they have started cleaning up.'

'So that's why you're still here. You're the next loose end that needs tidying up.'

He shrugged. 'I was as safe here as anywhere. I made some arrangements while I was detained, and I would probably have stayed a bit longer, but now we have my psychotic ex-girlfriend on her way. Ana is a fanatic. She does mean to kill me. I'm sure I could get the better of her, but it's all getting messy. Thank you for your hospitality but I think I'm ready to go.'

'You're safer here inside the building. She won't be able to get in.'

Boucher grinned. 'I agree that your defences present a challenge. But our training always tells us that the weak spot in any organisation is its people. Ana will be out there trying to find your weakest link. Any of your staff susceptible to a pretty girl with a sob story?'

Marcus. Bernard.

'Stay here. We can protect you, and deal with Ana.'

'Yes, and arrest me.' He reached for the door handle. 'I'd like to believe that you're just trying to help, Mona Whyte, but I think you are probably holding a grudge.' His smiled disappeared. 'And I strongly suggest that you give me time to leave the building before you start shouting for help. If I have to fight my way out of this building, I will.' He held up the letter opener. 'I don't want to have to stab the lovely young woman at your reception through the eye with this.'

With that he was gone, leaving Mona staring at the door. Her hands were beginning to turn white as the blood to them was restricted. She started furiously scraping the laces against the metal of the window catch, and after a minute or two the laces frayed and gave way. She raced down the stairs and found Marguerite still idling at the reception desk.

'Did Boucher just go past?'

'The nice man from earlier? Yeah, you just missed him. He blew me a kiss on the way past.'

'Fuck.'

12

'So where are we going?'

Bernard thought for a moment and realised the only thing he could do was tell Marcus the truth. 'I just need to pop into the restaurant and tell Lucy that I'm going to be late. I'm meeting her parents for the first time and I don't want to make a bad impression.' He thought for a second. 'Or at least any worse an impression that I can possibly help.' Whichever way he looked at it, not turning up for a meal with your girlfriend's parents didn't look good.

'No.' Ana grabbed his arm. 'This is not possible. Office first, then meal.'

He turned off the High Street onto Cockburn Street. 'That's the deal, take it or leave it.'

Ana let out a cry of frustration. He picked up his pace, eager to get his apologies over and done with. Ana kept pace with him, muttering to herself. Mostly she was grumbling in her own language, although he heard an occasional *we go now* in English. Marcus seemed to have disappeared. He looked back to see that he was ferreting about inside his rucksack.

'Come *on*, Marcus.'

'Sorry.' He came bounding after them, holding something fluffy and pink. 'When you mentioned Lucy, I remembered that you won this.' He held a large teddy bear in his direction.

'What?'

'You won Marguerite's raffle.'

'Please.' Ana stamped her foot. 'We must go.'

'OK, well, can you carry that please.' He waved the chocolates and flowers at them. 'No hands.'

Ana snatched it and started walking. 'We go faster, please.'

'No arguments there.' He strode on, determined that nothing else would interrupt them. He didn't even slow down when his phone rang, he just pulled it out of his pocket, saw Mona's name and declined the call. They were literally two minutes from the restaurant. Two minutes to explain what was going on to Lucy, another couple of minutes to find a cab, add another five driving time. He'd be at the office in ten minutes tops, so Mona could wait until then.

A blast of the Star Wars theme tune came from Marcus's inside pocket.

'If it's Mona, don't answer it.'

Marcus looked at his screen. 'It's Mona. I could just speak to her and tell her you're on your way?'

'No. Any conversation will just delay us.'

Marcus looked deeply uncomfortable with this suggested course of action, but did as he was asked.

'Restaurant is bad idea.' Ana glared at him.

'Yes, well, that's still what we're doing.'

'Bad people are looking for me. You want take them to your girlfriend, maybe?'

He stopped dead. He'd already be double locking his door tonight after Marcus had brought Ana to his home. He didn't want Lucy dragged into all this as well. 'Right, you two, in there.' He gestured into one of the many narrow alleyways that ran from Cockburn Street to the High Street. 'Hide yourself up there, the restaurant is on the other side of the road, I'll pop in and be straight back.'

Ana yelled something at him, which he suspected from the tone and arm gesture that accompanied it might have been a swear word, but he walked on, speeding up his pace. He heard his name being called and sighed. Could Marcus not, just for once, do what he'd told him to do? Was it too much to ask just to have five minutes to sort things out with Lucy? He spun round on his heel, then stopped in horror, taking several steps backward.

'Oh God, not you.'

'Guv, we've got a prob—' Mona broke off abruptly. In all the excitement, she'd forgotten Paterson's warning that Hunter was in the office. Thank God she hadn't bumped into Boucher on the stairs.

'Oh, hi, Ma'am.'

'Mona.'

'Ehm, Guv, could I have a word?'

Her boss stared malevolently back at her over the top of Hunter's head. She had a sense that whatever they'd been talking about it hadn't been a pleasant conversation, that Hunter hadn't just popped in to tell him what a bang-up job he was doing of managing the North Edinburgh HET. 'Yes, I think Ms Hunter was just leaving—'

Hunter looked furious. 'I'll decide when I'm leaving, thank you, John. Now, Mona, I believe you were about to say that you had a problem. Perhaps you could share what that problem might be?'

'Well, I ...' She faltered, looking at her superior officers, both of whom were glaring at her. She reluctantly decided that due to the seriousness of the situation she was going to have to confess.

'Boucher's gone.'

Paterson said, 'What do you mean gone?' at the same time as Hunter asked, 'Boucher was here?' She didn't have time to deal with both of them so focused on Paterson.

'When I went in to see him he threatened me with a, ehm, bladed implement, see.' She showed Paterson the cut on her neck. 'And then he—'

'What was Boucher doing here?'

'With all due respect, Ma'am, I don't have time to explain.' She turned back to Paterson. 'Ana Procházková isn't who we thought she was. She's not an innocent activist who's out of her depth, she's a well-trained operative and she is out there, I think targeting Bernard and Marcus, who may be in danger, and neither of them are answering their phone—'

'WILL SOMEONE PLEASE EXPLAIN TO ME WHAT IS GOING ON?' Hunter had turned purple. 'I am the senior officer here which no-one seems to recognise. You all answer to me.'

'Just tried them again, Guv,' Maitland spoke. Mona turned round in surprise. She'd been so focused on Paterson that she hadn't realised that Maitland and Carole were also in the office. 'Still no answer.'

Hunter threw her hands up in exasperation.

'OK, Ma'am,' said Paterson. 'From what I can make out, two of your staff members are in danger, I'm not sure entirely why, but I'm willing to trust Mona that time is of the essence. What do *you* think we should do?'

There was a very long pause, while everyone in the room stared at Hunter. 'Well, we should . . .' She tailed off.

'Right.' Paterson regained control of the situation. 'Anyone know where Bernard and Marcus are?'

'Marcus set off for Bernard's flat over an hour ago. He should have been there by now,' said Maitland. 'Why is he in danger?'

'According to Boucher, Ana P is heading this way intent on killing him—'

'How could he know that?' Hunter was trying to regain some leadership. 'And why?'

'Can you just take it on trust for the moment, Ma'am? She thinks he's still here, and I think she's going to spin Bernard or Marcus some line so that they let her into the building.'

'It could be OK,' said Paterson. 'If they do bring her here, we can be waiting for her.'

'Yeah, Guv,' said Mona. 'But there's always the possibility that Bernard will refuse to bring her here. He might think it's unethical, although I'm surprised he hasn't been in touch to tell us so.'

'He won't bring her here.' Carole spoke. 'At least, I don't think he'll come here directly.'

'Why?' Mona was surprised at how certain she sounded.

'It's his big night tonight. He's meeting Lucy's parents for the first time. He's not going to let anything interfere with that.'

Paterson swore. 'He's not stupid enough to detour to a restaurant before coming here. And why hasn't he phoned us?'

'Because he doesn't realise he's in any danger,' said Mona. 'He thinks that Ana P was the one we needed to worry about, a poor student who was in deep trouble. He's going to think that nipping into a restaurant to apologise to his in-laws isn't a problem.'

'Right.' Paterson had heard enough. 'Maitland, Carole, you both stay here. Do we know the restaurant he was going to?'

'Somewhere on Cockburn Street,' said Carole. 'I don't know the name.'

'We can work with that. Ma'am, can you arrange for police to be despatched both here and to Cockburn Street?'

Hunter didn't say anything.

'Ma'am, this is urgent.'

'The call might be better coming from you.' Their boss gave up any pretence that she was in charge and leaned against a desk. 'I have a feeling that if *I* make the call, it won't be prioritised.'

'OK, let's do it while we're moving.'

13

'Operation Trigon, Bernard.' Ian Jacobsen smiled at him, a tight little evil smile, that did not bode well for Bernard's future happiness. 'Remember that? That key piece of information that you were so keen to pass on to us? Well, we've looked at it every which way, and I don't think Bryce was ever anywhere near it.'

'Happy to discuss, but this isn't the time, Ian, believe me.' His eyes flicked in the direction of the restaurant. He was opposite it now, only the narrow, cobbled road separating him from Lucy. He hoped that she didn't look out of the window and seem him there, stopped for a chat when he was already late.

'So, my question for you is, did you know that was the case when you told me that Bryce was focusing on it?'

'I didn't say that, I just told you what I heard.' He took a step towards the pavement's edge. He could make a break for it. Maybe he could get into the restaurant and make his apologies before Ian realised what was going on. Although the chances were he'd follow him, and whatever he said to him in front of Lucy's parents it definitely wouldn't improve the situation.

'Really? Or what Bryce told you to say? You do know that your duff information meant the redirection of hundreds of hours of staff time, time that could have been more usefully spend dealing with other stuff, like this current disaster.'

He edged forward again. 'Yeah, about this current disaster—'

'So, Bob and I think it's time you came into Fettes and gave us a proper *interview* about all this.'

The emphasis Jacobsen was putting on the word interview made Bernard's blood run cold. He didn't want to think about what might happen to him in an out-of-the-way meeting room at police HQ. 'You'd need to talk to my line manager about that.'

'Not if I arrest you, I won't.' He pulled back his jacket just enough for Bernard to get sight of something large and metallic underneath it.

'Why are you armed?' Not for the first time he wondered who the HET/CID Liaison Officers really were. They didn't behave like HET staff, and they didn't behave like any other police officers he'd come across. The word that sprang into his head was enforcers, doing whatever it took to ensure that Carlotta Carmichael got her way.

'I'm armed because I need to be armed. You've no idea the scum that I need to deal with. So, why don't you resist arrest? Give me a reason to use this.'

Bernard looked round nervously. There were lots of people about. Surely Jacobsen wouldn't risk using a firearm in such a busy place? Yet there was a glint in his eye that suggested to Bernard, not for the first time, that Jacobsen had left a little bit of his sanity behind at the Plague Museum. He looked around for inspiration. It wasn't a great couple of options: go with Jacobsen and let him and Bob Ellis do what they wanted to him, or stand his ground and risk getting himself, and possibly some innocent bystanders shot.

A flurry of black appeared behind Jacobsen, and before Bernard could really register what was happening, Ana P had pulled a black bin bag over Jacobsen's head and pushed him to the ground. She gave him a swift boot between the legs, then punched him in the head. She turned to Bernard. 'Run, Bernard.'

He ran, mentally trying to work out which particular laws he had just broken. Hopefully Lucy would visit him in prison. He ran up the steps of *The Sizzling Pepper* and flung open the door.

'Bernard!' Lucy waved to him, then got up from her table and walked over. 'You're nearly half an hour late.'

'I know, I'm so sorry, and I can't stay.'

'What?' Lucy's face fell.

'It's a work thing. Introduce me to your parents and I'll explain.'

Mr Withington's expression communicated without the need for words that he had not expected to be kept waiting for this length of time. Mrs Withington just looked relieved that he was finally here. There was a bottle of wine on the table that had had three large glasses out of it, and a basket that may once have contained bread. They appeared to have held off ordering food until he arrived, and were quite probably starving. He hoped the rolls had kept the worst of the hunger pangs at bay.

'I'm so sorry I'm late, it was a work thing.' He held the flowers out in the direction of Mrs Withington who looked slightly mollified. 'And I'm afraid I can't stay, I need to get an, ehm, colleague escorted to our office.'

'Bernard, we go now.' Ana P appeared at his side and pulled on his arm.

Lucy was staring at her. 'I've never heard you mention this colleague before, Bernard.'

'Why are you carrying a teddy bear?' asked Mrs Withington.

'Bernard give it to me.'

Lucy looked distraught. 'I knew you were seeing someone else. You've been sneaking around for weeks. Has this been going on the whole time we've been together?'

'No!' He realised this was a bit ambiguous and clarified. 'Ana is not my girlfriend. Tell her, Ana.' He turned round to look at her, and saw she was unzipping the back of the teddy bear. He had a moment's idle curiosity about why a teddy bear would have a zip in it, which was quickly replaced by horror at the realisation of what she was pulling out of it. 'Oh, God, you stole Ian's gun.'

Ana pointed the gun at him. 'We go now.'

He turned his head slightly in the direction of Lucy. 'I told you she wasn't my girlfriend.' Lucy stared back at him, horrified. 'Although probably best we discuss that later.'

A blonde woman on the neighbouring table had caught sight of the gun and screamed, her alarm rippling out across the restaurant, and sparking a general stampede for the door. Within seconds the only people left in the restaurant were Bernard, Ana, the Withington family, and one bemused waiter.

'We go now, Bernard.'

He didn't move. 'Why do you want to see Boucher, Ana? It's not because you're scared, is it? Do you mean him harm?'

'We go. Before police come.'

'I can't take you there, Ana. I think you are planning to kill Boucher, and I'm not going to be any part of that.'

Mr Withington half rose in his seat. 'My daughter and wife will be leaving now.'

'No.' Ana stepped back and pointed the gun in Lucy's direction. 'Bernard, we go now, or I shoot her.'

Mrs Withington let out a small scream.

'Bernard,' said Lucy. 'What do I do?'

'Nothing. Just stay still.' He turned to Ana. 'Stop pointing the gun at her. I'll take you there.'

The bell above the door jangled as a figure half walked, half fell into the restaurant. 'No, you won't. Ana Procházková you're not going anywhere. And I'd like my gun back.'

'I think we may have found the place.' Paterson pointed to a crowd of people standing outside a restaurant called *The Sizzling Pepper*. It looked like exactly the kind of place Bernard frequented, low key with a heavy emphasis on plant-based cuisine. Unfortunately, the opaque frosted glass was stopping them getting a good view of what was happening inside.

There was a pall of anxiety hanging over the bystanders; their lack of jackets and bags suggested that they'd relocated in a hurry, giving Mona a moment of worry that they'd arrived too late. What had happened in the café to make them all flee? Yet the throng seemed to be remaining calm and maintaining a respectful distance back from the window, without any of the usual hysteria that invariably happened when something really bad had happened.

'Here's the police,' said Hunter.

'Excuse me.' Paterson began to push his way through the crowd, Hunter and Mona following close behind. His assertive forward motion had them at the front of the crowd in seconds, and they approached two uniformed officers, one of whom was getting a long story from a grey-haired man who had been inside the restaurant when it all kicked off.

'And then the woman produced a gun!'

'A gun?' said Mona.

'Can you step back please, ma'am?' said the PC, gesturing her and the other people away from the window.

'We're job, son,' said Paterson.

The officer turned round and did a slight double take. 'Oh, it's you, sir. Can you help in keeping people away from the window?'

'Yeah. Have you requested the Armed Response Team?'

'I'm on it, sir.' The other PC looked up from his radio.

'Have there been any shots fired?' Mona asked the man who had shared his story.

He shook his head. 'No, thank God.'

'Could you describe the person with the gun?'

'She was just a young girl.' He shook his head again, this time in disbelief. 'Younger than you, I'd say. Ordinary looking, long dark hair. How does someone like that end up holding up a restaurant? What was she after? Is it money for drugs?'

'We don't know, sir.'

The man was just getting into his stride. 'I don't understand the world any more. A man should be able to go out for a meal with his wife—' He broke off and looked around the crowd. 'I'd better see where she's got to. She was quite upset.'

'OK, sir, but please don't leave until you've given a full statement to one of the police officers.' He'd already disappeared into the crowd, which seemed to be growing by the minute. It would only get worse as people posted on social media, and yet more rubber-neckers turned up. Mona hoped the police reinforcements got here soon.

'I don't understand.' She felt a tug on her arm, and Hunter pulled her to one side. 'There was nothing in the intel I was shown to suggest that these people had access to guns. How can Ana P suddenly now be armed?'

'We don't know that either, Ma'am.'

'Mona, Ma'am.' A large presence loomed next to her, and she looked up to see Bob Ellis. She should have known the HET Liaison Officers would appear sooner or later, although she for one could have lived very happily never having to work with them again. She supposed it could have been worse – at least it wasn't Ian Jacobsen. 'Ms Hunter, there was a DCI looking for you. I think they're setting up a Command Centre in a shop over there.' He pointed further up Cockburn Street.

'Oh, OK, I suppose I should go and speak to them.' She turned and began to fight her way back through the crowd, moving considerably more slowly than when Paterson had been clearing the way.

Bob grabbed Mona's arm. 'We need to move fast, before Hunter realises that was a complete lie. I need your help, you and Paterson.'

She used her free hand to remove his digits from around her arm and took a very large step backwards. 'I'm not helping you with anything.'

'Don't be like that.' He looked exasperated, and she felt her irritation levels rise even further. 'It's about Bernard. He's in trouble.'

'You think? He's being held at gunpoint!' She waited, curious to know what Bob was talking about.

'Paterson.' Bob waved him over.

'What do you want?' Paterson had also adopted the HET's standard tone of voice for dealing with their liaison officers – an overtly hostile tenor that masked underlying concern at what Bob and Ian were up to this time.

'Ian Jacobsen's in there. He phoned me to say that Ana Procházková had jumped him and taken his gun.'

'That explains where she got it from,' said Paterson. 'Jacobsen should be able to sort this out then. One confused lassie shouldn't be beyond his powers to disarm.'

'Yeah, I agree. But ...' He pulled them further away from the crowd and closer to the restaurant. 'The problem is that Ian, well, he's not been himself since that incident between him and Bernard at the Plague Museum. I don't think he should be at work, to be honest, but, you know, nobody likes ratting out a colleague to Occupational Health.'

'So, he's holding a grudge against Bernard.' Mona looked at the frosted glass and wondered what was going on behind it.

'Bit more than that. Bernard passed us some information which he claimed he'd heard from Bryce. Turned out to be a big bust, and Ian's got it into his head that Bernard did it deliberately just to annoy him.' He gave a humourless little laugh. 'He's pretty obsessed with Bernard, to be honest. He phoned me about ten minutes ago to say that he'd been attacked by Ana P who had stolen his gun, aided and abetted by Bernard, and that he was going to track him down and, ehm, kill him.'

'That could just be a figure of speech?' Paterson's words were hopeful, but his tone was not.

'I'm not so sure, and do we really want to take that chance? We need to get in there.'

Mona looked up. 'Hunter's heading back this way.'

'Let's find another way in.'

14

Ana had insisted everyone sat down, so they'd grabbed a chair each and were now arranged in a long line, with the exception of the waiter who appeared to have fled. Bernard was sitting with Lucy on one side, and Ian Jacobsen on the other. Ian was breathing heavily and irregularly. Sneaking a look at him Bernard could see his face was badly bruised. Delighted as he was to have support to deal with Ana P, he really wasn't sure Ian was in any fit state to help.

'Are you OK, Ian?'

'Shut up.'

Bernard turned his attention back to Ana P, who was pacing around the restaurant, three steps in one direction, turn, back the other way. 'Ana, it would be better if you gave yourself up. You're not going to be able to get out of here. There will be armed police outside by now.'

She ignored him, talking to herself in a language he didn't understand. He tried to remember what country she came from, then concluded it didn't really matter, as his only claim to multilingual status was O-grade French and a small number of badminton-related phrases in a range of European languages, a legacy from his previous career.

'At least let these people go. They've got no part in all of this.'

She looked at him, and he could see the uncertainty on her face. He felt almost sorry for her; the evening's events had escalated pretty quickly, and not in a direction that she could have anticipated. 'The more people you have in here the more you have to keep control of.'

Eventually she nodded. 'You two' – she gestured to Mr and Mrs Withington – 'can go. But she stays here.' She pointed at Lucy.

'I'm not leaving without my daughter!' Nobody moved, although Mrs Withington burst into tears.

'Dad, just go. Get Mum out of here.'

After a second he got to his feet, holding on to his wife's arm. 'Come on, Emily.' He shot Bernard a look of extreme fury as he passed. Bernard attempted a smile in return. He really had set a world record in terms of the World's Worst Meeting of the Girlfriend's Parents for the First Time. It was going to take a lot more than flowers and chocolates to get back in Lucy's parents' good books.

'Lucy.' Bernard reached for her hand, which she moved out of his reach. He hesitated then decided to press on. 'I know this is probably not a good time to say it, but I have had a few problems in my personal life that I should have been open about. I just wanted to say that, well, I love you very much.'

Jacobsen rolled his eyes. 'Oh, God.'

Pointedly, Lucy turned away from Bernard.

'I'm so sorry about how tonight turned out, and I'd really like to meet your parents some other time, if that—'

'Right.' Jacobsen got to his feet. 'I'm not listening to any more of this shit.' He walked in Ana's direction. 'Give me my gun.'

Ana swung her arm away from them, facing Ian. Bernard saw an opportunity.

'Lucy, head for the back door.' He stood up, and held his hands out to the side, in a not particularly successful attempt to form a human shield for his girlfriend's escape.

The gun wavered between Bernard and Jacobsen, Ana looking increasingly upset. 'No, you stay. Everyone stay.'

'Lucy, keep low.'

She ducked under the serving hatch and into the relative safety of the bar.

'Stop.' Ana fired in her direction, hitting one of the bottles sitting above the bar, which shattered and gushed its contents onto the floor. Bernard felt for a minute as if he were in a Western, a shoot-out scene missing only a piano player. Jacobsen, however, was not wasting any time on such fancies and took the opportunity of Ana being distracted to seize her gun arm. There was a horrible crunching sound, and she cried out in pain. Ian grabbed the gun, then struck her twice on the head with it. She fell to the floor, and he kicked her as she lay there.

'Well done,' said Bernard, partly because he meant it, and partly to distract Jacobsen from meting out any further violence. From what he could see Ana no longer presented a threat to anyone. 'I'll go and get help.'

'No.'

'No?' Bernard stopped in his tracks. 'Why not?'

'Because first you and I are going to have a long-overdue conversation.' Jacobsen pointed his gun directly at Bernard's face. 'Sit.'

There was a dark-haired man in the close beside the restaurant, dressed in black trousers and waistcoat and white shirt. His level of agitation suggested he'd been involved in the events in the restaurant. He was muttering to himself in what sounded to Mona like Spanish or Italian, not that she spoke either language; he had his mobile phone in his hand. He spun round at their approach. 'You are police?'

'Yes. Are you from the restaurant?'

'Yes, yes.' He nodded repeatedly. 'There is woman with gun. She threaten people. I don't know what to do, so I try to phone police.'

'You did the right thing, sir.' Mona reassured the man. 'Can you tell us how we get into the restaurant?'

He pointed at an open door. 'This lead into kitchens.'

'Right, I'm going in to try to see what's happening,' said Bob. 'You two wait here.'

Mona and Paterson protested at this, but Bob waved their concerns away. 'I'm armed, you guys aren't.'

Mona turned to the waiter. 'Has anyone else come out of this door?'

He shook his head.

'Then there's another civilian in there – Bernard's girlfriend. You need someone with you to get her out.'

Bob thought this over. 'Has either of you met her?'

'I have,' said Mona.

'Right, you're with me. Paterson, you keep the people out front updated.'

'OK. Take care in there.' Paterson didn't look overjoyed at the thought of staying outside, but seemed to accept the situation. He placed a hand on the waiter's back, and shepherded him down the close.

The kitchen was small. A basket of bread rolls had been upended, its contents strewn across the floor suggesting that someone, possibly the waiter they had just met, had passed through in a hurry. She had a quick look around, but the kitchen staff seemed to have done a good job of at least turning off all the cookers before they took to their heels. Bob pointed at a door on the far side of the room, a sturdy white affair with a small diamond-shaped window. They manoeuvred round the bakery products on the floor and peered through the glass. The tables seemed to be have been moved to clear a space in the centre of the room. Bernard was on a chair, with Ian standing, his gun pointed firmly in her colleague's direction. Neither of them was speaking.

'That's not good,' Mona whispered.

'I need to talk to him.' Ellis was clearly frustrated at the limited vision the window provided. 'I don't see the girl though?'

'You talk to Ian. I'll find her.'

'OK but try and stay out of sight. Ian doesn't much like you either, and we don't want him taking a shot at you.'

'Good advice. Lead on.'

Bob pushed open the door and stepped into the bar. 'Ian, mate.'

Jacobsen swivelled round in surprise. 'Bob, glad you're here.'

He didn't look well. Even from this distance she could see the bruising on his face, the left side of his face swollen and purple. She had some doubt that he could see properly out of his eye, and there seemed to be a slight tremor in his gun arm. Bernard was as much at risk of being shot accidentally as killed on purpose.

'I tracked him down, Bob.' He gestured in Bernard's direction with the gun. 'He's working with the terrorists.'

'No I'm not!' Bernard sounded furious. She was glad that her colleague hadn't crumbled under the circumstances, but she sincerely hoped that he was going to have enough sense to keep his mouth shut. 'Ian's gone mad.'

'Shut up, Bernard,' said Bob, slowly lifting the hatchway between the bar and the restaurant and letting himself through. Bernard's eyes widened as he caught sight of Mona. She pressed her finger firmly across her lips, and he gave her a half nod in return.

'Ian, mate, what's going on here?'

'I tracked him down, Bob. I knew he was working with Boucher.'

'Well done. I know you'd had an eye on him for a while.' Bob stepped further into the room. 'I'll take him into custody.'

As Bob moved closer, Jacobsen caught sight of Mona. 'What's she doing here?' He swung the gun in her direction, and instinctively she ducked behind the bar. 'I wouldn't be surprised if she's working with Boucher too. You can't trust her.'

'Believe me, I don't, mate.'

There was broken glass and alcohol all over the floor. Mona caught sight of a foot sticking out from underneath the bar. She crawled forward, the glass crunching under her knees, and saw Lucy staring back at her, her eyes wide with fear. Mona put a finger to her lips, and Lucy nodded, hugging her arms around herself. In the background they could hear Ian rambling.

'They don't know, Bob. This is all just a game to them. A cushy job for a couple of years.'

Despite the situation, Mona felt prickles of irritation. Whatever her job was, *cushy* did not describe it. She picked a stray shard of glass off her palm.

'Yeah, agreed. Let's get them back to the station and find out what they've really been up to.'

'They think that these are the dying days for the Virus. A few more months of pretending to work, causing as much trouble for us as they can and it'll all be over. They don't know though, Bob, do they?'

'That's enough, Ian.' There was a sharper tone to Bob's voice. 'Let's get back to Fettes.'

Ian laughed. 'How would these lightweight fuckers react if they knew the Virus—'

A shot rang out, reverberating around the walls of the restaurant. Forgetting every bit of training she'd ever had, Mona shot to her feet. 'Bernard!'

Across the room her colleague looked back at her, a thin splatter of blood across his face and chest. At his feet lay the body of Ian Jacobsen, blood beginning to pool around his head like a halo.

'He was about to shoot,' said Bob. 'I could see his finger squeezing the trigger.'

Lucy scrambled to her feet. 'Oh, God!'

She clamped her hand across her mouth, and for a moment Mona worried she was about to be sick, but she was staring at the scene in front of her. Mona put an arm round her. 'Don't look, Lucy.'

Bob crouched down by Ian's body. He grabbed a napkin off an abandoned table and used it to pick up his gun. 'He was about to shoot Bernard, OK? Are we all clear on that?'

Mona nodded. Bernard's gaze was fixed on the body on the floor.

Bob stood up and took a step towards him. 'Bernard, are you clear on that?'

Eventually he gave a small nod. 'Yes.'

Bob didn't look entirely satisfied but didn't pursue this further. He crouched down beside Ana P, and checked her over. 'At least this one's still with us.' He stood up, ushering Mona and Lucy out. 'All right, let's get going. Everyone out of the front door, and remember to hold your hands up as you go.' His hand rested briefly on Mona's shoulder as she passed him. 'We don't want anyone else getting shot.'

FRIDAY

TAKEAWAYS

I

Mona was pounding the streets, anger fuelling her every step. Her rage was widespread and encompassed just about everyone she had spoken to since she left the restaurant, with a particular depth of ire directed at Bob and the two unnamed men who had interviewed her for the best part of three hours. They'd said they were police, but she didn't recognise them, and they certainly hadn't held to any of the niceties of a normal Police Scotland interview. She'd been offered neither food nor drink and had had to plead for a comfort break. Bob had escorted her to the ladies' toilets and back again in, she assumed, an attempt to stop her contacting the outside world. No-one had explained who they were, and any attempts to persuade them that she needed to talk to her line manager or the Head of SHEP were rebuffed, with a continual emphasis on the fact that she had to just answer their questions.

And they'd had a lot of questions. They'd gone over and over not just the events of the evening but the investigation leading up to it.

Why was the HET looking for Ana P?

Because she was a Health Defaulter, with no record of a Health Check in her home country.

Who authorised this search?

Fraser Mauchline, Deputy Head of SHEP.

Who had they spoken to in their pursuit of Ana P?

Florian Boucher. Some volunteers at a Food Bank.

What information had their discussions with Florian Boucher and Ana P yielded?

Very little of use to our Health Defaulter search.

How did you arrive on the scene of Dieter Lange's suicide?

A tip off from a newspaper.

So, why was the HET *really* looking for Ana P?

Because she was a Health Defaulter.

On and on the questions went, round and round, and back again. The men, whoever they were, had clearly had a good idea what the HET had been up to over the past week. Was the questioning to find out more, or just to see if she would trip herself up, say something that they knew to be untrue? It was exhausting, and she'd had to bite her tongue to make sure she didn't reveal anything they didn't already know. Like, it would appear, the fact that Boucher had been in the Cathcart Building.

Mona booted a stone along the street, and tried very hard to hold on to her anger. If her fury died, she'd give in to fear, and there was a lot she should be afraid of. If Bob Ellis was willing to shoot Ian Jacobsen, with whom he'd had a long working relationship, he wasn't going to have a moment's hesitation about shooting her, or Bernard, or anyone else from the HET, if he was required to.

But why had he shot Ian? Why now? She racked her brain to think what Ian had been saying just before he was shot. She'd been distracted, tending to Lucy, but her memory was that he'd been berating them for not understanding the true nature of the Virus. Had he been about to back up Bryce's theory that the Virus was manmade? Was that the kind of revelation that would get someone killed, or was it Ian's general flakiness that made him a

266

security risk? Either way she found it difficult to believe that Bob had made a spontaneous decision to shoot to kill. He'd gone into that restaurant armed with permission to silence Ian permanently.

Her pace was slowing, and despite her best attempts to stay mad, she could feel fear beginning to worm its way into her brain. Had they spoken to Paterson? Had their stories contradicted each other? Being found out in a lie would have consequences, she knew that; the only unknown was the magnitude of the reprisals. She didn't think that she presented enough of a threat to the powers that be that they would want to see her dead, but there were lots of other less drastic options for them to take. Her mind was drawn back to Hunter's comments about misuse of public office. If Hunter wanted to do some digging, she was sure she'd find plenty she could use. Every single cupboard in the Cathcart Building contained a skeleton.

She stopped. She'd reached her destination. Her familiar pilgrimage through the stone-built villas of the Grange had ended as it always did, with a dark and silent house. The garden gate screeched as she threw it wide and ran up the path past the Professor's half-dead roses, stopping to press long and hard on the bell. She swivelled round to look at the street, but her attempts to summon the Professor resulted in no movement, either in the house, or in the cars and dwellings nearby.

What now? She sat on the Professor's doorstep taking small shallow breaths, resetting both body and mind as she tried to recover. Liz's suggestion that she take it easy had been well and truly ignored over the past couple of days. Not that Liz had ever thought her advice would be taken, but she probably had had some hope that someone recovering from a traumatic head injury would have refrained temporarily from scenarios involving kidnap, stabbing threats and shootings. But then Liz hadn't ever experienced working for the HET.

Where was Bircham-Fowler? A five-minute conversation with the Professor could have straightened out all the confusion in her brain.

Mona, of course the Virus isn't manmade. Where did you get this nonsense? Listening to Bryce? Well, he was clearly mad, wasn't he? Saying all sorts of things just to upset you.

But then there was always the other possibility. If the Professor confirmed Bryce's theory, if they were all at risk, if someone, some organisation, was doing this to the world deliberately. If, if, if. But to her mind, whatever the situation was, she'd rather know the truth than live in ignorance.

She took one last deep breath and got to her feet. If she couldn't talk to somebody who understood the medical side of what was going on, she could at least talk to someone who could explain to her, firmly, and probably with quite a bit of swearing, the politics of it all.

Stuttle's house, in contrast to the Professor's, had a warm and welcoming light glowing in a downstairs room. This gave her some relief; even under the current circumstances, she hadn't relished getting her former boss out of his bed at 2am, or even worse, getting her former boss's *wife* out of her bed.

Her hand still lingered before pressing the doorbell. What if the Stuttles had guests? She didn't want to crash the party. Or what if Stuttle was alone and drunk, watching crap TV and rueing the decisions that had led to his fall from grace? She steeled herself, gave a tentative press, and held her breath until the door opened.

'Well, well, well, Mona Whyte. You must be psychic.' Fraser Mauchline smiled back at her. 'This saves us a phone call. So, the Stasi finally let you go?'

'The Stasi?' She followed him into the hall.

He closed the door behind her. 'I think that's as good a description of them as anything. They certainly aren't Police Scotland, and they didn't feel the need to explain themselves to the likes of me. As soon as I heard Bob Ellis had you in his clutches I headed over to Fettes, but they wouldn't let me anywhere near you.'

'Really?' Mona processed this. 'How much trouble am I in?'

'Oh, shitloads.' He gave an airy wave of his hand. 'Fortunately, we've got a crack team working on it.'

'Great! And I think I might have come up with a way to put pressure on Carlotta—'

She walked into the living room and stopped dead at the sight of who was in the room. Stuttle pointed in the direction of an occupied armchair. 'Can I assume you don't need an introduction?'

2

It was late and Bernard should have been tired. He needed a good night's sleep. Carlotta Carmichael's office had texted him, and he assumed the rest of the North Edinburgh HET, at 11.50pm to summon them to a debriefing session at their office, 9am, tomorrow. Except tomorrow was now today, and due to the massive amounts of adrenaline remaining in his system he knew that sleep was still several hours away.

Only part of the adrenaline was due to him facing down a madman with a gun. The hours after the shooting had been, if anything, more stressful that the brief period when he thought his life was about to end. First, he'd had to walk out into a welcoming committee of armed police, who had taken some convincing that they should lower their weapons. Then he'd tried to speak to Lucy again, only to have her father appear and hustle her away. And finally, there had been the interview about the events of that evening, an interrogation that had lasted several hours and had not, in his opinion, shown due deference to the fact that he had just had a very traumatic experience.

They had separated them out immediately, with Bob, Mona, Lucy (her protective father in tow) and himself all taken to separate rooms at police HQ. He hadn't had a chance to speak to Mona about the events, to hear what she had seen. Bob had been very clear on what had happened – Ian's finger had been about to squeeze the trigger. Under the circumstances he should be grateful that Bob had acted so quickly, saving Bernard's life at the expense of his close colleague's. The only thing was, from where he had been sitting, at the point just before Ian had been shot, his face had been turned towards Bob. If anything, his grasp on the gun had slackened. In the seconds before Ian's death, Bernard's main concern had been that Ian might have dropped the gun so that it went off accidentally.

He'd said none of this in the interview. Contradicting Bob's point of view would, he was sure, bring a world of pain down upon him. At the same time, he wasn't keen to back up Bob's lies, so he'd taken the only option he could think of. He'd told them he'd been so terrified by the events that he'd had his eyes closed the whole time. The police interviewing him seemed to have believed this. No-one had, as yet, offered him any counselling.

There would be a reckoning for all of this, he was sure. Not just for the events of the previous day, although he was sure Bob wasn't done with him yet. But Bryce was also still pulling their strings, despite Mona's insistence he was dead. Someone was still messing with them, and his money was on Blair Taylor. Blair, whose parents were living through the hell of not knowing whether their son was dead or alive, and he, Bernard, was doing nothing to help them. If there was to be a reckoning, some part of it, no doubt, was heading his way.

He surveyed the contents of his kitchen, in pursuit of something to calm his nerves and help him sleep. He was not in the mood for herbal tea, and he didn't have enough milk in his fridge for hot chocolate. After a moment's indecision, he headed for the single bottle of wine in his underused wine rack. Drinking alcohol at this time of night was a bad idea. Getting drunk would give him a couple of hours' sleep before he woke, his mind racing and unable to doze off again. However, a couple of hours' sleep was better than nothing, which would be his sum total of rest if he couldn't find some way to relax.

He poured himself a large glass of red, sat on the sofa, and scrolled through his phone in the hope that Lucy had answered one of his texts. He'd phoned her the second he'd been released, but she hadn't picked up. He'd followed that up with a number of texts enquiring about her wellbeing, all of which had been met with zero response. He stared at his phone and tried to remember if Lucy actually had her phone on her when she left the restaurant. Maybe it was lying on the floor of *The Sizzling Pepper*, ringing and beeping to an empty room. Maybe she had reacted to stress differently from him, and had gone home exhausted and fallen into a very deep sleep. Or maybe the Withingtons had decided *en famille* that he was very bad news and absolutely, definitely, not boyfriend material. He stood up and plugged his phone into its charger. He didn't want to have a dead phone when she did eventually make contact, whatever she was planning to say to him.

There was a long buzzing sound. He paused with his hand on the plug, and stared at his entry phone, a slow feeling of dread stealing over him. The best-case scenario was that Mona had come over to see how he was, and to compare experiences. He was all for that, although he would prefer that he had an (increasingly unlikely) good night's sleep before he spoke to her. The worst-case scenario was that it was Bob Ellis, eager to check that Bernard had backed up his story. No doubt that conversation would happen at some point, but it wasn't happening when he was on his own in his flat if he could possibly avoid it. He decided to sit tight and hope they went away.

His phone beeped to announce a new text message. Could they not just leave him be? Were Ellis and his colleagues trying to deprive him of sleep? Pick up their questioning when he was at his most vulnerable and likely to say the wrong thing? He closed his eyes and reached for his phone. Opening one eye, he looked at the screen and saw Lucy's name.

Are you still awake? I'm at your front door.

He threw himself in the direction of the entry phone, and pressed down on it for a long time, just to be sure she could get in, then headed out to his front door to watch her climb the stairs. He tried to ascertain from her gait whether this was a *Dear John* situation, or something more hopeful. It was clarified when she reached the landing and threw her arms around him.

'I'm so glad you're OK, Bernard.'

'And I'm so glad you're here.'

He shepherded her into the flat, and poured her a large glass of wine, which she took gratefully. 'I've just left my parents. They were trying to insist I stayed over but I said I wanted to get back to my flat.'

'I owe them a huge apology.'

'It wasn't your fault, though, was it?'

Bernard had the feeling that it wasn't the first time that she'd made that point since she left the restaurant. 'Are your parents mad at me?'

'Furious. They're pretty much insisting that I never see you again.'

'Ah.' His heart sank. 'That doesn't seem unreasonable seeing as I nearly got your whole family shot.'

'Again, not your fault.'

'In hindsight, I really shouldn't have come to the restaurant. I was just so keen to meet them, and I wanted to apologise in person.'

She nodded. 'I know.'

'I hope the police interview was OK.'

'Yes, they were all really nice. Who was that woman, anyway?'

'She's ...' He thought about the best way to describe Ana, and decided there was only one way to go. 'She's classified, I'm afraid.'

'And the man who was shot? Is that also classified?'

'For now at least.' He'd literally no idea what to say about Ian Jacobsen, but no doubt he'd be told what the official version was at the 9am briefing.

Lucy nodded again, her eyes wide. 'Of course. Your job is so dangerous, Bernard.'

She seemed worryingly excited by this thought. He didn't know how to tell her that his job should not be dangerous. It should not be exciting. It should not even be particularly interesting. Yet somehow, along with his colleagues, he seemed to end up in these situations. He'd always blamed Stuttle for this, yet he was gone, and inexplicably the chaos had carried on.

'You've finished your wine. Would you like some more?' He held up the bottle. 'Or are you hungry? Would you like something to eat?'

She laughed. 'I was well fed at my mum's, believe me. I think it was a reaction to stress. She all but cooked us a three-course meal at nearly midnight. Anyway, it's getting late.'

'I could call you a taxi?'

There was the briefest of pauses. 'Actually, I thought I might stay.'

A small fiesta of joy took place in Bernard's head. Unfortunately, his conscience was making a concerted effort to elbow the mariachi band out of the way. 'I'd love that, but I need to tell you something first.'

Lucy slumped back into the corner of the sofa. He decided to keep going before he lost his nerve. 'I know that you think I've been up to something, and I suppose in a way I have. My wife is pregnant.'

She looked horrified.

'With someone else's child,' he hurriedly clarified. 'She's having the baby alone, and her blood pressure has gone through the roof, so I've given her some support, taking her to appointments and things like that. I really should have told you, but it's a bit of an awkward situation.'

He couldn't quite read Lucy's expression. She was staring down at her wine glass, then suddenly looked up, staring straight at him. 'Just be honest with me, Bernard. Are you and your wife going to get back together?'

'No! Absolutely not.' He took her hand. 'I love you. I know we've not been together very long, but I could really see a future for us together, a long, happy future.'

She looked relieved, and his heart did a little jump for joy.

'Well, at least you've done your bit helping your wife, and you can leave her to get on with her new life now.'

Bernard thought that this would probably be a very good time to discuss the implications of pre-eclampsia, and the fact that his wife was very vulnerable, and didn't have a lot of other sources of support, which meant that he would have to continue giving a teeny bit of support to her in an entirely platonic fashion.

But Lucy's lips were on his, soft and wine-stained, and right then that was the only thing that mattered.

3

Mona checked the time on her phone, then pressed long and hard on Bernard's buzzer. She suspected he'd had a sleepless night, and given his sudden inclination to tardiness she wanted to make sure he didn't sleep right through the meeting with Carlotta Carmichael. At least, that was part of her motivation. The other motive was finding out exactly what he'd been asked in his interview. She hoped to God his answers were close enough to what she'd said.

'Hello, who's there?'

The voice at the other end of the buzzer sounded surprisingly alert, bordering on chipper.

'It's Mona. Did you get the message that we all need to come into the office for 9am?'

'Yes. We were just leaving. See you in a minute.'

We?

Bernard's surprisingly good mood was explained when he emerged from the tenement with Lucy in tow. She gave Mona a little wave, pecked Bernard on the cheek, and set off down the street. Bernard turned to Mona, trying, and largely failing, to hide a smile that could only be described as smug.

'Last night not all bad then, Bernard?'

'Apart from the bit where I nearly got shot, and the part where I alienated Lucy's parents for ever, it was great.'

As they fell into step, Mona started with her list of questions. 'What did the police ask in your interview?'

'They wanted to know how we'd ended up in the restaurant, so I told them all about Marcus being stalked and bringing Ana P to my flat—'

'Good one, Marcus.'

'Yes, not a great idea. Someone really needs to have a word with him, but anyway, I explained that we were on the way to the office, and I'd just popped into the restaurant for a moment.'

'Did they say anything about that? I mean, it's not a great idea to take a terrorist suspect to a restaurant to meet your girlfriend's parents.'

He grimaced. 'I kind of expected that to be raised, but no, they didn't. The only thing they really seemed concerned about was whether I could back up Bob's story that Ian was about to shoot me.'

'And could you?'

She watched his face contort as he thought through the events of the previous evening. 'The thing is, Mona, I don't think he was about to fire. He was rather distracted, you know, by you and Bob appearing. He'd turned towards you and his gun was kind of ...' He mimed a gun being held at a slightly downward angle.

Mona stared at him, her anxiety rising. 'Did you tell them that?'

'No. I said I had my eyes shut the whole time.' He stopped walking. 'Do you think I should have told the truth?'

'No! I thought Ian Jacobsen was the resident psychopath in the HET Liaison Unit until I saw Bob Ellis kill a man without a second thought. Who knows what would happen to us if we started saying Bob executed one of his colleagues?'

'So, you think we just witnessed a murder?' Every inch of Bernard's face was begging her to say *no, of course not.*

She disappointed him. 'I don't know, Bernard. Can you remember what Jacobsen was saying just before he got shot?'

'I don't know, something about us being snowflakes, not really understanding the Virus?' He frowned. 'You don't think that's why Bob shot him? He was about to reveal something we're not supposed to know?'

She shrugged. 'I don't know. I think Jacobsen's been a walking security risk ever since the Museum incident, maybe even before. They were probably glad of an excuse to get rid of him.' She smiled. 'I hate to break it to you, but I don't think Bob likes you enough to shoot his colleague just to save your life.'

'Yes, I'd kind of worked that out for myself.' Bernard stopped walking, 'I need to tell you something else.'

'OK.' She was slightly concerned by the worry on her colleague's face. 'But we need to keep walking.'

He started moving. 'You remember the surveillance files that Marcus uncovered? There were two lists of names, which we are assuming was a list of real people and their aliases?'

She nodded.

'Well, I had a good look at the list of aliases that the people were using, and ...' He sighed. 'One of them was Robert Ellis.'

'Robert Ellis?' It took a moment for the penny to drop. '*Bob* Ellis?'

He nodded, mournfully. 'When I saw Robert Ellis listed I actually thought it was funny, because we now know that Bob is an alias and the list revealed his real name. But I'm sure he wouldn't want us or anyone else to know that. And after the way he behaved last night, I'm thinking—'

'That it's dangerous information to know.' Despite her earlier urging Bernard to keep moving, she found she had come to an involuntary halt. 'It might not be him, of course.'

'Of course. It's a common enough name. So it could just be a coincidence.'

'Albeit a big one. So, what is Bob's real name?'

'Russell Fitzsimmons. Does that mean anything to you?' She shook her head. A thought struck her. 'Was Ian Jacobsen's name on the list?'

'No. Which supports the coincidence theory, as they usually come as a pair.' He thought for a minute. 'Or maybe Jacobsen got so flaky that he just couldn't be trusted with ... with whatever all this means'

'Have you told anyone this?'

He shook his head.

'Good. Keep it to yourself.' They started walking again.

'*I* won't mention it, but Marcus is all over these files. He's going to pick it up at some point, and you know he doesn't have a tactful bone in his body. I don't know how to warn him about how dangerous Bob could be without discussing what happened last night.'

'I need to think about this, Bernard.' Already her brain was starting to hurt, a dull ache behind her eyes. What should they do? Ignore it, and hope that Marcus didn't twig? Pass it on to Stuttle and let him decide how to proceed? There were dangers either way. But then, even doing nothing could be dangerous, if Mr Russell Fitsimmons decided that he didn't want them knowing how his mum referred to him. 'Let's just get through this meeting and talk again.'

'Well, we're here.' He paused, with one foot on the steps up to the door of the Cathcart Building. 'Ready to face an irate politician?'

'Who knows, Bernard, maybe she's come to say thank you?'

Marguerite was behind the reception desk, wearing, if it were possible, even more make-up than the previous day. 'Is your French visitor coming in again?' she asked, hopefully.

Mona considered mentioning the use that the front desk letter opener had been put to yesterday but decided it could wait. 'He's Belgian, and no, he isn't. But if he does appear, be sure to let us know immediately.'

'Where do you think Boucher is?' asked Bernard, quietly.

'Long gone. Either his friends will have worked out a way to get him out of Scotland, or his employers will have caught up with him.'

'Who are his employers?'

'I have no idea, but I think they are the kind of people who don't take kindly to you messing up on a mission.' She updated Bernard about Boucher losing the keys to the lorry, and her discussions with him at the Cathcart Building. 'So, I'm pretty sure that as far as our legal system goes, Ana P is going to carry the can for everything that happened with the lorry.'

Bernard pushed open the door to the office and was met with a barrage of swearing from Maitland.

He smiled sweetly in return. 'Hello to you too.'

'It's so unfair! You and Mona got all the excitement last night and Carole and I got stuck here waiting for an activist that was never going to show.'

Carole looked up. 'Can I just say I am quite happy to have avoided all the excitement?'

'I'd have been quite happy to avoid it too,' said Bernard. 'Aside from thinking that I was going to die, I'm pretty sure Lucy's parents are never, ever, going to speak to me again.'

Maitland looked slightly mollified that Bernard hadn't enjoyed the experience. 'Well, next time there's some action, I'm going to be there, not sitting on my arse miles away.'

'Very happy to volunteer you for any activity where you might get shot.'

'Morning all.' Paterson swept in, Marcus trailing in his wake.

'You OK, Mona?' He leaned in as he passed her. 'Prepared?'

She patted her bag. 'Yes, Guv.'

'I hear footsteps.' Marcus looked worried. He sat down at the nearest desk, opening up his laptop to put a barrier between him and the upper echelons of the SHEP management structure.

'Good morning.' Jennifer Hunter pushed open the office door. She looked happier than she had all week, and there was a spring in her step. Even her hair looked glossier. The minister and a young civil servant followed her in. Mona was relieved to see that Bob Ellis wasn't with them.

Carlotta didn't offer any salutations, just looked round the room with an air of disgust. She sniffed. 'There is a distinct odour in here.'

'Yes, Ms Carmichael,' said Paterson. 'That's what you get if you leave unrefrigerated prawns and steaks lying around for three days. A lingering smell.'

'I'll open a window.' The junior civil servant emerged from Carlotta's shadow. He fumbled with the catch for a while, until Carole took pity on him and helped.

'The collection and disposal of the food was a simple task. Yet another straightforward job that the North Edinburgh HET has made an unnecessary meal of.'

Marcus laughed, then realised that the Minister's pun had been unintentional. She glared at him and he retreated behind his screen.

'With all due respect, Mrs Carmichael, it may have been a simple task but it shouldn't have been our task at all,' said Paterson.

'John,' said Hunter. 'I don't think that this is the time. Mrs Carmichael has just popped in briefly to ask for your discretion around the events of the past few days—'

'I'm not asking for their discretion! I'm here to impress upon them the national security implications of the events and to make it clear that I will take a very dim view of any leaks to the paper, particularly that odious Cassandra woman, about anything that has occurred recently.' She shook her head in disbelief that anyone could think she was asking them for a favour. 'When you are confirmed in post, Jennifer, I hope you are going to be taking a firmer hand with this team than Cameron Stuttle ever managed.'

'No.'

'No?' Everyone in the room looked at Hunter in surprise, except Paterson. Mona was trying not to smile. There had been several hours of preparation for this moment, all done in the early hours of the morning at Stuttle's house. When she'd seen Hunter sitting in Stuttle's living room, sipping one of his finer whiskies, Mona had let fly a volley of accusations, questioning Hunter's knowledge, abilities and ethics, climaxing with a rather unfortunate comment about her dress sense. Hunter had responded by pouring her a large dram, and telling her to sit down, shut up, and listen. She'd downed the malt, listened to what they had to say, rubbished their plan, and presented a better one of her own, which was currently being put into action.

'No, Mrs Carmichael. I've decided I'm going to return to my substantive post. I can't manage the HETs. It needs to be someone with a police background.'

The politician's eyebrows rippled as she took in this suggestion. 'Nonsense. The HETs are as much about health as they are about law enforcement.'

'Except they're not.' Hunter stood her ground. 'HET officers risk life and limb every day. They're threatened with violence. Actually experience violence. They're also being blackmailed.' She gestured in Carole's direction. 'And what are we doing in return? We're demonising them for wanting to leave. Threatening them. Finding ways to punish them. They need to be supported properly, and I'm not the person to do that. As of Monday, I'm returning to my old job.'

Carlotta looked furious. 'You can't do that. Get on the phone to HR, Paul.' She realised her mistake and clicked her fingers at the new boy. 'Get on the phone to HR, ehm . . .'

'Dylan.' He pulled nervously at his shirt collar. 'Er, what am I asking them?'

'You're not asking them anything,' said Hunter. 'I've spoken to them and they said I'm entitled to do so.'

'You will do the job that I ask of you,' said Carlotta.

'I can go quietly, Mrs Carmichael, or I can be extremely honest about the circumstances under which I'm leaving.' The two women stared at each other. 'You need to get Stuttle back.'

'Hell will freeze over before that happens,' Carlotta snapped.

'Will it, Mrs Carmichael?' Mona dug into her bag and produced Elaine's William Morris notebook. 'Do you recognise this?'

The Minister looked confused. 'Should I?'

'It's Paul Shore's diary.'

Carlotta's face was a mixture of panic and disbelief. 'Paul didn't keep a diary.'

This was probably true, but Mona pulled on every acting skill she possessed. 'Oh, but he did, Mrs Carmichael. And we're not sure quite what it says yet given that it's in code, but we've got our best people working on it.'

Everyone looked at Marcus, and Mona had a moment of dismay that he was going to pipe up that he had no idea what she was talking about. Fortunately, he was engrossed in whatever it was he was doing on his laptop, his fingers flying over the keys. Mona hoped that Carlotta would assume he was busy with some de-encryption software.

'If that diary relates to his time at the Scottish Government, then it's the Scottish Government's property.' She snapped her fingers in Mona's direction. 'Hand it over.'

Mona wondered if anyone, anywhere, had ever done something because someone snapped their fingers. She sincerely hoped not. 'Actually, Mrs Carmichael, this is Paul's private property, which he asked Mr Paterson and me to look after for him when we visited him in hospital, where he was, we thought, recuperating from his injuries.'

Paterson nodded his agreement. Carlotta's eyes narrowed as she considered the plausibility of this. Her gaze switched to the book, and Mona felt a little internal burst of joy. She was buying it.

'Paul was in a very sensitive position. I have to insist that you hand that over. Dylan!' She snapped her fingers again and gestured from her assistant to the diary. Looking deeply uncomfortable, he took a hesitant step towards Mona, as if he was considering making a grab for it.

Paterson took control of the situation, by moving his large bulk in Dylan's direction. 'Don't go doing anything stupid, son.'

Stymied, Carlotta turned her attention in Hunter's direction. 'Please instruct your staff member to hand that diary over to me.'

Hunter smiled mirthlessly at her boss. 'I'm afraid I share their view that this is Paul Shore's personal property, which he has clearly indicated he wishes Mona to hold on to. I had quite an argument with Cameron Stuttle on the issue.'

'Stuttle? When did you speak to Stuttle?'

'I believe Mona had raised the issue with him, and he contacted me out of the blue, making a very similar argument to yourself about the potential security issues relating to the contents of the book. He was all for destroying it unread.'

Carlotta rolled her eyes. Whatever her other faults, she was quick on the uptake. She knew when she was being blackmailed.

'I wouldn't feel comfortable trusting anyone other than Mr Stuttle to deal with this, Mrs Carmichael.' Mona smiled at her.

'Of course you wouldn't.' Carlotta's expression was grim. 'And no doubt he would destroy the diary, and hang on to the translated version.'

She gestured in Marcus's direction, and he looked up. 'What?'

Paterson stepped in. 'On with your work, Marcus.' Marcus looked confused but kept typing.

'Doesn't count for much without the original in Paul's handwriting. It would just be a series of typewritten notes. Anyway, we haven't decoded it . . . yet.'

Abruptly, Carlotta turned on her heel. 'Dylan, come on. You too, Jennifer. I believe you are still working for SHEP for the moment, at least.'

She stormed out. Dylan hurried after her, giving Paterson a conspicuously wide berth as he went. Hunter gave them a little wave, and Paterson followed her over to the door, closing it firmly behind her.

'What was all that about?' asked Maitland. 'That's book's nothing to do with Paul, is it?'

'That was our best attempt to get Stuttle his job back,' said Mona. She turned to Paterson. 'Do you think she bought it?'

'She's rattled, definitely. My guess is that she's straight out of here talking to Bob Ellis about what she can do. Wouldn't be surprised if both the HET and your flat get broken into in the next couple of days.'

'Well, this really is very interesting.' Marcus finally looked up from his laptop. 'Not what I would have expected at all.'

'You've found out something about those files that were released?' Paterson hurried round to Marcus's side. Mona looked over at Bernard, who stared back at her in dismay. She took a half step towards Marcus, wondering if there was anything she could do to stop him blurting out what he'd found.

'Oh, for God's sake.' To her surprise, Paterson stepped away from Marcus's side, laughing. 'That's what you were so busy with?'

'I think it is a legitimate area of interest,' said Marcus.

'What's he on about, Guv?' asked Maitland. 'Is it something we should know?'

'Probably,' said Paterson. 'Go, on Marcus. Tell them.'

'Well, after all the food got stolen, I had a sudden thought that Mrs Carmichael was going to have to come up with two hundred alternative dinners, and I kind of wondered how she'd manage it. So, I sent out emails to a few IT acquaintances and I got an answer.'

'Which was?' Maitland was clearly losing patience.

'Stovies.'

There was a moment's silence while everyone took this in. Carole was the first to speak. 'You mean Mrs

Carmichael fed the great and the good from the eight most powerful countries in the world a dish that's made out of mashed potatoes and beef? It's not exactly haute cuisine, is it?'

'Apparently she gave a long speech about how it was a traditional Scottish delicacy.' Marcus thought for a second. 'And there were oatcakes on the side.'

'Stovies and oatcakes,' said Paterson. 'I bet they couldn't get out of here quick enough!'

'At least she didn't deep-fry anything,' said Bernard.

Deep within her bag Mona's phone started to ring. She turned away from the laughter and pulled it out, looking at the screen as she did so. It was a number she didn't recognise.

'Hello?'

'Mona.' A familiar voice spoke. 'Sandy Bircham-Fowler here. How are you?'

She nearly dropped the phone in surprise. 'Professor! I've been trying to get hold of you.'

'Yes, Tess and I were laying low for a bit. We're back now, and I need to speak to you about something.'

She stepped away from her colleagues. 'OK.'

'Have you seen the news today?'

'No, not yet.' She walked over to Marcus. 'Can you call up the BBC News webpage?'

He nodded and obliged. She stared at the screen. She could hear the Professor talking away in her ear, but she wasn't listening. All she could focus on was the headline.

New Outbreak of the Virus in Haiti. Potential New Variant Identified.

'Professor.' She cut across the conversation.

'Yes?'

'Tell me where you are.' She pulled on her jacket. 'I'm on my way.'

'I'm at Tess's. I'm afraid things don't look good, Mona.'

She hung up and ran out of the building, ignoring the questions from her colleagues, ignoring Marguerite's attempts to speak to her, ignoring Carlotta Carmichael and Hunter, who were having a set-to on the stairs outside the building.

Bryce was right.

The Virus was manmade.

She stuck out her hand for a taxi and jumped in, staring back at the Cathcart Building as they sped away. No amount of Health Checks could stop a Virus that could be mutated at will. No health promotion campaigns or vaccines could stop it re-emerging in a different form. The Professor was the only person she knew who might be able to stop it, and if there was anything she could do to help, anything at all, she'd be at his side.

Even if it killed her.

Acknowledgements

Thanks to everyone at Sandstone Press, particularly Moira Forsyth for her support and editing, and Ceris Jones for her inventive promotion of the books!

I'm indebted to Paul Allera at the Road Haulage Association and Phil Monger at the Petrol Retailers' Association for answering my questions about lorries and petrol stations. I hope I got it right.

I'm grateful to everyone who has taken the time to read the books, particularly to my sons' friends who have gone where my sons fear to tread.

Love, as always, to Gordon.

And yes, there really is a quiz in Edinburgh that always has a Belgian question. Thanks for all the entertainment, Quizmaster Dave.

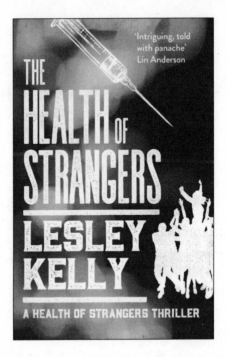

'Intriguing, told with panache'
Lin Anderson

THE HEALTH OF STRANGERS

LESLEY KELLY

A HEALTH OF STRANGERS THRILLER

The Epidemic is spreading. Monthly health checks are mandatory.

Enter the Health Enforcement Team, an uneasy mix of police and health service staff. Stuck with colleagues they don't like, politicians they don't trust and civil servants undermining them, Mona and Bernard are fighting more than one losing battle.

'An intriguing tale of crime in a post viral Edinburgh, told with panache.'   LIN ANDERSON

'Moves along at a cracking pace ... a really well constructed and extremely entertaining thriller.'
Undiscovered Scotland

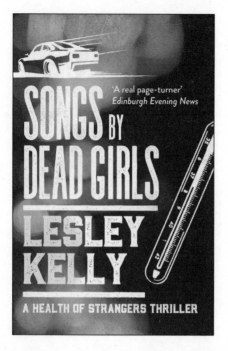

'A real page-turner'
Edinburgh Evening News

SONGS BY DEAD GIRLS

LESLEY KELLY

A HEALTH OF STRANGERS THRILLER

A deadly flu virus. A missing academic with a head full of secrets that could embarrass the government. A prostitute on the run. And a music-loving drug baron who needs a favour.

All in a day's work for the North Edinburgh Health Enforcement Team.

'Laced with dark humour, there's a mesmeric quality to Kelly's writing that ensures this book, like its predecessor, is a real page turner.'

LIAM RUDDEN, *Edinburgh Evening News*

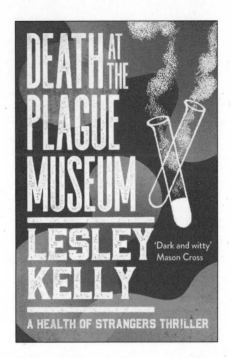

DEATH AT THE PLAGUE MUSEUM

LESLEY KELLY

'Dark and witty'
Mason Cross

A HEALTH OF STRANGERS THRILLER

On Friday, three civil servants leading epidemic policy hold a secret meeting at the Museum of Plagues and Pandemics. By Monday, two are dead and one is missing.

It's up to Mona and Bernard of the Health Enforcement Team to find the missing official before panic hits the streets.

'A dark, witty mystery with a unique take on Edinburgh – great stuff!'
MASON CROSS

'Really entertaining'
Ian Rankin

MURDER AT THE MUSIC FACTORY

LESLEY KELLY

A HEALTH OF STRANGERS THRILLER

The body of Paul Shore toppled onto him, a stream of blood pooling around them on the concrete. Bernard lay back and waited to see if he too was going to die.

An undercover agent gone rogue is threatening to shoot a civil servant a day. As panic reigns, the Health Enforcement Team race against time to track him down – before someone turns the gun on them.

'The book also kept me hooked, and guessing all the way, with its race-against-the-clock plot.' JACKIE MCLEAN

www.sandstonepress.com

Subscribe to our weekly newsletter for events information,
author news, paperback and e-book deals, and the occasional
photo of authors' pets!
bit.ly/SandstonePress

 facebook.com/SandstonePress/

 @SandstonePress